Kasia's Love Purpose

Kasia's Love Purpose

Dear Pam,
Thank you so much!!
Truly hope you enjoy!

Todd Love Ball Jr.

Life is good
love [signature]

Strategic Book Publishing and Rights Co.

Strategic Book Publishing and Rights Co., LLC
USA
www.sbpra.net

For information about special discounts for bulk purchases, please contact Strategic Book Publishing and Rights Co. Special Sales at bookorder@sbpra.net.

ISBN: 978-1-68235-747-7

Dedication

To my beautiful wife Kasia! There isn't enough ink to write down my love for you. This book is a dedication to what you have given me in all aspects of our life. Remember when we first got married and I would write love letters to you? Well, view this as a long love letter to you with a message through a story. Twenty years teaching me how to be a good father, turning me into the best husband, giving me a whole different culture, making me be the best person every day. I want you to know that when you read a detail of how beautiful something is, or how special or magical something is, I always had you as my foundation to go back to if I ever got lost. You will read this and know we have so many inside jokes and stories. Writing this book was a reminder of all you have given me in this world and spiritually. Don't just love you but I'm in love with you.

Love,
your Tadeusz

To my Polish community and family...

When I met my wife I could have never known the enormity of what I was getting – another culture. I fell in love with the culture as I fell in love with my wife. While you read this book I hope that you can see your culture from a fresh set of eyes—not just a different set of eyes, but a set of eyes in love with everything about your way of life. After twenty years of experience with the culture with my wife, I still learn something new every day. Sit back and enjoy the beauty of your culture.

Todd Love Ball Jr.

To all my clients,

You have listened to me talk about the book, but you have supported me more in life! Much love and respect to you all and will always remember you!

Coach Ball

Soundtrack to the Book

I have complied a list of songs and what chapters they go best with. You do not have to listen to the music or have the playlist. It just gives you an idea of the mood and the ambiance for those parts I was trying to set.

Prologue: "In Exile" by Lisa Gerrard from the album *The Silver Tree*.

Chapter 1: "A Lovely Place to Be" by Patrick O' Hearn from the album *So the Flow Current*. Played throughout the chapters during the explanation parts. This song is the main setting for the book.

"See the Sun" by Lisa Gerrard and Pieter Bourke from the *Ali* soundtrack. Played during the letters.

Chapter 27: "Get You" by Daniel Caesar from the album *Freudian*. Played during dance scenes.

"The Unfolding" by Lisa Gerrard and Peter Bourke from the album *Duality*. Played during the farm parts and throughout the book background.

Chapter 31: "Motion" by Khalid from the album *Suncity*.

Chapters 38 and 39: "Always and Forever" by Heatwave from the album *Too Hot to Handle*.

Chapter 41: "Say Something" by Brooklyn Duo from the album *Brooklyn VII Sessions*.

Chapter 42: "Ribbon in the Sky" by Stevie Wonder from the album *At the Close of a Century*.

"Shape of My Heart" by Sting from the album *The Best of 25 Years*. Played during the close out.

"Pearls" by Sade from the album *love Deluxe*. Played starting at page 249.

Prologue

Me and Grandpa Charlie sit in an intense game of Monopoly arguing over trading Park Place or Boardwalk. He, of course, is killing me in the game. He's a cool guy, and I have been coming to visit him more often lately. But there is something different about him this day.

I suddenly get a strange feeling in my stomach, when all of a sudden he stops and grabs his chest. I run over to him as he slumps over the couch. As I grab my phone and start to dial 911, he quickly grabs my wrist with a grip so strong it's painful. Then Charlie's eyes roll to the back of his head. I try to pull away but can't. His grip gets so tight I start to scream for him to let go, but he continues to convulse and his eyes are just white.

A bright flash goes off and I black out. I am out but can still feel what is going on. It feels like I'm falling. My heart rate spikes and I start to lose my breath. My heart feels like it's going to explode. My eyes open but everything is pitch black, and it still feels like I'm falling for a few moments. It feels like I am falling into deep water, and it begins to get even harder to breathe. Right when I feel like I can't breathe anymore, I sit up and finally catch my breath. It was like I was underwater for minutes and just came up for air. I look around as I gather myself and discover I am no longer at my Grandpa Charlie's house. *What the hell is happening?* I wonder.

I stand up in the middle of some forest or something. I have no idea where I am. It is warm and sunny and all I can see are trees and brush for miles around me. Suddenly, I break out of my lostness and see a younger-looking version of my Grandpa Charlie running through the forest with some woman. He has on a military outfit and the woman looks like she is wearing some traditional European garb, a dress with green and red colors. They are holding hands and it looks like they are running for their lives as they weave through tree brush after tree brush. They run right through me. About two seconds later about eight men come screaming by on horses. I can't understand what they are saying; it's in a different language and I can't make out what language it is. For some reason, no one can see me so I follow behind. *It must be a dream but it feels so real,* I think.

I finally catch up to my grandpa and the mysterious lady he's with. They had found some bunker or something and are hiding inside, hoping no one followed them there. If they did it wouldn't end well, because there is no way out of this hidden, what looks like a war bunker. I follow them down to the bottom where they sit together in a circular room. They hug and hold hands. He kisses her so gently and stares into her eyes. For some reason I can feel them; I have some strong feeling, but I don't know what it is.

My Grandpa Charlie starts to glow. It is a light of gold that forms around him as he pulls the young lady closer. I can hear the men climbing off their horses and making their way into the bunker. Charlie and the woman pay them no attention. As my grandpa pulls her closer she also starts to glow. I can tell she seems scared but Charlie seems at ease, almost like he is happy.

"Charlie, what's happening?"

"I'm in love with you ... that's all I can explain right now because I don't know what's going on either. I had to tell you

I love you before those men come in here and do something bad to me. Whatever happens I'm glad I risked my life for you. I would rather have these stolen moments with you than to live life and never have known what love is."

The eight men come blasting through the doorway. They circle them but Charlie and the woman pay them no attention. The glow of gold and light shines bright around them. One of the men yells for the woman to back up before she gets hurt. Another man yells at my grandfather that he better let go if he doesn't want the woman he's with to get hurt. For some reason, even though it was said in a different language I can now understand them. Charlie and the woman still do not react. I can feel my heart rate starting to spike again. My grandfather locks eyes with the woman and smiles. He whispers, "I love you."

One of the men, who looks like the leader of the pack, walks up to my grandpa and stands behind him, looking at the other men in the room. They all look confused. The man gives Charlie one more warning and screams with all his might for him to let the woman go. Strangely, I can feel her heart beat. The man shakes his shoulders and lifts up a pole he was holding and swings with all his might. Right before he makes contact there is a bright flash. I can't breathe again, my stomach is in knots, and I feel like I'm falling. Then everything goes black and I feel like I am back in the dark water again. As I come to I gasp and reach for air.

I am back in my Grandpa Charlie's house, sitting on the floor. I am in a full sweat, my clothes soaked. I get up and Charlie is sitting at the table, still in front of the Monopoly game. I look around lost and then back at him. He doesn't say much; he just looks at me. For some reason my tears start falling uncontrollably. I try to talk but no words come out. Charlie just sits there and gives me a weird look. I am still sweating profusely and my tears are matched with an uncontrollable wail of a cry. I can't control any of my emotions then. I feel every emotion at once. I am extremely happy, yet I felt a deep sadness hitting me in my stomach. I feel excited yet extremely nervous. I can feel myself shaking and I can't stop.

I feel out of my own body as I look at myself just sitting there while a spirit of myself walks around me. Grandpa Charlie just sits there, watching me. I feel like I am screaming at him but he can't hear me. Finally, after a few minutes of all the emotions going through my body, I start to calm down. I feel my heart rate come down and I finally start to feel like I'm not going to throw up. I finally am able to move my body. I cough to see if I have my voice and finally I am back. I look into my grandpa's eyes, who hasn't stopped looking at me.

"What was that, Grandpa?"

"I can't answer your questions, my child. You'll have to go through your journey to find your power. All I can say is love."

"What does that mean?"

"You are love and my end has come, which means your destiny has started."

Chapter 1

I finally get to the point in my life where I feel I have everything figured out. At twenty-eight-years-old, I'm on top of my world at work. My finance company pays me pretty well, and all I have to do is find companies for them to buy up and chop down. I love what I do. Making six figures was my initial goal, but I can actually see myself getting to the seven-figure mark if I stick to the plan when I get older. My years at the University of Wisconsin have paid off. Funny part is my major was agriculture. I thought I wanted to be a farmer, but then the numbers made more sense in the finance department. I purchased my first home already and got a great deal on a place by the lake in Chicago. Never considered myself a suburban guy, but my house feels like I'm living the suburban life. It's a little too much house for me and my puppy, Maxine—a four bedroom, two-story colonial— but my client got me a steal for the price.

I have given myself to the world. I volunteer time at foster homes and mentor the kids. I even have my own foundation called Life's Love that helps kids without families get ahead in life. I teamed up with Big Brothers Big Sisters of America and have changed the lives of a lot of kids. My fortunate life allows me the opportunities to do well financially and I feel a duty to give back. I have traveled across the U.S. for work and seen the beauty in the country (and the ugly, for that matter). My hopes are to travel outside the country soon to see the rest of the world.

I'm the youngest of three brothers. Most in the family would say I'm the loudest, that I was a mistake, but I would just say they're jealous because Mom loves me most. I hope. I have had a few girlfriends here and there but nothing too serious. Nothing has panned out to the point of marriage and kids, though I'm not even sure I want any of that. I'm a solo rider and like being by myself, and I'm not sure how it will change. I was very respectful to all the girls in my past and would consider myself a good catch. If you ask all my ex-girlfriends, they would say I'm afraid of commitment. I just haven't found the one yet. I'm not even sure I know what love is.

I'm rambling on, talking about nothing, because I'm searching my soul for answers. I'm sitting in front of my Grandfather Charlie's house, who just passed away. I feel like I just lost a friend and a mentor who I didn't get enough time with. I'm so lost for words; things just feel off and strange things have been happening to me. To make the weight heavier, he left the house to me. Only to me. I'm his youngest grandson and I wasn't the closest to him out of all the kids. Even my family is confused, and my dad is hurt his father didn't leave it to him. I spent a lot of time with Grandpa Charlie, but it was just recently after chasing my dreams, and I was, by far, not the favorite. It was such a shock that I even tried to give it to the family, but in his will he prevented anyone but me from having it first.

I feel horrible because he made me promise to keep the legacy of the house in the family. I figured the only reason he left the house to me was because he knew I could afford to do what's best for the family. Maybe he figured I could invest in it or something. I'm not sure; I didn't get a lot of answers before he died. I still help out some in the family financially, so maybe he wanted me to turn it into a home for those down-and-out in life? Still guessing.

Charlie was a smart man and had a good grasp on life, so I'm trying to figure his angle in leaving me the house. There has to be a reason. My family has chastised me because they think I got close to him and got in his head before he died. It's just confusing because they know I didn't want the house and, if anything, I'm just following the patriarch of the family's wish. I spent the last year just getting to know Charlie so I could know the family history line and know where we come from. He was such a good soul; there was something different about him, something magical I couldn't explain. He once told me I was the only one that could feel and see that power. He would always look at me like he wanted to say something but couldn't just yet. Or didn't know what to say or how to say it. It was like he was from another planet or lived a different life before here. He seemed to be waiting for the next phase in life or something to happen that never did.

The last few conversations I had with Grandpa, he told me, "You have love in your heart, Grandson. I can feel it; you have something that is magical in you. You don't know this yet, Trev, but you will finish a legacy and finish a lineage that was supposed to start years ago. You are one of God's angels. Unfortunately, back in my day, the world wasn't ready for a love like my queen and I. I won't go into any details because it would be disrespectful to your Grandma Betty and the world she gave me with you and your siblings. I will say, though, you should know that I had a different life before you, before it was forced to end. You don't know a lot about my time during the war, because there were some tough things and I choose not to remember those, but I left an angel, a treasure that I should have never left. I'm truly hoping that when I die you find that treasure and she shows the way to fulfill your destiny. I know you will find her because it's written in your lifeline. Please promise me one thing.

Promise to tell her that I never stopped loving her. I had to do what I thought was best at the time, and I had seen too much lost already, so I made the choice to get on that train. But she always held a spot in my heart. Promise that if she is still alive she hears that. Please, promise me, Trev!"

Of course I made my promise and plan to keep it. I just don't know how and, to be honest, I just think he was being a little crazy before he died. That was one of our last conversations. That was the first time he had made mention of the woman I saw in my flash. Weird things have been happening to me, and I'm just chalking it up to Charlie's death and me being tired. I'm a realist and don't believe in all the spiritual stuff, so this Grandpa Charlie I saw towards the end … I just assumed he was losing his mind as he got older. He never really talked about his time during the war, so it made his comments about the mystery woman even more far-fetched. The few times he did talk about the war, it wasn't a pretty picture. It's funny, I got good grades in history class. I was so enamored with World War II because of Granddad that I wanted to know more about what he went through. I learned so much; it felt like I was supposed to.

I'm back to reality at my Grandpa Charlie's house again. It's in the middle of nowhere Illinois in a city called Rockford. Not sure, other than the resale value, why my family would think I would want this home—it's nothing compared to my downtown flat. Aside from being in the middle of nowhere, it's old and needs a lot of updating. It's just plain rusty. A few miles off I-90, it's about a two-hour drive away from my home downtown. The house is in such an old town that there are only a few stores on a strip of their town they call downtown. A liquor store, a video shop, a Subway, and a dollar store make up the strip of shops in town. Shoot, along this line of stores there is only one stop light. A trip to Walmart, which is a few miles away, is the way the town gets their home goods. The town reminds me of an old western movie.

At least Charlie kept everything working and up to date. The foundation, like the roof, the basement, and the walls, are all in great condition so the resale value should be good when it comes that time. The backyard is nice because one of Grandpa's hobbies was gardening. Not sure where this black man got a green thumb from, but he loved his homegrown veggies and fruits. He had everything growing back here, from tomatoes to strawberries. He had little greenhouses spread out throughout the big one-acre backyard. As I look at his growth in the backyard, he must not have known a heart attack was going to take his life; the strawberries are almost ripe for the picking. No doubt he knew his death was close because he updated his will a year ago, about the time I met him for that Monopoly game. Not sure where he got the green thumb from, being that our family was raised in the city and I never saw anyone with a garden. Again, no question he knew something was close because you don't update your will for no reason. Not a coincidence.

As I sit here looking at this vast garden, I'm tempted to just to say the hell with it and leave it to the family to figure out, but something inside me tells me I should follow Charlie's last wishes. Plus, I have to find out why he left me, and only me, the house. I'm confused at what the right thing to do would be.

After collecting all the veggies and fruits I could to take home, it's time for me to comb through the house and wrap up the paperwork and documents. He basically left everything as is. Call me crazy, but I swear the coffee mug I put away is still warm from coffee. One side of me feels like he knew it was coming, the other side of me looks at the house the way it was left and wonders if was he ready go. I spend the majority of the rest of the day organizing the house and getting all the mail, documents, bills, and the like in order. It feels weird putting all of his stuff in boxes ready for storage. Artwork and drawings and little doodles he left around the house all going to storage.

The night falls quickly as I lose track of time. The house actually feels nice at night. You can feel the breeze from the lake and the night sky is clear as ever from here. At night I get a feel of what Grandpa used to love about this house. I'm just about done wrapping everything up, and as I put the last few boxes in the car, I notice a light on in the attic. I start to leave anyway, but wonder why there would be a light on in the attic. I turn off the car when the thought comes across my mind that the only way up to the attic was with a ladder, so how did that light get on? It would have been a miracle if Charlie was the last one up there, because he would never had made it up the ladder with his old butt. His back and knees wouldn't even let him get to the first steps. My next thought made me walk back. *Who needed to check the attic anyway?* I wonder. *I'm sure there's nothing up there. All of Charlie's belongings are in the basement anyway.*

My curiosity got the best of me. I grab the ladder and make my way up. I get to the top where the door is and try pushing through, but it's stuck. After a few tugs and a struggle it finally budges open. I thought something was on top of the door, but it's just heavy and old. Even more of a mystery of how Grandpa got up here, or whoever was up here.

The attic is big and bright and unfinished, completely empty other than a big box sitting in the middle of the floor. I look around as I walk in, trying to figure out how this light got on. Something feels off in here. On the side of the dusty old box in big black letters is a phrase that reads, "My Dear Love Kasia."

I open up the box and discover a pile of old letters. I guess I thought I would open up the box and find some long-lost treasure or something. Maybe cash, or maybe some birth pictures, or something a little more dramatic. Shoot, Grandpa mentioned something about a treasure he left in Europe, so I thought there would maybe be a treasure map or something. Nope, dusty old letters. There has to be at least twenty to thirty letters here. All of the envelopes have writing on them that reads, "To my love Charlie." I pick up one of the letters that reads "My *Chanuntka*" on it. I pulled it open to read a little ...

My dear Chanuntka,

> *It has been too long that I have seen your face. Yes, a few weeks but still. These letters allow me to still feel close to you when they send you away on missions. Miss your chocolate-brown skin; it reminds me of my morning coffee. Maybe it's the sinfulness in our relationship that turns me on about your skin tone. I wanted to apologize that you had to run away and hide when some of the elders came into town. I wished we lived in a time where our relationship would be seen as right, but unfortunately our love remains a secret. It's a shame because I saw how much you and my father got along and if it wasn't for my stubborn culture, you two would get along so well. I am praying for the day when the war is completely over, your military duties are over, and we can possibly find a country or a nation that will accept our love ...*

I put the letter down for a second, because I didn't feel too good. Not sure if I'm just tired from the day or maybe Charlie's death has me more emotional than I thought. I feel something pulling me as I read this letter. I can't explain it. I'm confused at the gravity pull of this letter, or maybe the gravity of what this letter means if this is really Charlie's. It just hit me like a bag of bricks of what was going on here. Every time I go back to read it, my heart starts pounding, I lose my breath, and I start sweating. I keep getting these flashes in my head of some woman and my Grandpa Charlie. Another flash and I can see them kissing passionately. Another flash and it's Charlie riding on a horse into a flash of light.

I drop the letter and the sound of the letter hitting the floor brings me back to reality. I'm now in a full sweat. I check my watch and only one minute has gone by, though it felt like an hour. I pick up the letter again and look at the back. It's dated January 10, 1946. My memory of my history class is pretty hazy, but I'm pretty sure that was a few months after World War II was over. Again, the few times Charlie talked about the war it was about the gruesome atrocities he saw. He never mentioned the side stories, and this would have been a pretty big side story.

I sit there for a second trying to get myself together. It feels like I have been working out. I look over at the box and there is this gravitational pull, pulling me towards the letters. It's like the box is talking to me. I stand up and walk over to the box; for such an old, dusty box it feels so powerful. The closer I get to the box the faster my heart rate gets. I pull out another letter and the date reads June 1945. I think it's old and smudged. Again, my details on the war are slim, but I believe that's the summer when the rescue efforts of the war were in full force and the war was coming to an end. I try reading a little …

Dear Charlie,

I hope this finds you and I hope this is how you spell your name. You told me where you were staying, but I know they move you around a lot so I really hope this reaches you. Also my English is so bad. I have been studying but it is the British English, so I am learning and your accent was hard to understand sometimes.

But I am writing to you because I understand good souls and from the moment you walked into my nursing tent our first meeting was nothing short of magic …

Suddenly, the room goes dark and I black out. Then a loud boom and a flash go off and I'm in a bright ray of light. I can't tell what's going on, but it feels like I'm falling. My heart rate spikes to the point where it feels like my chest is going to explode. I'm trying to catch my breath, but it feels like the harder I try the harder it gets to breathe. Right when it feels like I'm about to drown, another flash goes off and I sit up, catching my breath. When I finally get myself together I realize I'm no longer in my grandpa's attic. I'm sitting outside some kind of tent. It looks like a big army medical tent. I must be dreaming but again it feels so real. I damn near fall out of my pants when a man on a horse comes zipping by my face. I fall over into the mud as another two men follow. I wave my hand in front of the two men but they don't react; they can't see me. Then in slow motion as I see a younger version of my Grandpa Charlie jumping off a horse and walking right at me. He looks like a young Will Smith, but darker. He walks right through me as he heads for the tent.

I take a look around and judging by the clothes I'm in some time warp or something. Charlie is in his army fatigues as he leads the two men into the tent. My mind is trying to grasp what's going on here. I'm sure it's a dream but I'm alert and it feels so real for some reason. Instincts and reflexes make me reach out and say something to Grandpa but he doesn't even flinch. Actually no one does. No one can see or hear me. I try yelling and screaming and jumping but no one reacts. I follow Charlie into the tent and try waving my hand in front of his face. He stops like I got his attention but when I talk he stares right through me. I turn around to see what he's staring at, and her beauty hits me as hard as it probably hit Charlie. There was that mystery woman I saw in my vision that day with Grandpa. She is so beautiful, regal almost. I could see my grandpa lost in her hazel eyes as everyone in the room gets lost in them, staring at each other. She stands confident and in control of the room. Her hair is so long, tied in a braid; the color of her hair is golden brown. I'm not sure if anyone else could see it, but she has a golden glow around her. I come back to whatever reality I'm in when Charlie clears his throat to introduce himself.

"We can stare at each other all day, sir, but these people urgently need help," she speaks with such confidence.

"My apologies, ma'am, but I'm awestruck by your beauty. My name is Charles." He reaches out his hand, as she stares him up and down like she's sizing him up. She doesn't return the handshake.

"Okay, Charles, as you can see this is no place and no time to admire beauty. These people are starving to death and face horrible things. They want nothing more than to get to their families and find some type of normalcy in their lives, whatever that may be. So while you take the time to admire beauty they are missing out on valuable time." If the hands on the hips aren't indicators of how in control she is, then it's definitely a sign of the attitude.

"Well, ma'am, before I prove your theory wrong, I would at least like to know your name." Charlie's not intimidated by her zest.

"Sir, you are borderline crossing boundaries here, and I'm not sure my name matters because most likely I will never see you again … it's how war works, you know."

"Well, while you sit here on your pedestal as if you've done something noble, I've spent the last few months moving dead bodies into ditches and watching mothers search for their deceased kids. I've seen body parts strewn across a field. I have carried three people to safety who I thought were children but were just starving adults. We're from a group called the Liberators and we risk our lives to rescue others, all while bullets are flying at our heads. Let me tell you that doesn't depress me; instead, it gives me my calling of helping people. After I rescued that first person, I committed the rest of my time to helping get people their lives back. Some of the atrocities that I've seen over the last few months … this world is a dark place. Do you know what it's like to let bullets fly past your face and risk your life for someone you just met and, like you said, will never see again? So excuse me for taking a second to admire beauty when for the last few months I've seen nothing but hell …" He's almost in tears. "So excuse me, ma'am."

Everyone in the tent sits in silence. I feel gratefulness from some of the survivors sitting in their beds. I scream hello again just to make sure no one could see me or hear me. This is too detailed and too long to be a dream. I wish I knew exactly where we are and how I got here. The room remains silent as everyone sizes each other up. Charlie looks so good. I always figured him to be a confident guy but this personality is superhero confidence. Plus, Charlie was always quiet, and this is the most I've ever heard him talk. He's just a different person. The family always pegged him for quiet Grandpa Charlie, just a laid back, chill kind of guy, but this doesn't seem like the Charlie the family knew.

He shrugs his shoulders and looks at the two soldiers who appear like they have been through hell. The gentlemen all look around at the survivors in the beds. There are about ten beds total and a few of them have two people in them. They all look on the brink of death. There are only a few ladies in the tent to help all these people. The room seems desperate, but Charlie picks spirits up a little just with his love and his confidence to help.

"Kasia," the woman says softly. Her strong demeanor is now shaken, it seems.

"I am sorry, ma'am. What did you say?" It's so unreal to hear Charlie talk – well, the younger version of him talking.

"My name is Kasia. My real name is Katarzyna Romanowski, but my friends and family simply call me Kasia. It's easier to pronounce." She gives a little curtsy, as a nice to meet you. She is drop dead gorgeous even in her dirty nurse's outfit.

"Okay, Kasia. Wow, a name as pretty as the person. Ma'am, let me apologize for my rudeness. As you know now, I'm Charlie. I'm sergeant in command of this group here. I'm from the Liberators group, secondary unit Tuskegee group, and we are coming from Italy. Our mission is to find survivors and then help the situation become established. Our coordinates are here, and we are to keep tight until further notice. Judging by the set-up here, you either didn't know we were coming or something changed."

"Yes, you are correct. Things have changed. I was sent in to help from a hospital in town. I'm not supposed to be here, but I'm here to help. I have no idea who's in charge or what the plan is. I just came here a few days ago and started treating people. No time to ask questions when people are dying. Whatever the original plan was or whoever was in charge before me just left. I was told by a preceding officer there was a dire need somewhere else that required more resources. I assumed he felt things were under control here … but obviously not." She seems exhausted.

"Ma'am, I'm sorry you are in this predicament. How can we help stabilize the situation?"

"Excuse me?" She appears confused. I'm squinting trying to understand every word, but her accent is very strong. It's either Russian or Polish or some Slovakian language. It sounds like Polish; I'm from Chicago and I hear a lot of Polish.

"Well, ma'am – Kasia – it has been a long trip getting here. I have lost a few of my men on the way here. Our efforts were to save as many people as possible, and it seems you still have a volatile situation here. I've only been taught to fix what is in front of me. It will benefit my men anyway; we need a space to reset camp, and you need manpower. This camp and camp area look like they need updating. My last word from my higher-ups was that help will arrive, hopefully, in five to six days. That is, if they didn't forget about us. So that means you have five to six days of help. Where would you like my men to start?"

Kasia stands there and contemplates for a second as she looks around. "Well, our water sources have been compromised, and this tent is over capacity. We have another tent this big but haven't had the manpower to put it up. It's been very cold and we need a room or area that has a source of heat, and this tent has holes in it … that is just for starters." For such a young girl, she's so in control of herself and situation. I can tell she's been thrust into this situation, yet she seems strong.

"Well, you heard her, gentlemen. Let's get to work." He waves his hand and a few of the soldiers start running around.

"Can I see you outside for a moment, Mr. Charles?"

"Gentlemen, get all the jobs done this young lady asked for. Private John, you will help the other nurse with whatever she needs." Kasia and Charlie make their way outside the tent and I follow; the heavy plastic zip door flies right through me. Everything feels so real, but I'm brought back to this reality when a soldier runs right through my body. Grandpa Charlie stands at the edge of the tent out of sight where no one can see them. Kasia walks around Charlie and looks him up and down. It's like she's about to interrogate him. She looks confused, sad, and angry all at the same time. I'm not sure; I can't read her.

13

"Charlie, sir ... I appreciate your help, but I must be honest with you, I don't trust anybody and we have had visitors before and they all have taken advantage. Every time we get sucked dry of supplies, and each time we take a hit it gets harder and harder to hang on. Our food supply is very low, people are very sick. This isn't a rest stop for the weak and ..."

"Kasia, please ease your heart. It's been a long trip. I've seen nothing but death and hatred. I want nothing more than to ease the situation you are in, and I hope after our few days here you are better off than when we arrived. I promise you that."

Charlie grabs her hand to go in for a handshake, but the long stare turns into a hug that seems much needed. She begins to say something, but a blast and a bright flash go off, and I fall from the sky all of a sudden. My heart rate spikes and my breaths start getting heavier as the bright lights start to go black. Now I feel like I'm falling into a black hole. I can breathe, but right when I feel I'm about to drown I spike back up, gasping for air. I'm back in the attic, lying on my back in a full sweat with the letter sitting on my chest ...

... and I knew as I held your hand that first day in the tent something special was going to happen between us. I look forward to seeing you again. I just feel different around you.

Sincerely,
Kasia

I quickly check my watch as the attic light flickers wildly. Only five minutes have passed, but it feels like I was away for at least two hours. Actually, I'm positive that had to be more than two hours. I look at the old box of letters and feel this magical pull. What is happening?

Chapter 2

I felt like I was in a drug haze the whole next day. I'm a very smart man I like to believe I've gotten far in life due to my intellect, but sometimes in life there are unexplainable things and I'm smart enough to know that wasn't a dream. Moments like this you would talk to a friend or someone who might understand, but I'm afraid I made a name for myself as a realist amongst my friends and family, and everyone would think I was crazy, so I can't say anything to anyone. I wish I could call Charlie and ask him what the hell is going on here. I almost called my Grandma Betty but realized the gravity of what I would have to ask her, so I declined to go that route. To think when I was driving to Charlie's house before the start of the weekend I was going over ways in my head to get rid of it. Now, my heart spikes just thinking of the promises he wanted me to make before he died. I always considered myself to be spiritual, not a church or religious thing, but I consider myself spiritual. But this is different; I'm actually seeing spirits. This is magic, which I don't believe in, and I'm so lost I'm questioning my existence.

The weekend flies by and it's back to work Monday, of course. But my haze over the weekend carries over into work, and I'm such a mess I don't get much work done—so much so my boss sends me home and says I don't seem like myself. I've never been sent home from work before. I must look like death. I fought to stay since I've been doing so well, but she insisted I'd been working hard and I should finish up today and tomorrow at home. I hope I didn't make a mistake or something. I just need to go home, take a nap, and relax. Maybe I need to find someone to talk to. I'm going to grab some pizza and beer and watch the Sox game, and I can finish the work tomorrow.

I'm so caught up in my thoughts on the day that before I realize it I'm halfway to Rockford and my Grandpa Charlie's house. There's a pull that I can't fight. The tired, sleepy lostness exchanges for a curiosity that I've never felt before. I should go get some work done, but I feel like I wouldn't be able to focus on work until I scratch this itch. Just a few weeks ago I still needed Google Maps to get to Charlie's house, but like a zombie I drive right up to it without directions. I pull up to the house and it seems different, almost like it was renovated a little. I look up and notice the attic light is on. I'm positive I turned it off when I left last time. Sure of it. Unless there's some sort of squatter here, there must be some sort of mechanical glitch or something up there. Or it could be just a part of me losing my mind. I swear the last time I was here the gravel was falling apart in the driveway, with cracks and holes in the lot. But now I'm met with a freshly paved lot leading into the garage. Now, the dead roots are gone and there's detailed landscaping bringing together the front door to the garage opening. The stairway leading up to the door wasn't just updated, it's upgraded with in-the-ground lighting and polished wood railings that wrap around the front porch. The porch that wasn't there yesterday is fully furnished with a nice couch set and another set of custom lighting. There are brand new windows shutters with wood trim, and the old coverings have been removed, and I'm sure that adds a tone of light into the house. I'm questioning my memory when the tree in the front is more to the side of the house now. What used to be a hill of dead grass is now a flat plain of freshly cut commercial grass, like for golfing. The attic window has been replaced by a skylight. There are new roof shingles, new gutters, new siding … shoot, even new trash cans on the side of the garage. It seems like a new house. I have to check the address again just to make sure I came to the right place.

I stand there in shock in front of the house, looking around to see if anyone's playing a trick on me or if someone is standing with a video camera, but the only image I get is an old lady sitting in front of her house across the way. She just waves and smiles. *She had to see something*, I think. There's no way all this work was done over the weekend without anyone seeing anything.

I finally make my way to the door, which now matches the decor of the rest of the landscaping. Gone are those old, big, white double doors with the old gold door handles, replaced with a big wooden cathedral door that matches the wood trim on the windows. I close my eyes before opening the door, expecting something different or new; instead, when I open my eyes I'm greeted with the same old dusty house that I came to growing up – its good old self. Wonder what Grandpa would think of the new look in front of the house? I make my way up to the attic almost as if I'm running. For a dusty old box, it sure feels magnetic. Part of my pull is I'm so interested in this history of Grandpa, and because he didn't say anything to anyone about it or at least mention to me why he left me in charge of this.

As I reach the attic I don't know where to start, or should I say restart. My heart rate starts racing again and I'm getting anxious. Oh damn, who am I kidding? Why am I scared? Nothing happened to me last time, other than feeling like I was going to drown. I close my eyes and grab a random letter. It's dated 1945, but I can't read the month or day because it's water damaged. I open it up and anxiety starts kicking in as I start reading …

My dear love Chanuntka,

My heart broke when I heard you had to go to Italy to get your stay approved. It just takes possible time away from seeing you. To answer your question you asked me the other day, I must start by saying I felt in love with you from the day you walked into the tent. You have something that I felt from day one that captured me. Your question, though, was what was my favorite moment in the months we've been seeing each other? I wanted to wait to tell you my favorite moment and write it to you so you can have something to remember me by and something to look forward to reading on your trip. I want you and hope you miss me as much as I miss you and your presence. So now, my favorite moment of our time together so far was when ...

A flash hit me so hard I feel like I got punched in the face. Everything goes bright white. I can't even open my eyes. I black out but I'm aware of my surroundings somehow. I was falling again and the bright light turned into complete darkness. My heart rate is at the max and I feel my breath getting shorter and shorter. Right when I feel like I'm going to explode and lose my breath, I snap out of it, searching for air. After catching my breath, I jump up, look around, and I'm at some farm in the middle of the forest. There's nothing else in sight for miles, just brush and trees, tall, amazing forest trees. In the middle of it all is an old wooden farm-like home, very small and modest. I can smell the wood chips and sheep, and I can feel the farm for some reason. The snow falls heavy, and I'm even able to catch a snowflake on my tongue. I'm dressed in my pajamas yet I don't feel cold. My guess is I'm either in Poland or Ukraine.

I'm broken out of my thoughts when I see my Grandpa Charlie walk past me into the cabin. Following him into the cabin I can smell the fire and what smells like firewood. I can also smell the aroma of fresh bread. This place is so peaceful and serene; I feel such a calmness here. As I follow Charlie past the cabin around the bend over a hill behind a set of trees, I'm surprised to see three small wooden houses a few hundred yards apart. Two of the houses are empty but had small fires going in the middle of them. The biggest house of the three is lit up like there's a party going inside as a big cloud of smoke pours out from the chimney. It seems as though Grandpa is a little nervous as I follow him into the big farm house.

As he walks through the door I walk through the side wall. I look at my body as I walk through the woods. It's a funny feeling, like it's scratching me. I could get used to this reality. I stop in my tracks as I see ten people or so all sitting around a table singing a song. I giggle a little because my reaction is the same as Charlie's, surprised at all the people he obviously doesn't know. He stands there as everyone stops singing and just stares at him. It's at least ten seconds before that familiar face of Kasia's comes over to greet us—oops, I mean to greet Charlie. Still getting used to this, I guess. This woman is so regal – it's amazing how she captures the room. I feel a connection to her. I wonder why. Her smile says she's extremely happy to see Charlie; she runs up and embraces him in a hug as the room watches. There are looks of hate or surprise, I can't tell which, but just then my grandad screams out "*Dzien dobry!*" and triumphantly raises his hands in the air with a big smile. The whole room screams back and cheers in unison. I don't know what he just said, but it felt like "What's up, everyone?"

The group continues to sing as Charlie grabs—the angel, I will call her—Kasia and starts to dance. The smile and look on my grandad's face says it all; he's so happy and comfortable. I now know we're in Poland because I hear Charlie whisper into her ear he's in love with Poland and the culture. They party like there's no tomorrow. Charlie dances and takes shots of moonshine—at least that's what it looks like. Now, I can smell the stench of vodka. I'm actually shocked because my dad told me Grandpa Charlie didn't drink. After about an hour or two of spirits and hanging out, I see Kasia ask Charlie to step outside. It's freezing outside and I'm not sure what could be so important. They hug and kiss as they stumble and walk to the small cabin next door. A candle and the cooking fire pit light the room. Everything seems to slow down. As they embrace and sit down with each other, there's a light glow that circles them. They don't move for a few moments and just stare at each other. I can hear a humming, but it feels like it's music.

"My sweet *Chanuntka*, thank you so much for all you have done to help my family and this farm. Even the elders are grateful, I'm sure of it," she says, rubbing his face.

"It's the least I can do."

"No, Charlie, you went above and beyond. You had your soldiers help fix up my family cabins. It was beyond needed. I mean, new water system, fixing the roofs, upgrading the floors, all the while being a gentleman about it with my community. I'm sure that all of this is against your military rules and you can get in trouble ..."

"Ah, I'm always in trouble anyway so ..."

"Please let me finish, Charlie. I know at first my family was cold to you, but you kept that smile and charm and won them over in weeks. Even though you can't understand one word they are saying, you've even managed to get my uncle to like you. The Polish language is tough but you hold that positivity. If you were to leave and I were never to see you again, the impact of what you did for the farm, even keeping my family's spirits up, will last a lifetime. Mr. Charlie Johnson, I'm trying to tell you that you're a great man."

He picks her up and puts her on his lap. She leans into his shoulder.

"I haven't had the chance to tell you why I joined the U.S. Army. I was running. I felt like nothing could be worse than the atrocities America was doing to my people. Being black in America right now is like walking around with a target on your back. The first moment we kicked the door down to one of those camps, I realized how good I had it back at home. I felt I had a weak heart back home because I cared too much. I felt the same weakness when I walked some of the survivors out of one of the camps. I automatically started to care too much, like I was responsible for saving them. The moment I saw you in the tent I knew I cared deeply for you. I care too much already, but this feeling was different. I already felt my heart tug differently. When we hugged outside the tent, after just meeting moments before, I knew this was different. What I'm trying to say is, Katarzyna Romanowski, you are a special woman. And I'm falling in love with you."

"What?" Her demeanor stiffened a little.

"Look, I'm barely out of my teens, so what do I know about love? But I know whatever I'm feeling has to be love. You told me I was out of line and you were right, but I wasn't acting like myself and it was you who made me this way. You made me lose who I am, and I love the person you made me become. I'm not sure what my military future holds with the war still in limbo. I don't know where my future will take me, but it makes me nervous now because whatever the option is it takes me from you. So yes, I love you."

Kasia turns herself on his lap to face him. She softly kisses him on the forehead and takes off her blouse. She starts to speak, but a bright flash goes off. My heart rate spikes again and I black out. I'm falling and it's hard to breathe. I smack right into the ground and finally get my breath back. When the dust settles, I'm back in the attic at Charlie's house. The light flickers on and off as the letter I'm reading falls onto my forehead …

I knew I was falling in love with you before that night. But that was my favorite moment of ours because it confirmed my love and my heart was yours as yours was mine. Until next time, my love.

> *Sincerely,*
> *Kasia*

Chapter 3

I can't sleep. I'm so confused. I have so many questions, not to mention the fact that I'm questioning my reality. I can tell what happened really happened, but it brings up so many questions. The obvious one in my head is *why me?* Then I think about my family matriarch, my Grandma Betty. At what point did Charlie meet her and does she know about this Kasia woman? My grandma's still grieving her husband, so it's not like I can ask her. Not sure I would ask even if she wasn't grieving. Does anyone in the family know about his time overseas? The love I felt and saw in those letters is real. Something must have happened, but how do I find out more? If I try to match the dates up when Charlie and Betty met and the end of the war World War II, there's a two year gap. I haven't put the letters in order yet, but the ones I grabbed I believe were dated two years after the war ended, so there would be a little overlap from him coming home and receiving letters to when he met Betty. At least this is all according to the information left by Charlie. I'm beginning to understand another reason why he didn't talk about the war.

Still, this comes back to *why me?* Why am I reliving all of Charlie's memories? I have to talk to someone, but who? Then there's the other side of this: the mysterious woman named Kasia. I wouldn't even know where to begin to investigate. I'm not sure there would be a point, because it would be like finding a needle in a haystack. I would have to get lucky. Even if she was alive, what do I say to her? "Hey, I'm Trevor and I'm your ex-boyfriend's grandson, you know, the one from the war." I guess the only thing she could answer is some of the questions about Charlie.

Let's not talk about the elephant in the room, which is me falling back in time inside these letters and magical things happening to the house. I feel different. Something's happening to me, but I don't what it is. There's a reason for this and I have to figure it out. I'll have to go back and organize the letters by date, get a timeline, and put the whole story together. Then maybe it will give me some answers. Then I can do some research and figure things out. It's the only thing on my mind right now. I can hear my grandpa screaming at me to find her and keep my promise.

"Find her, Trevor. She will answer all your questions."

Chapter 4

I make plans to go stay the weekend at Grandpa Charlie's house and just dive in and finish the letters. Before that, I'm planning to get together with my family, which we do once a month on a Thursday, at my uncle's house. The tradition is we watch whatever game is going to be on that day, whether it's the Bears, Cubs, Bulls, or White Sox. We gather as a family and each time someone brings food. Tonight, I'm getting some steaks and fish catered to the house. One of my clients owns a catering business and was nice enough to set me up for the occasion. I used to hate these forced get-togethers, but after college I had a different perspective. I now look forward to seeing the family and getting updates from everyone. Family is worth all life. Nothing like sitting watching my family flow. There's always a fight for the video games amongst my nephews.

Being the youngest of the three boys, and much younger than the other two, gives me a perspective on what to do in life and what not to do in life. I'm twenty-eight; next up is Tray and he's thirty-two. He's a stand-up guy, married with two kids, and is a manager at a UPS warehouse. He's also a good dad, church-going, and just does everything right. I'm sure my parents want me to be like him, personality-wise. I would guess I'm the closest with him. He rides me a lot, says I'm the family favorite, but he always jabs me in good humor. Then there is my brother Tony. He is thirty-six and divorced with one child. He got married out of high school and they had my niece when they were very young. It just never materialized into a good relationship. I love my niece Taylor; she sneaks and hangs out at my downtown home sometimes to get away from her dad. My parents named us all with the letter T as the first letter of our names. It's me, Trevor, Tray, and Tony, and this is in honor of my father Tom. My mother's name is Pamela. This is the gist of my family. There are friends and distant cousins that stop by for the occasional Thursday get-togethers, but the core group is my brothers, Mom, and Dad.

This Thursday's a little different than all the others because this is the first without Grandpa Charlie. I thought it would be somber, but instead we celebrate him, laugh about his best jokes, and shed tears over his memory. Everyone gets up and tells their favorite memory of Charlie. Even one of my little cousins has something to say. Everyone says he was just plain old school and mellow and made everyone feel important. There's so much gratitude in the room. The best speech of the night comes from my Grandma Betty, who stands up out of her wheelchair to tell funny stories about her late husband. She's very sharp and witty for ninety-six-years-old, a jokester actually. She's obviously down but she's putting on a good face for everyone. Wonder if she still has the same will to live? Damn.

As I'm lost in my thoughts staring at Betty, I see Kasia's face flash and merge with my grandma's. I stood up and spilled my drink, causing everyone to look at me. I apologize as I run to clean everything up. I try shaking it, but when I look back at Betty, Kasia's face flashes again. My mind races back to all the questions as I watch my grandma sit back down gingerly in her wheelchair. At one point when we sit down for dinner, Kasia appears, sitting next to Betty at the table as if she's going to get a plate. I have to get off the table, run to the bathroom, and throw water on my face. I'm getting up to dry my face and fall over the toilet when I see Kasia's reflection right behind mine in the bathroom mirror. Once I gather myself, I still see Kasia there in the reflection and she just smiles at me. I need to get my shit together.

Time warps and letters, and now I'm seeing a freaking ghost. What the hell is wrong with me? I'm shaken back to reality when my nephew knocks on the door screaming he needs to go pee. The night goes on and starts to settle down. It's time for my Grandma Betty to go lay down; it's way past her bedtime. I jump at the bid to walk her to her room. Everyone looks at me like I'm crazy because I've never done it before. I've always been nervous about that, because while I developed a late relationship with Charlie, I could never figure Grandma Betty out. Not to mention there's medicine and a procedure that needs to be done before she retires, and I always ran from the responsibility. I can see the surprised look on my dad's face. He whispers the words, "Are you okay?" I can see a smile on his face as I walk his mom through the door.

Once we are in the room, I sit her down in her chair. She gives me a puzzled look. Maybe she's confused as to why after all this time I'm doing this. To be honest I don't know either. Maybe she can give me some insight on Charlie. She looks like she wants to say something but doesn't know how to say it.

"You seem like you're searching for answers, my grandson. You're still a little lost and down since Charlie passed, huh?" Damn, she's so sharp at that young age of ninety-six. I guess I'm not hiding my thoughts at all. I don't know where to start or what to ask. I'm afraid to ask the wrong thing.

"How did you and Grandpa meet?" is all I can muster up. I figure maybe it can give me insight on what Charlie was like when he came back.

"Honey, we were high school sweethearts." The shocked look on my face must have startled her because she jumps a little. High school sweethearts?! Damn, wasn't expecting that. That explains why no one could know about the mysterious woman Kasia. This is not just about Charlie's time overseas. Do I call him a cheater or a cheater of life? I feel conflicted. He never struck me as that guy, but we all have skeletons in the closet. Why didn't Charlie mention anything to me about that? I'm sure no one in the family would think that. I actually don't believe it; there has to be an explanation. I had questions coming into tonight, and now I will for sure have many more. I'm starting to feel like I won't get any answers from my family.

"Wow, Grandma, that's great. Do you have a favorite memory of him for just you two?" I ask as I get my mind together and try to process things.

"There are so many, Trevor. Your grandad was a great man. I wouldn't be able to narrow it down. I would just say his biggest trait was he gave himself to others. I don't mean just being a nice guy or helping a little, I mean he gave himself to others and always felt like he had to save someone. He had to make people smile in bad moments, because he wanted people to feel good when they were down. He was a savior. I can't explain it, but my Charlie had a magical presence about him. Did you know during his time in the war his mission was to rescue people?"

I pause for a second because I have to catch myself from saying, *Yeah, I saw it in a vision from a letter.* "Yeah, Grandma, he told me stories about the people he saved. It was a terrible time in human history."

I just stare at her for a moment as she gazes off in memory. I'm sure Charlie didn't give her the whole story—not that he could have or should have, now that I think about it. One thing my grandma says strikes a chord: she mentioned that Grandpa was magical and she couldn't explain it. There's been nothing but magical things happening to me since his death. There's so much unexplained, but the family seems content with the Charlie they know or knew. They haven't seen the letters like me. I'm hit with a weight: *I'll have to bury the secret with me as Charlie went to the grave with it.*

"Grandma Betty, I know you're tired so I'm going to go, but I have one more question."

"Sure, honey, this is so lovely. Your grandad would love you putting me to bed like this, so I'm enjoying your stay." She holds my hand and all of a sudden for some reason I feel like crying.

"Grandma, why did Charlie leave the house to me? There are so many family members that could have used the house, but he chooses his youngest grandson. It doesn't make sense. The family thinks I had something to do with it, and I'm losing sleep over it. I was hoping he said something to you or at least gave an explanation … something." I can feel her squeeze tighter.

"I mentioned your grandpa had a magical side about him. Well, it was a double-edged sword, honey, because I could never figure him out 100 percent. He would say things like his life wasn't his and he was sent down from heaven to save people and spread love. He used to say this world just wasn't ready for a spirit like his. He never told me what happened, but he said something happened to him before he returned from the war that stole his soul and ripped him apart. He mentioned that it showed him that the world was not ready for a spirit or a love like his. He never spoke a word of it once we got married, out of respect for me and our marriage. He kept that promise of not talking about it our whole life together, until about a year ago when he found out he was sick. I believe he'd just seen you the day before; you visited him to play a game or something. He woke up that next morning like I had seen him for the first time when we first got married. He was smiling from ear to ear, happier than I had seen in a long time.

"When I asked Charlie what was going on, he told me that you were going to get the house when he dies because you are the only one in the family that has his soul, that carries a special trait. He swore you would fulfill some destiny that he couldn't. He said he saw a sign that night before that told him it was his time to die and your time to become who you're supposed to be. He said the world was now ready for a love of life like he was destined to have … I never brought it up because I never understood his crazy talk and I always assumed he was just a little off." Then she starts to doze off.

"Wait, Grandma, please explain. I need more. I honestly haven't been able to get a good night's sleep since Charlie died and I can't figure out why. Things have been happening to me, magical, unexplainable things. I need to know why."

"Oh, honey, that's all I got. That's all he gave me. I'm sure if there's more, you will figure it out, baby."

She falls into a deep sleep before I can even get out another word. I want to wake her up so badly, but obviously she's too old and I'm already being disrespectful. Her husband just died, and this is one thing he took to his grave. I wouldn't begin to know what it feels like to not fully know your spouse but be married for life. Now my only hope for answers lies within the ink of those letters. Before I even turn my vehicle on, Grandpa Charlie's address showed up in my Cadillac truck.

Chapter 5

I drive past the house at first because of those unexplained renovations. Or maybe I'm still in my head trying to figure out what's happening. The place looks so beautiful from the outside now. Even more so at night; everything just seems in the right place. I'm actually looking forward to getting that feeling of Grandpa when I walk in. I need that old smelly house to bring back some good old memories. Unfortunately (or fortunately, depending on your point of view), the inside has been renovated when I walk through the doors. No more walls separating all the rooms – now just one big, open living room space that connects to the brand new kitchen. There are custom appliances, with a new stove, a new fridge, and a new oven-microwave combo. The old glass door to the backyard is replaced with wall-to-wall, ceiling-to-floor windows. So modern yet with a hint of the classic. The whole floor is a gloss cement—which is exactly what I was going to put at my house downtown. The island in the middle of the kitchen stretches all the way across into the seating area. The living room, which you can see from the beautiful sink area, is big and open and centered with a wrap-around couch. The seventy-inch TV sits atop a wooden mantel that perches over a big beauty of a fireplace. Shoot, there's even a fire already going. I can't believe how much this place has changed. I feel like I'm on one of those renovation shows; this is straight out of a magazine. I'm caught admiring this, but should I be worried? I still don't know what the hell is happening here.

I quickly run outside but there's nothing—no trash left over, no dust or dirt, no semblance of construction at all. I look across the street and there's that same old lady, out at this time of night. She just waves and smiles. I start to walk towards her to ask questions but she just gets up and walks in the house. Weird. I need to get some answers.

I practically run upstairs to the attic. I'm expecting the light to be on this time and it is. The other day I thought about calling an electrician, but I think I now know the reason the light has been on, and I'm starting to accept this reality. While everything else inside the house has been renovated, the attic remains that same blank slate and that old box is still sitting in the middle of the attic. Every time I come close to that box, I feel a powerful pull.

My plan is organized—all the letters are sorted by date or storyline—so I pour them all out on the floor. All the envelopes are old and the same, but one big yellow one is different from them all. It seems newer as well. I laugh to myself, thinking, *Well, it will just make sense to start with that one.* I'm waiting for one of those crazy reactions, like losing my breath or something, but instead I'm surprised to see the letter is addressed to me. It was signed by Grandpa Charlie ...

Dear Trevor,

I just realized as I wrote this that it's the first time I called you Trevor. From the day you were born I have always called you Trev. I know things in your life have been crazy or seem like a dream now, but I promise you it's all real. You are a real life angel. I can't write the map out for you or tell you

32

what your destiny calls for—it's written for you already—but you have to go through the journey so you can learn your full potential. I will say this: you have something special, something like a power that was passed down from me. It can't be explained to human beings because they will never understand you.

I can give you one bit of information and I can tell you that you were put on this earth with a purpose, and you have a power that's only fully seen when you love. My power was the power of saving. When I was saving people, things just happened in my life that were good. I never felt like I couldn't get or do what I wanted in life because I always did what I was put on Earth to do. The same will happen to you. As long as you follow your destiny good things will happen to you, my child.

You will have to get over the fact that not many people will understand you fully. It was a curse of mine that no one told me about. I'm sure when you see family everyone will say good things about me, but I think you now know that wasn't the real me. I would see things that couldn't be explained but had no one to talk to about it. The family never really understood me. If I said anything, I would have come off as crazy. I tried a few times to talk to your Grandma Betty, but she just thought I was nuts so I didn't bring it up. Poor Betty; our marriage was me rescuing her depressed soul and it was my destiny to save her and keep my family.

It was tough sometimes living where no one could see your power or understand or see what you see ... you see, that's why these letters are so powerful. Kasia was the only one that saw me for me. For some reason she could feel my magic; for some reason she was the only one who saw the things around me that I saw. She was willing to risk everything for us even though everyone saw her as crazy. She ran through the impossible for me. She went through terrible times that shaped her life, I am sure, because she fought for our love. Unfortunately, the world wasn't ready for a love like mine and Kasia's.

I was sent home on some political stuff. I'm sure race played a part, and the fact that I looked happy – they made it a point to make sure I went home. But to be honest with you, I would have had to leave eventually anyway. The more me and Kasia fell in love, the more problems we encountered. I was responsible for all the heartache and pain Kasia went through, so I had to leave. It was a sign to me ... she was the only person I couldn't save. It wasn't meant to be. A belief that haunted me my whole life. I should have fought for her.

I felt a little of my magic leave when I was forced out of Europe. God must have had a different plan for me, Trev, but your journey will be different. You will finish what I started, I promise. I am sorry, I know it feels like I'm not answering any questions. I'll leave you with this, my grandson: you will start to see more things that are unexplainable. You can now take the surprise out and know it's part of your journey. Unfortunately, you won't be able to talk to anyone about it because no one will understand.

Remember, love is your power. I know you have questions about that, but you will have to learn on your own. If ever you come across someone who can understand you or see the magic you possess in some way ... never let go of that person, for it's one thing I did and it changed my life and I lost my power for it. I love you and the family is right: you were my favorite because I knew you had God's gift, that I was given, in you.

Love,
Charlie

34

P.S. If she is still alive, go find Kasia. She might be able to help you answer a few questions, but at the very least, she will see you for you.

What the hell is this? What is going on? I don't understand any of this. In fact, I'm questioning if someone's playing a sick joke on me. This letter doesn't sound like Grandpa Charlie. This sounds nuts. Yes, crazy things have been happening, so I shouldn't be surprised, but he talked about God's spirit and magic, and he called me an angel. An angel of love at that. I don't even know what love is, let alone being an angel. I've never loved anyone in my life other than family. I'm not even sure what to do now. Maybe I'm upset because I'm confused and know now for sure I have no one to talk to about this. I was sure these letters were going to answer all my questions once I got them organized, but now I'm questioning my sanity even more. I fall down to the ground after looking up from the letter. I'm caught off guard because the whole attic has been renovated and changed under my feet. Damn, I couldn't have been that caught up in the letter from Charlie to not notice all of this.

A glaring change I should have noticed right away was the new skylight from the exterior. It's now bigger and lets in the light of the moon and stars. As I push myself back and fall up against the wall, I look around the room. A beautiful, long brown table sits in the middle of the room right where the night light hits. It has such craftsmanship and detail. The box of letters sits atop the table. The blank wood, four-by-fours, is now replaced with brick walls that have beautiful artwork. I'm no auditor or anything, but these pieces look expensive. There's a glass case with what looks like old war artifacts and history pieces. The bare floors have been replaced with dark wood flooring. The once-hanging light has been swapped out with recessed lighting and controlled sensor lighting trails along the floor on the wallboards. The attic now looks like the office of a world traveler looking for a treasure hunt. A big globe sits on the table next to the box of letters. When I finish surveying the room, the globe starts to spin in a circle.

I'm lost. I feel the sense of magic Charlie talked about, but I also feel this sense of loneliness. I have so many questions yet, like Grandpa said, no one will understand. Shoot, I can barely figure out if I'm dreaming or not. I can only imagine me telling my friends, *Hey, when I read these letters my grandfather left me, I fall into memories of those moments in the letters.* They would send me to the crazy house immediately. I can't think of any scenario where they would believe me. If someone came over right now and asked about the renovations, I can't just tell them I showed up and the house was like this. Come on, Charlie, you should have given me more instructions. Instead, you left me with more questions and hurdles. I guess my only way is to look for answers in these letters and hope they point me in the direction of this mysterious Kasia—if she does exist.

Chapter 6

I spend the night organizing all the letters by date. I guess about right: there are thirty letters overall. Some of the dates and writing were a little destroyed, so I have to guess where to put them in order. It's crazy. They all just seem like plain old letters, but when I touch them I can feel something. I'm still shaking off Charlie's letter that left more questions. After contemplating, I think maybe I'm not being open-minded enough. I should be by now, with all the things that have already happened, but in some way I'm trying to hold on to my sanity. It turns out the first full letter I read was the first. The war was coming to an end and the dates line up, I think; as the war aftermath died down this relationship started. When I was in high school studying World War II, I'm glad I was paying attention. When I jump into some of these letters it will be good to know some details. It will help me navigate.

When I wake up in the morning I spend the whole Saturday diving into the letters. When I say diving, I literally mean diving, so much so my body is sore from jumping from past to present. My sense of time is all over the place: with some letters it's only been minutes when I return, after some letters it's been hours. After reading one of the letters, I lost about eight hours. Every letter pulls me back to the past. I feel every moment, every expression, every breath. My senses have been heightened; I feel everything a little more.

All the letters are from the angel Kasia. With each letter I dive into, the more connection I feel to her. I swore one time during one of the memories she saw me and responded to me, but it was just a glitch. She and Charlie spent so many great moments together. It was such a different time back then, with not so many worldly distractions; they just seemed to love different. Call it an old school love, one I only hear about in the movies and read in books. There was no Instagram or Facebook or dating apps, just the simple hurdles of everyday life. They took secret picnics in the dark under starlight and horseback rides far into the woods to set up camping tents near the water to spend the night. They went skinny dipping in the river water, not knowing what was in the water, or even worried about it, for that matter. It gave me so much joy to watch Grandpa Charlie act like a child when Kasia took him to secret castles that had been built centuries ago. I'm surprised to see how handy Grandpa was, helping basically build a house in the middle of some farm. I mean, the house came with its own outhouse and water supply, which was huge back then, especially in this area. He helped change Kasia's life on the farm they visited frequently.

I'm along for the ride when Charlie and Kasia hide and dodge some lost German soldiers. It's an intense moment, but they laugh and kiss the whole time with their lives in imminent danger. I make sure to remove myself from sexual moments she loves to write about. This kind of love is unheard of to me. The way they look into each other's eyes, there's something different there. Maybe it's because all my senses are really sensitive, but it feels like every time they hold hands they do it like it could be their last time. With all the dangers, just to keep their relationship private … it's so tough to imagine building a love this strong with such hate and strife around you. The majority of the time has been spent around this ten-mile radius of forest and bush. It seems so far removed from civilization, almost like another country itself. Actually, this doesn't do it justice; it feels like another planet to me.

Most of this area is covered in forest trees mixed with jungle-style trenches throughout. It's such a murky area, it's a wonder they're even able to find this place and set up here. Not many soldiers made their way out here, which makes it even a wonder Charlie and his team made it out this way and found them on the outskirts of the forest farm. If you go deep enough into this forest, it opens up into a big circle clearing and you are taken into a little city almost. A few cabins spread out, almost camouflaged, mixed into the trees. It's a little community that's sustained by helping each other out. Sometimes when I'm walking with them in a memory, when we are on the farm, I feel this sense of belonging. A few times, I swear, Kasia can see me when I'm at the farm while reading those letters.

I'm starting to get tired. I'm through twelve letters now and still not any closer to finding out why I'm seeing all these things. I look at the time and it's midnight; I have been going at the letters for over eighteen hours now. I feel like I spent days with Kasia and Charlie. I'm trying to maybe sneak in one more letter, but I can't keep my eyes open and my forehead feels heavy. I fall asleep right there on the brand new, big wooden table.

Chapter 7

I wake up with letter thirteen across my forehead. I had been dead asleep on the floor of the attic. Last thing I remember I looked up at the skylight as the sun was setting. Damn. That was about 6 p.m., and now it's the next day. I just lost about eighteen hours, dead to the world.

It's just midnight and now I'm sitting here like I got drugged. I check my phone after plugging it in and see a few missed calls and texts from friends and family. Not sure how the phone died. It was still at ninety percent when I started to fall asleep, and there weren't that many calls. I'm trying to shake off the sleepiness. I feel very strange. Then I realize either someone is cooking downstairs or I'm just that hungry, but I smell food. I run downstairs as if I'm going to catch someone moving around the kitchen. Instead, I'm greeted to a feast of food—steak and potatoes mixed with cornbread and grilled broccoli. It's my favorite meal Grandpa Charlie used to make. Damn, this feels so real but it has to be a dream. How in the hell would someone be able to sneak in here and cook a meal like this without me knowing or hearing a thing?

The oven timer beeps and I run over and open it. There's a pie that was just freshly made. Steam is still rising from the pot of food left on the stove. I run out front to see if I could catch a car driving off or something, but nothing. Instead, I meet eyes with that lady again and she just waves and smiles. I start to say something but she just gets up and walks inside again. I run out back thinking maybe they went out back but was left with the sight of Charlie's old backyard garden—the one thing that hasn't changed about the house, yet. It's getting old now, thinking I'm feeling crazy or need someone to talk to. If I'm going to try and solve this, I have to believe the things that are happening to me and figure it out. While I think it over, I sit down and enjoy the wonderful meal someone made and sent down from the heavens, apparently. I knew I was hungry, but I ate three servings and was returning for the next plate. I'm still getting used to feeling different. My body feels stronger now that I'm full.

I take my sixth beer upstairs to the attic. I must be feeling good because I'm usually a weak drinker and three would have me over the top. I have to get used to everything being different and the new feeling in my body and mind. I'm once again shaken by how quickly I forgot the attic renovations and, again, I remind myself to try and get used to it. This attic is amazing, especially at night with the lighting and the skylight giving the room the feel of being outside. Wish I could compliment the carpenter. Before I read letter number thirteen, I drink another beer and I'm starting to feel hungry again, so I go and grab a piece of that pie that was baking. It's still warm. Strawberry rhubarb, so good. Another beer washes down my pie and here we go ...

Dear Chanuntka,

Let me apologize about your last visit. There is no explanation for their behavior, but I will try to explain because I think you deserve one. You see, that man you had the encounter with is named Pawel. He and everyone else thought growing up he was going to be my husband, but I always viewed him as a friend. He was too small-town-

41

village-minded. I had visions of something more special, something magical. When you walked into that tent, I knew right away; I could feel you were different. I had dreams of a fairytale-style meeting and it was you who saved the damsel in distress. I knew from day one Pawel would not meet my urge for something different in life. Even the way you handle yourself in such turmoil, it was almost regal; even they felt it, I know it. Even though you walked away with your dignity and grace, I feel you should know the how and why that happened to you. Word got out to Pawel that I was running around spending time with you, and well ...

Oh, man, here we go again. There's a loud boom and a flash follows. Everything goes bright and it feels like I'm falling again through solid darkness. Once again, my heart rate increases almost to exploding. I get to the point of almost drowning and I pop up, gasping for air before I figure out where I am. The routine has been the same, and I think my body and mind are starting to get used to it. My mind doesn't get too far, knowing the end game won't kill me.

I'm shaken back to my current reality when I see Grandpa Charlie riding a horse next to Kasia while they hold hands. It looks like we are somewhere lost in one of the corners of the forest area enclosing the farm. Again, it's that feeling of being in the middle of nowhere, on another planet. They ride along in the sunset, holding hands, laughing and kissing, and they can't take their eyes off each other. I'm young and haven't figured out what love is just yet, but this has to be it. If this isn't love, I don't know what is. I know those eyes of Charlie's and they never shined the way they are shining at this moment. That look is love.

I'm shaken out of my love delirium when I see a group of men approaching on their horses. They are riding straight at Charlie and Kasia. When they get close enough to be recognized, I can see Kasia's face change and feel fear in her heart. I actually feel my heart rate jump a little. We are connected in some way. The men get close and circle them, with their horses kicking up dust all over.

"*Co to do dibla*, Kasia?" Even though it's in Polish I can understand him for some reason. When he speaks, the words just translated into English. I can tell Charlie's searching and can't understand him though. The guy asks Kasia, "What the hell is going on here?" I think. It wasn't in a loving way.

"Pawel, what are you doing here?" Kasia is angry and nervous, I can feel it.

"*Mowisz do mnie po Angielsku? Dlaczego to małpa może to zrozumieć?*" I believe he just said something to the extent of Kasia speaking English, "so this monkey can understand." They all stand around in silence, posturing. One of the men spit at the feet of my grandpa, but he doesn't react. He stands his ground and smiles.

"*Dzien dobry*," Charlie says out loud. They all look at each other and start to laugh.

"You know what, Kasia? You are right. We should speak English. It would be rude for this tribal villager to try and speak our beautiful language ..."

"Pawel, please don't do this." Concern is strewn across her face.

"No, no, it's okay. I actually must thank him. He helped to build our future home together. Did Kasia not tell you, my tribal friend, that she has a future husband?"

"Pawel, are you crazy?! You will never ..."

"Shut up, Kasia, *byc calkiem* ... can't you see men are talking right now?"

"It's okay, Kasia. I can handle myself."

"Yeah, Kasia, he can handle himself. Back up, please, so you don't get dirty." Two of the men pull Kasia back while the rest circle Charlie.

"Pawel is your name, right? No, she didn't mention anything about being married or mention anything about you. She sure didn't act like she was about to get married over the last few months we spent together."

The look on the Pawel's face says it all: trouble was coming. He almost turns red. Kasia screams for them to stop but one of the men grabs her and puts his hand over her mouth. Charlie still holds that smile and confidence.

"Do you think something is funny?" Pawel pretty much spits in my grandad's face.

"Not at all, Pawel. I'm truly sorry it didn't work for you and Kasia. You seem like a great guy, and there's someone out there for you that will respect you and treat you right."

At first none of the men move; they all just look in confusion at each other. Even I'm not expecting that. Pawel jumps off his horse and walks right up to Charlie.

"Why don't you just go back to the villages of Africa where you came from?" He's now so close to Charlie's face that little droplets of spit are getting on his cheeks.

"Pawel, do you think this is the way to win my heart? This is showing why you were never worthy of my heart or love!" Kasia yells and screams, but it falls on deaf ears.

"I am actually from the USA. Pawel, you should open your horizons. I can't believe you don't have more knowledge about my people." I'm not sure how, but Charlie keeps his composure the whole time. I, on the other hand, am jumping out of my pants.

"Ha, even worse. Do you think your country loves or cares about your people? They sent you over here in foreign land on suicide missions. You have no home."

"You're right. This could be true. But it's still my home and my missions over here are to liberate all the people over here, including some of your comrades. My home is wherever God calls me to be, and I have done my duty as a human on this earth." They all stare at each other with no one knowing how to react.

"You're a noble one, huh? *To yest povasne?*" Pawel asks if Charlie is serious while he looks at his crew.

"Not noble. I just happen to know what my calling on this earth is. I was put on this earth to save people, simple as that. Even people who hate me, like you." His smile stops, but he remains calm and confident.

"Well, isn't that very brave of you? So let me ask you, who is to save you from me and my guys here kicking your teeth in?" They all climb off their horses as Kasia starts to go crazy, screaming and pulling, trying to get away from the guy holding her.

"Let me answer your question before you proceed with whatever it is you guys plan on doing. I'm already saved. Like I said, I found my calling. I'm even going to save you after this," Charlie says as they all start to get closer, but I can tell some of them are conflicted.

"Yeah, monkey, how do you plan on saving me?" Pawel asks. They all are starting to look unsure about themselves.

All this time, Charlie shows no hostility to them. "I already did. You see, I just saved you and your boys from hate … If I were to react the way you had in your head, or you expected me to hate you, it would feed your belief that because my skin is different than yours, we should hate each other. You can call me monkey, but I'm your brother in blood. We are just different colors. So now whatever you do, or whatever your move is, you will know when you look in the mirror that it's you who has an ugly heart.

I think I just opened the eyes of your friends here that if you do what you plan to do, it will be just your ugly jealousy, not their actual feelings. They'll know that it's their dignity that will be tarnished, not mine. I've saved you from going down the rest of your life without knowing who you truly are. It's a big burden I have helped you with, because it's more tiresome to have hate than it is to have love."

They all stand and look at each other. The silence is broken when Pawel punches Grandpa Charlie in the gut and he falls to the ground. I scream out, forgetting they can't see me. I swear Kasia hears me, or at least reacts from my screaming when no one else did. She screams for them to stop. I can feel she felt me there. Pawel bounces around like a boxer before my grandpa struggles to his feet. Pawel braces for a fight, but Charlie just stands in front of him and looks into his eyes.

"It's okay, Pawel, go ahead if it makes you feel better. I know you don't know what to do with your emotions right now."

Pawel looks around, and the men in the group at this point just stop and stand there. Everyone looks confused. I can see one of the men shake his head no. Pawel looks as if he wants to start crying in frustration. He reaches back and swings so hard, but instead of punching Charlie he punches the ground and screams. My grandpa didn't even flinch. He grabs Pawel and hugs him. The men jump back on their horses and take off as it starts to rain. As Pawel lays back and cries, Charlie just pats him on his shoulder. Pawel pushes my grandpa back, looks at him, and then shakes his head. He screams out, "You will pay!" then stares at Kasia with a desperate look before taking off on his horse. Then Kasia runs to embrace Charlie ...

Boom. It's the routine that I'm used to—the no breath, the almost drowning darkness as I'm falling into the night. My grandad had such a different personality during that time than the Charlie I got to know. I must keep going. I check my phone and only five minutes have gone by. It's for sure been at least five hours since that moment with Charlie.

Chapter 8

After wrapping up some work emails and doing a few conference calls, I jump back into the letters again. It seems the stronger their love got for each other, the more problems they went through. It starts to feel like it's not meant to be. The more I read the bigger the hurdles, it just seems they can't catch a break. It's like spirits are working against them almost—another thing I can't explain. The realist in me gets challenged every day now. The day flies by and I'm inside this next set of letters for eight hours. I'm sure the situations I'm in with Kasia and Charlie expanded over three days at the very least. I laugh out loud as I picture myself telling my friends what's going on in my life now; they would get a good kick out of this. Once again, I'm starving like I haven't eaten for days. Maybe my brain isn't used to the time switch, so mentally it feels like I haven't eaten in days. I don't know. And just as the hunger kicks in, the smell of food hits from downstairs again. The first time I'm nervous and scared but I'm taking Charlie's advice and I'm not going to be surprised anymore.

It's still a wonder how the food is just showing up though. I run downstairs and the whole table and kitchen island are filled with food. There are all different types of finger foods. Pierogi, deviled eggs, Polish sausage, mini bites of cheese and pickles, and some kind of meat all put together on a toothpick. Mashed potatoes with spices on top, cabbage, and there are a few dishes I'm not familiar with or can't pronounce as well. Raw fish backs, mini hotdogs wrapped in croissants, and all different types of bread. Lots of bread. If I wasn't from Chicago, I wouldn't know that this is Polish food, but I have a few Polish friends and some work associates. There are two million Polish people in Illinois, and everyone knows a Polish person. I've actually never tried any of this food, but it all looks so good that I don't know where to start. This is for sure some kind of magic, or voodoo for that matter, because no one in my family or no one I'm close enough with has ever cooked Polish food like this. I just jump in and try everything. It's all good. Not sure what this is called, but this cabbage wrapped around meat and rice and spices is my favorite. I could just be starving, but this sausage is the best I've ever had. I'm deep in heaven on my way for my third serving, I'm so hungry. I'm so into my meals that I didn't notice a woman cooking in the kitchen.

I drop my drink and fall out of my chair when the woman turns around singing. It was Kasia. This Kasia looks different. She looks to be about my age now, and her hair is a darker brown. She looks tired. This is a different Kasia than the young nurse I saw in the first letter. She's humming some Polish church song. Not sure how or why, but I can understand her.

"Umm, excuse me, ma'am." I'm not sure if this is one of those dreams or not, but I'm not reading a letter. When she reacts to my voice, right away it feels different.

"Oh, hey, Trev, I'm glad to see you're hungry after your nap. How was school today?" Holy crap. Not only did she hear me, she called me Trev. She asked how school was, so something is definitely off.

"I'm sorry ... I know this is a dream and you have the wrong person. I'm twenty-eight-years-old and now working. I have been out of school for years now," I tell her.

There she is, this magical angel in my kitchen calling me Trev. During all of these visions and memories in the letters no one was able to hear me or see me, but now Kasia is here in Grandpa's house. No letter, no magical blast, my heart rate is normal and I can breathe. She just appears in my kitchen. It's official: I'm losing my mind.

"Trevor, have you had a bad dream or something? What's wrong with you? You're talking crazy and you're worrying me."

She hears me is my first reaction. She responds, "You have to take a deep breath and try to get it together. Something special is happening."

I can hear my Grandpa Charlie's letter ringing in my ear. "Just get over it. Things will happen that are magical. You must accept them and move on."

It's so hard. In all of these letters this woman was some mystical figure that only felt like dreams. Now she's here in this renovated house that I don't even know how it was renovated. Once again so I'm lost, but I guess I must figure out how to play along. Maybe it will give me some answers. As I sit here trying to figure out what I need to do, or what I am supposed to do, Kasia is standing closer to me now, looking at me with concern in her face.

"But this all seems so unreal" is all I can muster up.

"Oh, honey, you think it's really good, huh? I make this for you and Charlie all the time, so I'm not sure why today is different. Speaking of Charlie ... Mr. Johnson, would you come over here and eat? What are you doing?" she yells across the house.

I quickly look around in anticipation, because either a zombie version of Charlie is going to walk around the corner, or the Will Smith-lookalike version will come walking through. Either way, I'm starting to lose my breath as I hear footsteps starting to walk towards us.

"Oh, man, I'm starving. Hope you made those beef pierogis that you make. Those are my favorite." There he is, this time looking more like my grandad, just a younger version. The Will Smith look is now traded for a young Morgan Freeman look. A long, gray beard makes him look tired. I believe he and Kasia are the same age but he looks like he aged a lot faster than her, like he went through war. He walks over and embraces Kasia with a big hug and a long kiss, like they haven't seen each other in a while. "Oh, hey, Trev, you joining us for dinner? That's great. What a good surprise."

Good surprise? I think to myself. I laugh a little as I sit there and stare at him for second. I can't talk. What do I say? I want to ask so many questions but I don't know what to ask, because I don't know who or what I'm talking to. It'd be redundant to ask what the hell is going on.

"Hey."

"Are you okay, Trev?" Even as Charlie speaks, I still feel numb.

"I'm good, Grandpa Charlie. I mean, Charlie … just a long day." I have to try and play along, maybe get some answers. I'm either going to wake up from this dream or vision or whatever it is, or I'm going to figure it out.

"You seem shaken by something," Kasia says, walking over and rubbing my shoulders.

"Just tired, Kasia," I tell her as she kisses me on the forehead.

"You look like you had a long night. I'm glad you are at least enjoying your pierogis. You know in Poland, it was Charlie's favorite thing for me to make."

"Oh, yeah, Trev, I love these. The first time Kasia made them for me it was the potato pierogi, and I think I ate like twenty of them."

"Well, I love cooking them for you so it works out."

"I love your accent. Sometimes I can barely understand what you are saying, but it sounds so beautiful."

They embrace in another long hug and soft kisses. I'm not sure what alternate universe I'm in, but I can feel the love and magic. I can't figure out the moment; I'm not sure if I'm supposed to be their son or what this is. I call him Grandpa Charlie and he doesn't flinch. Kasia asks me about school, so I must be younger in their eyes. They stop and look at me as if I'm messing up their make-out session.

"Sorry, Trev, sometimes we forget other people are in this world with us." He smiles but never takes his eyes off of Kasia. In all my years with Grandpa Charlie, I've never seen him smile like that.

"What about Betty, Grandpa Charlie?" I'm tired of playing along. I have to test my reality for now. I figure I'll get some answers by asking real-time reality questions.

"I'm sorry, Trev, who are you talking about? What are you talking about? And why do you keep calling me Grandpa?" They both stare in confusion, which answers my question of what the situation is. Now I'm scrambling because I didn't think of response.

"Oh, I'm sorry. I was thinking of something at work. I got confused. I'm just tired and a little off."

"Well, son, I didn't know you had a job. You're sixteen-years-old and you should be focusing on your schooling and grades." I hear what he said, but it's still registering in my head. He called me son and said I was sixteen. I think I'm figuring out this dream or vision or reality or whatever it is.

"Did you call me son?"

"Umm, yes, Trevor. Your mom Kasia gave birth to you sixteen years ago. I was in the hospital room, so I'm pretty sure you're my son."

Right after he says Kasia is my mom I get up and run to the bathroom. Just as I expect, I look like a totally different person in the mirror. I'm myself but my skin is about three shades lighter and my dark brown eyes have been replaced with hazel eyes. My forehead is a little bigger and my eyebrows are much thicker. I look ten years younger and feel that way as I flex in the mirror. It's so strange to see myself like this. I look like a good mix of Kasia and Charlie. *Okay, come on, Trevor. Get it together.* I have to because I can feel Charlie and Kasia on the other side of this bathroom door. There must be a reason I'm seeing this reality, so I'm going to try and put a better acting job together.

"Trev, are you okay, honey?" It's Kasia's voice through the door. She sounds so soothing. In all these letters I looked at her like some mystical figure, and now she's at my Grandpa Charlie's bathroom door. But it's not my Grandpa Charlie standing at the door, it's my father? Another tap on the door and my think time is over.

"I'm fine. My nose is really running and I wanted to catch before it got on my shirt." I race past the two of them before they have time to inspect me. They both have looks of concern on their faces.

"I know you said you were tired and didn't feel good, son, but you are sure you're okay? You have been acting very strange and your mom is getting a little worried." I flinch at hearing him call Kasia my mom.

"No, really, Charlie … I mean, Dad." Calling him Grandpa is just habit.

"Alright, come sit down and have some dessert with us. Your mom made some delicious pie." He inspects me up and down with his eyes.

"Sure."

We sit down at the table for dessert and have small talk. Kasia sets out at least five different types of desserts and some coffee and tea. You would've thought we were expecting company with the spread she had set up. I'm able to throw them off my back by making up some fake talk about high school drama. Acting like a sulking teen allows them to think things are normal.

After having conversations with them and listening to them talk for the last half hour, I believe I have this reality figured out. This version of life occurs when Kasia comes to the U.S. with Charlie after the war. I'm the son they had when he got back. He sounds like he got a good engineering job after he talked about the stress at work. Kasia is a nurse at some local hospital. I'm able to get the gist of their routine listening to them talk to each other. I'm so impressed with how they are with each other. They laugh and joke like they're best friends. They feed each other like they're on a date, even though I'm sure this is just an average day for them. It's just small pecks on the cheek, but when they kiss each other it's passionate. This is love. There's no definition for this; it can't be explained. Before all the letters, and all these things happening now, I didn't know what love was. I can truly say I'm starting to get an understanding of what love is and what it means. As much as I'm caught up in this love, this isn't real and thoughts of my Grandma Betty and my mom come across my mind. It reminds me that I'm only letting this vision ride because I'm trying to get answers. When a moment of silence comes, I want to confirm the way they met.

"Hey, Mom, Dad ... how did you guys meet?"

They both pause and stop laughing for a moment. Kasia grabs Charlie's hand and smiles. "Your dad was like a commando as he walked into my tent. He commanded the room. I actually called him rude, and at first I was resistant. But it didn't take long for me to see his magic and the love your dad carried. All he talked about was his calling to save as many people as possible. It's all he talked about from day one. I figured someone as selfless and caring as that had to be worthy of receiving my love. It was love at first sight, as you say ... what made you ask, son?" She goes from nostalgic to having a worried look on her face.

"Oh, I was just wondering … just feel like I'm dreaming. It's so amazing, you two together. I know I seem off right now, so I guess just getting some history would help clear my mind … wait, what year is it again?"

"Trevor, are you kidding? It's 1962." Charlie seems perplexed. I just want to confirm my thoughts.

"Trevor, you're starting to scare me." Kasia walks over and puts her hand on my shoulder.

"I'm good, really, this has been good for me mentally. One more question … when you guys came public with your love … let me rephrase that … did you have hurdles getting here, Kasia, sorry, Mom? I'm assuming it wasn't that easy to get here. I'm assuming when you were pregnant with me it was hard to get here, post-war. I'm just thinking of a few things that don't add up here. Interracial marriage is illegal until 1969, yet here we sit in 1962 and you guys are comfortably married and happy in this house … so I'm just trying to figure out some things here."

They both pause and don't move. I can see Charlie start to shake a little bit. Kasia covers her eyes as she starts to cry. When she removes her hands, blood fills her eyes and blood streaks run down her cheeks. I jump up and fall over a chair in the corner as I push back up against the wall. What the hell just happened? I look over at Charlie and he too is crying now, but his tears are just black, some sort of black oil or something. They both get up and walk towards each other as the tears of blood and black oil pour down their cheeks.

Charlie gets down on one knee in front of Kasia and just starts kissing her stomach and crying uncontrollably. They both get up and start walking towards me slowly; they look like zombies. I try to get up and move but my body's stuck. I start to get scared a little and there's fear in my heart. They both get up close enough to touch me but just stop and stare at me. Kasia goes to touch my cheek and I flinch a little. She quickly jumps at me and hugs me. The more she cries, the stronger the hug gets. It's starting to hurt. It gets to the point where I'm starting to panic a little and I scream out, "You're choking me!" She hugs me harder and harder until I'm almost out of breath. Right before I pass out, she stops and just keeps saying she's sorry over and over again. As I catch my breath, she hugs me tight one last time and turns to dust. I quickly dust off my clothes and get myself up. Charlie stands there motionless with that black oil in his eyes.

"Just find her, Trevor. Finish your destiny." He touches my shoulder and turns to dust.

As soon as the dust settles, I black out and start falling into air, losing my breath as a big flash goes off.

Chapter 9

I sit up and catch my breath. My clothes are soaked in sweat ... and blood?! Once I get my breath back, I sprint downstairs and the newly renovated kitchen is cleaned. It's still daylight out; sure feels like a long Sunday. I check the stove clock and it's four in the afternoon. I feel so tired, like I took a long nap or woke up from coma. I'm full and can still taste the pierogis, so I know that it wasn't just a dream or some kind of vision. But, of course, this leaves more confusion in my head. Why did that last memory or vision—or whatever that was—just happen? All the letters I've read up to this point were positive and about love and joy and laughter. But this was very different. It was dark, actually scary, to me. I saw the love, then something changed after I asked about their marriage and how Kasia got over here. The blood and mud in their eyes was horrifying, but I'm afraid when I find out why their eyes were like that, I'll find out a more horrifying thing. The biggest takeaway from that vision is that it feels like a message. I felt their emotions for a reason. In all the letters, no one could see or hear me but this memory ... the situation was the focal point.

I take a big stretch as I walk to the bathroom, and for some reason I feel sore, like I worked out. I look in the mirror and I have a six-pack and muscles that weren't there before. I still look like my good old self, the twenty-eight-year-old businessman, with my chocolate skin back. I won't complain or research why

I'm getting these muscles. *I think I'll just enjoy them for now before they go away*, I think, laughing to myself as I flex in the mirror.

I have to get back to the letters and try and finish them while I still have some time Sunday. I grab my phone and have to plug it in to charge again. I think I will get a new phone because there's no reason for the power to keep going out—it's the latest version of the iPhone. When I plug my phone in, I'm hit with thirty missed calls. At first the calls are from work, then it's family ... damn, then the police?! Just ten minutes ago. Shit. I quickly call the police station back making sure they know things are good, and it's just a family matter. Then I call my father first.

"Hey, Pops, what's wrong? It seems everyone has been looking for me."

"Oh, my God, you're okay!" I can hear my mom in the background screaming, "Oh, my God, is that him?"

"Of course I'm okay. What happened? What did I miss?" Their panic sounds real and I'm getting a little nervous. With all this craziness going on, who knows what this could be.

"Are you high or on drugs or something? Where have you been for the last forty-eight hours? Your job was calling, and your friends have been calling and sending messages ... Where the hell are you and what the hell have you been doing?" The worried voice is exchanged for the angry father voice.

"What's wrong with you guys? I've been at Grandpa Charlie's house going through a few things and cleaning up his house. Sorry I had my phone off. But with that being said, I'm a grown-ass man."

"Why wouldn't you call your work or ..."

"Wait, did you say forty-eight hours? What day is it?"

"It's Tuesday, boy. Have you lost your damn mind!?"

"Dad, I have to call you back. Tell everyone I'm having a hard time dealing with Charlie's death or something but I'm good."

I hang up the phone but I can hear him telling me to wait and talk to him.

Damn it. I was in that flash reality since Sunday? It's impossible. It was only at dinner; it couldn't have been longer than three hours at most. Maybe I was so tired from the situation I just slept that long. It does feel like I've been out a long time, sleep-wise. I have to get myself and my life together, so I call my boss to make sure I still have a job. Luckily for me, my boss found out I lost my grandfather and she feels sympathy for me. She actually tells me I've done a lot for the company and I should finish the rest of the work week at home. I can hear real concern in her voice for me. Weird, I know I've been doing okay for the company for the last few years, but I always thought she didn't like me. This is such a change. She makes a point to tell me to call her if I feel like I need more time.

I call all my friends and all of them have already been contacted by my dad and the sympathy about Charlie grows. I feel sorry for using Charlie's death in vain, but I'm not sure anyone would believe me if I told the truth and what I was really doing for the last forty-eight hours. I spend another hour making sure everyone knows I'm okay and there's not an APB out for me. The moment the last call is finished, I'm running back to the attic. It's like a drug; I can't stop. My life has been turned upside-down. I feel like to get my life back I have to finish these letters and figure out why these things keep happening. I'm already at the table in the attic when I see two sets of lights pulling up in the driveway through the attic window. With everything going on I'm hoping it's just mail or something, but I'm quickly brought to my feet when I hear my mom yell out, "Oh, my God, it looks so amazing!"

I run downstairs to see my parents and my brothers walking around the house with shocked looks on their faces. It looks like they're the guests for a home renovation show and they just got the big reveal. I see a tear come to my father's eyes. Dad and Mom both walk up and give me a big hug but don't really look at me; I think they are amazed at the renovations. Shoot, I've seen it a few weeks now and I'm still amazed as well. I'm actually relieved a little bit because now that my family's here I see that these new renovations aren't a figment of my imagination. As I gather my thoughts and peel my mom off me at the doorway, I see that lady sitting across the street again. Same spot, same chair, same wave and smile. She had to see something. I'm snapped out of my thoughts because my mom is standing at the doorway staring at me with a weird look.

"Are you okay, son? Did Charlie's death affect you that much where you have to shut everyone out?" As she says this, I realize that could be the story I stick to, because no one is going to believe what really happened. I'm still questioning the truth.

"Yeah, I didn't think it would affect me like this, but I've been having a hard time." If she only knew.

"It's okay, honey. You were Charlie's favorite and everyone knew it. You can mourn all you want, honey." She just keeps hugging me and staring at me.

"I'm okay, Mom." Her look goes from worrisome to confused.

"You look different … I can't put my finger on it, but you look different." She rubs my face and my shoulders.

"I said I'm good, Mom."

"Are you wearing contacts?" Damn. I forgot about the changes to my eyes.

"Nah, my eyes have just been burning a lot. I've been reading and stuff for work from home, you know."

"It's okay, honey. You can admit you have been crying."

I giggle to myself a little because ever since his death I haven't even thought about crying. I'm happy he's not in any pain. I can probably cry now because of the all the questions and things happening to me. To be honest, other than the last vision, positive things have been happening to me. I still come back to when he first died, and I wasn't even considered the closest one to him. I'm starting to cave in to the belief that there's magic and spirits involved, but I still need answers.

"Little bro, I know you have been working out, but damn, your arms look big. And when did you get that six-pack, boy?" my brother Trey says as he comes up and taps my stomach.

"Ah, you know, I just ramped up my cardio a bit." Damn, they keep asking all these questions. Eventually they will catch me in one I can't answer. All little lies.

"Okay, little brotha, I see you. Let me get in on your workout system. Bring me with you to the gym next time you go." He never wants to hang, so we'll see what happens.

"Not sure you can keep up with me, brotha, but we'll see." We wrestle around a little as we both get down for some push-ups.

"Son, I know you are doing well at your banking job and making good money at twenty-eight-years-old, but wow, the renovations must have cost you up to at least $100,000 … at least!" My dad walks around in amazement, touching some of the craftsmanship and the artwork on the wall.

"Oh, you know, Pops, a few friends in the industry made it happen. I helped a few companies get financing for their businesses so some owed me some favors. It was time to cash in on a few of those favors. Things came out much nicer than I thought they would." None of this represents my personality, so I can see why my family is struggling with it.

"Damn, son, I think I was just here no more than three weeks ago. I believe you just got the keys two weeks ago … did your connections work overnight?" It doesn't seem like he's questioning me. He's more in shock trying to figure out how renovations this good got done so quickly.

"Well, Pops, like I said, I made people good money and, as a favor, I'm sure they wanted to get it done and not stop production. I have good connections and money talks."

We all stand in silence as my mom just walks around the kitchen, opening cabinets and checking everything. My dad just keeps shaking his head. He has that look on his face that I've had over the last few weeks ... so many questions.

"I'm just making sure things are good, son. What brought on all this change? When my dad first died, and everyone read his will, everyone was shocked to see it was you who he left the house to. You will also admit that when we had our one and only conversation about it, you said you wanted to get rid of the house and wanted nothing to do with it. Now, here, a few weeks later, and $100,000 later, is this beautiful home I grew up in and don't recognize. More importantly, you've been here spending time, which you never did growing up. Once you got to high school, we had to drag you here. I can see the time spent here has affected you ... so can you understand the shock from us?"

I don't respond at first. We all just stand there as our thoughts fill the room. I don't respond because I literally don't know what to say. He's right; this all looks so extraordinary. For a moment I think about just telling the truth and telling them what's been going on in my life. I have second thoughts about that as I look up and see anticipation on their faces. My silence pays off because my dad just comes over and gives me a hug. I hoped everyone would just chalk up my behavior to me really missing Charlie. It just comes with bad moments, as this awkward hug carried into awkward time now.

"Son, do you want to know the last thing my dad said to me before he died?"

I start to say it's okay, but I can see in his face he needs to tell me. "No, what, Pops?"

"I could feel it was going to be our last conversation, and I know he knew it was our last talk as well. The conversation wasn't what I thought it was going to be. I was expecting, 'Hey, son, do right by your kids and wife and leave a legacy of a good family man.' Nah, he didn't mention anything about the will. He didn't tell me anything about my mom and the great relationship they had. He didn't say anything about his work or his friends. He didn't say how proud he was of me or any motivational things to leave his son with ... Do you want to know what the last thing he said to me was?" He's almost in tears.

"What was that, Dad?"

"He could barely talk for days and then all of a sudden on his deathbed he began talking clearly like he was thirty years old ... He spoke about you."

"Why me?" I wish I could act surprised, but instead I'm just interested in any information that can help me find some peace.

"He said to make sure that no one gets in the way of your destiny. He told me you are a miracle and your destiny will happen no matter how hard you fight. He said you are magical and your legacy started almost sixty years ago. I know it sounds like crazy talk, right? At first, I pushed it off as crazy, but to be honest something was different. He went from not even being able to eat on his own or talk or go to the bathroom on his own to clearly talking and being himself. Something wasn't right. He spoke with such clarity. He was serious and it seemed like he saved his last bit of energy just to tell me this stuff. I just longed for him to say he loved me and my brothers and my mom, which rarely he did. I hoped that on his deathbed he was going to apologize for being mentally absent all these years. He always made it feel like my brothers and I and my mom weren't where his heart was ... I could never get the answers I wanted or understand what was in his head. Even after I had you and your brothers, I was hoping for some kind of approval or at least an 'I love you' every now and then. But nothing. Trevor, the one day I felt like he was truly happy was the day you were born. He looked at you differently. The first time he held you, he just sat and cried. It was like he had seen you before and lost you or something. I can't put my finger on it but I know …"

"Dad, I'm …"

"Hold on, son. Let me finish. My dad, your Grandpa Charlie, was a savior. He only seemed to be happy helping other people. Unfortunately, he didn't know how to show love – or at least show his family love. He didn't know how to show love once the person was rescued. He even admitted to me out loud a few times that it was hard for him. I asked him why he got married, and he said he was just saving my mom and it was the right thing to do at the time. He told me everyone got married and had kids and left legacies. Our relationship was a stalemate until the day you were born, and he looked at you with such glee in his eyes. He had a smile on his face that I had never seen, not even when your brothers were born. He looked at you in the hospital and said you were the definition of love. He said you were the reason he knew his legacy would continue. He never explained any of that; he only told me that you were going to be everything he was not … I found solace in that, son. At least I did something right: something I created he loved. You were the one reason me and my dad had a relationship. He had never been nicer to me after we left the hospital and kept being that way to his deathbed. Anyway, when I walked in here and saw how much money you put into this place and how much love you put in, I know he would have been so happy … I know I'm happy with it and the fact you're keeping it." My mom puts her hand on his shoulder and he's trying to hold back tears.

"Dad, I'm sorry I didn't know about your and Charlie's relationship. I have to admit that the house renovations were ..."

"No need to explain, son. It's beautiful and I'm happy it's you that got this house."

"Thank you, Pops."

"Oh, and I didn't finish telling you his last words. After talking about you he said, 'Go find her, it's the only way you will find peace.'"

"Wait ... what?" My worst fear is that my reality and my visions are separate, but my father's last comments mean it's as real as it gets.

"That's it. I thought it was crazy talk as he died, but I figured I would tell you anyway ... told him to elaborate, but he said you would know what he was talking about ... then he died."

Chapter 10

I spend the rest of that day just catching up with my mom and dad. It's actually refreshing. My dad tells me stories of Charlie's stubbornness and some of his weird quirks and sayings. As he speaks, I realize I have a totally different picture of what my family sees as quirks and weirdness. I'm able to just sit and talk with my mom heart-to-heart about life. At the end of the conversation she kisses me on my forehead and tells me I'm easy to love and talk to. She rubs me on my head as if I'm a puppy. My dad keeps walking around and looking at the architectural touches of the house. He just keeps shaking his head and whispering, "It's just perfect." I've tried a few times to tell him it wasn't me, but he thinks I'm just being modest. I even once told him the truth and said that I just showed up and it was like this, he looked at me and started laughing so hard tears were coming out.

While the brief moments of family love took my mind off the letters, it's not long before they start calling me again. It's not a sound or anything like that; it's something spiritual pulling me to the attic. There are some crazy things happening here. It's interesting that this is the first time I feel like I had a heartfelt conversation with my parents. It's also the first time my brother wanted to work out and hang with his little brother. He seemed different to me, and he gave me different vibes. Almost like he looked up to me or something.

They say their goodbyes and I'm practically pushing them out the door as my mom holds on for a long hug. As I wave bye to the family, that lady is on the porch again, smiling like usual. I wave back and say hello and her smile gets bigger.

As soon as the door closes, I run upstairs—the letters are calling me. Letter number thirteen is sitting on the table right where I left it before family came. I catch myself panting and realize how excited I am to jump into the next letter. My life has become entrenched in figuring out this puzzle of mysterious things happening. There's a twinge of guilt in me because I love my dad and Grandma and my family, but I can't help but fall in love with the love my Grandpa Charlie and this mystery woman Kasia share. The new layer to all this is that I feel a stronger connection to this angel after every letter. The guilt comes because I know if things did work out the way they wanted back then, I wouldn't be sitting here. I pull out the letter and start to read ...

Moj Chanuntka,

It was so hard to tell you the news knowing there was a good chance you wouldn't have enough time to react, but to be honest, I had to tell you because I felt there could be a chance, though it would be an uphill battle for you to get permission to stay. I was also very scared to tell you I would be having a baby, and you were going to be a father, because I wasn't sure how you would react. It all happened so fast. With everything going on with the world and cleanup of the war, I was worried that you ... or I don't know ... Charlie, we barely got to know each other. Of course, the few times you were able to visit it's love and magic, but this is real life and structure is different and the future is so uncertain. Luckily for me you were an angel with your reaction and your face said it all ...

There's a flash and a big bang. I'm suddenly falling and there goes my heart rate spiking to the point of me not being able to breathe again, although this time I'm a little bit more in control and can actually look around and recognize the situation. Again, the more letters I read, the easier the process gets, and, *boom*, I'm sitting up catching my air again, trying to figure out where I am.

I'm in a beautiful, old broken down castle. Nothing in my history books have anything that would resemble the historical perspective of this place. It looks ancient but for some reason I can feel it's thousands of years old. I know I'm in Poland, but just don't know what part. The castle sits atop a big hill and looks over a wasteland of forest trees and brush. Big holes plague the exterior wall. They look like cannonball holes, but I'm just guessing. A big wooden gate, maybe twenty feet high, leads me across a big water moat that circles the entrance to the castle. The place has been empty for centuries but it still holds its prestige and valor. It's very majestic in a historical kind of way, and I can feel the presence of those who have passed on.

I'm shaken out of my visions as I see two figures running up a set of stairs past me. They walk quickly through the foyer of the castle holding hands. As I get closer, I can see it's Charlie and Kasia once again in that loving embrace. I'm learning quickly why most of their meeting places are in remote hidden gems. As I think back to my reality, interracial couples weren't even legally allowed to get married until 1969. I can only imagine what they were going through. If only everyone knew what love could do … damn, listen to me. I obviously know this love affair comes to an end, but now I'm starting to wonder what would make them give up after such a strong love. Whatever comes after me reading these letters, I know I will accept nothing less for love in my life.

"Okay, okay, okay, my cocoa ... please sit down. I have something very important I need to tell you." Her accent is so strong and amazing, I can barely understand her sometimes. Did she just call Charlie "my cocoa"? I laugh a little at that.

"Okay, fine, but if it requires me to eat those fish skins again, I'll have to choose another option please." She smacks him on the shoulder then kisses him on the forehead.

"I thought you liked my mom's fish? No, seriously, I have something to say, but before I do promise me something."

"Oh, okay, you haven't been this serious with me since day one ... What's bothering you, my love?"

"Promise me that you are that magical angel I have come to know. You are something special and different. I'm afraid of you changing after you hear the news ... I want the same Charlie."

"Kasia, now you're scaring me ... I will always be me. God put me on this earth to save people. I'm happy and see good things in my future. It's a powerful thing when you know your purpose in life. I would hope, if anything, I've earned your trust by now."

"I'm pregnant."

Wow, not in a million years did I expect that. I can see it hits Grandpa like a ton of bricks. When she mentioned the baby in the letter, I figured she couldn't be talking about Charlie's child.

"Oh, my God, that's great ... how ... what about ..."

"Relax, take a deep breath. I know it's overwhelming."

"Are you sure? We haven't been together that long ..."

"It's not long. Just the beginning, but I can feel it."

"No, I'm so excited. It's a dream I never thought about. It's just all so sudden, and we ..."

"I know ... the future's not written clearly for us. We are young. I'm not sure how I would get into your country unless we did it illegally somehow. Not to mention we're not married, which my family will kill me for. Your time of being able to come back and forth to visit me will be up soon … I don't know what we thought was going to happen. Now, we have no plan."

"We have love, Kasia. Love is a good foundation to build on. Again, I felt in love from day one and was always thinking of how we're going to make it work … now, it will be of the most importance we figure it out. We'll have to make it work."

"Oh, thank God … I love you …"

"Were you worried? About what?"

"Oh, *kocham*, we've had a love affair for less than a year and were caught up in the zest of it all. We didn't take time to get to know the small things. We never talked about kids, of course, because it would have been crazy. Well, now it's here. How was I to know how you would react? We are from two different countries, two different cultures, two different worlds. It's an impossible situation. You must forgive me if I have my doubts." She starts to tear up. They seem like tears of fear.

"Kasia, my Polish queen. You said I was magical and there was something different about me that you couldn't explain. The truth is, I wasn't like this until I met you. You changed me. I've always felt a calling, but you have brought out that calling in me, and since I fell for you, things just feel different for me. So we must accept our fate and love and figure it out."

"I love you. We are going to have a long battle, but I feel I can do anything with you by my side."

They embrace. They don't speak for a while; they just snuggle in each other's arms. My Grandpa Charlie looks nervous and shocked. Kasia seems to be in heaven for the moment as she hugs him tight. As I get closer to them, I can see Charlie almost take a deep sigh, as if he knows the outcome isn't going to be good.

A big bright light and loud flash goes off and my heart rate spikes. I'm falling into complete darkness. I sit up after catching my breath and now I'm back in my reality. Not sure what's reality anymore. Since I'm here I obviously know something happened, but now I know it must have been terrible to make my grandpa make a switch and leave.

Chapter 11

I have learned not to read more than three letters in a day. That's when I lose days and things start going crazy. I finally catch up with myself in life. I haven't spent much time with my dog, Maxine, so I take my girl to the dog park and the lake. I clean up my house downtown a little and for some reason it doesn't feel like home any more. I'm able to not only catch up at work but I get ahead and strike a few good deals for my company. My boss says she has been pleased with the work I've done from home over the last few weeks. She tells me I should keep it up for a promotion and a bigger cut of my deals. It's funny because I thought I was doing bad at home and losing time because of being lost in the letters, but I will take the push at work. It feels really good to clear my head with normal life stuff. I was starting to forget who I was.

I have a lunch get-together with some of my boys. It's so good to just sit back and talk sports, girls, work, and drink too much. Everyone I greet looks at me differently; they all say something changed and something is different in a good way. Of course, they all tease me about my new workout routine being the reason they haven't seen me lately. After a few beers and celebratory shots, I'm feeling brave and want to tell the crew the truth. I'm drunk and need the release, so I tell them everything.

I start with the way I found the letters at Charlie's house after his death, telling them that every time I read the letters, I fall back in time to see what was going on during these letters. Although I tell them that I have been feeling different lately, I feel stronger physically and I've felt at ease mentally—almost a confidence that things will work out in life. I admit that, really, I haven't worked out in months and after reading the letters I just woke up one day with a six-pack. I tell them I feel like I'm going to be able to have powers once I figure out my power of love. I brag about the beautiful renovations to the house and how I just showed up from work one day and everything was brand new. It's strange, I tell them, because the house is exactly the way I would have designed it. Maybe a few color changes and different artwork, but otherwise it's perfect.

I laugh out loud to myself as I tell them about the old lady next door who's always outside smiling and waving at me. It feels so good just to get it out and talk about it to someone.

I'm so relieved that I don't even notice all my guys staring at me like I'm crazy. They all sit in silence. After a few seconds, one of my guys comes over and puts his hand my shoulder and apologizes for me losing Charlie and says he didn't know it affected me this much. Then I look around at everyone and just burst out laughing, and they all follow suit. We laugh until tears come out. One of the other guys comes up and says, "I thought we were going to have to put you in the looney bin for a few weeks to recover," then I laugh even harder. Everyone chalks up the stories to me being drunk and emotional. It all does sound crazy, but it still feels good to talk about it out loud.

Chapter 12

It's been a few days off from the letters and the pull has gotten stronger. I was able to dive into work even more and get ahead so I would have quality time to dive into the letters again. I feel so energized; I've never felt healthier. I pull back up to Grandpa Charlie's house and the feeling is still new, pulling up seeing it renovated like this. I keep thinking one of these times it's going to be that old rusty house that I remember. It would be a sad day, actually, because I'm really starting to like this new home.

As I pull up to the driveway, I notice all the lights on in the kitchen and the whole downstairs area. I'm not surprised anymore. Now it's replaced with anticipation about what I'm going to run into, or what vision or adventure will I get into next. I expect surprises now. I'm sure I locked the door and turned everything off, so this will definitely be a surprise. When I walk in, the smell of baked goods fills the room. I can hear some kind of traditional Polish music playing over the house speakers. Huh, those speakers must be new because I don't remember them the last time I was here. When I walk around the corner, there's Kasia cooking, dancing, and humming to the music. It smells like cookies and cake, so good. She sometimes moves in slow motion to me; there's something so mesmerizing about her. She jumps when she turns around and sees me standing there. This is another one of those visions because this for sure isn't a letter and she can once again see me.

"Oh, hey, Trevor. You startled me." Her smile makes me relax.

"Hello, Kasia." By now I know playing along works best, and I've actually reached the point where I'm just trying to enjoy the moments. Or at least be in the moment.

"Still mad, huh? You don't have to call me Mom because I'm still confused. Your journey's the same as my spiritual one, so bear with me."

"It's okay, I like Kasia anyway. It's such a beautiful name," I tell her, then a smile returns back to her face.

"I'm glad you came back, or it maybe I'm glad I came back. I'm still not in control of when I show up in this state, but I'm still figuring things out. I need to apologize for what happened last time with the blood in the eyes and the fear and things. I felt it too. To be honest, I have to apologize for a lot of things." She turns serious.

"No need to apologize. I get small windows of time with you it seems, and I'm figuring out things happening to me as well. I assume I've been seeing visions of you for a reason." I've decided to do what I would do if this was my reality and that would be to ask questions.

"Please be calm and take deep breaths ... I have to apologize because I never got the chance to."

"When would you have had the chance?"

"Just listen to me, child ... I am so sorry I couldn't protect you from them, my family, from the world. Charlie and I fell in love against all odds, and the world just wasn't ready. I couldn't protect your soul, so I was punished. Your Charlie was punished. I wasn't ready to deal with a loss so precious. I should have known it was all going to work against us. You aren't my long-lost son, but for some reason you are my punishment. I must do right by your soul, but I'm at a loss what to do. I'm at a loss what you are to me. I can only see sadness."

"What are you talking about? I'm right here ..."

Before I could finish my sentence, a sharp pain hit my stomach. It hurts so bad I can't catch my breath, but this is different. It feels like I need to throw up; instead, foam starts coming out of my mouth, and I'm back to that lost feeling of questioning what's happening to me again. I try getting up to move to the bathroom, but the pain hits me harder in the stomach and I knock over a vase trying to save myself from falling. I feel no control over my body and more foam comes spilling out of my mouth as Kasia kneels over me. She cries her heart out as she holds me and rocks me back and forth.

"I know, Trevor. It hurts. Try and breathe ... I'm so sorry, honey. I didn't think they would stoop that low. Sorry, I can't help you now. You have to go through this to feel our pain, to rectify our wrongs. Charlie couldn't handle it and gave up. He felt like his magic couldn't rescue the most important soul of all ... Please find it in your heart to forgive me."

I'm drowning in my own acid saliva. It feels like I'm burning on the inside of my body, like someone is poisoning me. I can feel my heart rate slow down. I'm dying, I can feel it. In my head I'm telling myself it's not reality, but this pain is so real. I can feel Kasia's tears fall on me and everything starts moving in slow motion. I can feel something leaving my body as I hold on to my last breaths.

"Please find the answers and fulfill your destiny ... It will save my soul before I die ... Come find me."

My eyes shut but I can still hear Kasia. She starts saying a prayer, then starts singing a lullaby. I try to get up but my last breath comes out.

Chapter 13

I wake up with a deep exhale as if I've been underwater for a while and I'm finally able to breathe. I'm very groggy and I wipe my forehead full of sweat. I look down at my shirt and see throw up or foam or something, and I'm quickly reminded of my vision. The letters were, so far, about love and caring and just a vision of the good times with Kasia and Charlie. Why are these new visions so dark?

I look around and I'm back in the attic again. Not sure how I got here, but I'm sure when I went into that coma that I was downstairs. I think to run downstairs again to see if I can find something, but I'm thrown off when the big globe sitting on the table starts spinning. There's no window open and I'm the only one here. I'm no longer surprised by anything, but I'm more cautious now, so I walk over to the globe slowly. The closer I get to it, the faster it spins. I grab it and it comes to a stop. There's a big red dot that wasn't there before. I take a good look and it sits on Poland. No city, no address, not even an airport to point me in the right direction, just Poland. I have never had Poland on my bucket list of places to visit, but it feels like it has always been leading this way. I know nothing about Poland, but I feel like I've been there just by the letters and the visits to the past. I can't tell you the name of the cities, but I can feel its presence.

As I run through what my plan would be in Poland if I could go there, I look at the table and letters fourteen through twenty are sitting there. This is different. I check the time to make sure I'm keeping ahead of my life schedule. These letters make my real time unpredictable. I've gotten into a safe zone of setting an alarm in hopes that I don't stay too long in one of the letters. I've also gotten used to checking in with everything in my real world after every letter. I'm starting to get afraid of losing my reality chasing answers, so I'm trying to get some type of routine. I catch up on all emails, change my voicemail to say I'm out until Monday, check in with family and friends just in case, then it's time to dive back into the letters.

I'm starting to think that the visions were a warning, as I read and jump through the experiences of letter fourteen through twenty. Up to this point, all the letters were all positive and the future looked bright – or at least had hope. But in these six letters things take a turn for the worse: they have to fight to keep their love more. It's almost as if they're fighting against destiny and they disagree with what destiny's telling them. I can feel the love being drained from them as they try to figure out who they can trust and what they will do about the baby. It's a plethora of hurdles. Charlie deals with racism from both sides, including all the Polish counterparts who he thought he made friends with and his own army comrades who didn't like his intentions for some reason. He fights and begs to be stationed in Poland until the last person leaves, but is denied by his higher-ups at every angle. They won't even listen to his request. Kasia has to deal with the same hate. After seeing it isn't going to work for Charlie to stay, she starts trying to find ways to go to America. Unfortunately, her pleas fall on deaf ears and she's turned away at every corner. Love is strong, but it doesn't win against hate unless it has help.

They both get desperate in their attempts to find a way to stay together. Charlie goes to one of his higher-ups who he thinks he had made an impression on and tells him the truth about Kasia being pregnant. Unfortunately, that man couldn't care less and squashes any thought of Charlie staying. There's a timeline on his departure. Charlie makes the decision to fight to stay even if he has to hide or do something illegal. The last straw is the fight over how to tell the family about the pregnancy. Charlie feels there are still options to fight and sees if he could stay or she could come to America. Kasia really thinks if she tells her family about the pregnancy, they can figure out how to make it work and figure a way to keep Charlie in Poland as a last result.

While the first letters are about love and showing me the meaning of really being in love, these last few letters have been what I've come to know is this thing we call life, which is just a struggle to live and then grasp on to moments of happiness. I understand this love affair comes to an end because of my family being here, but I'm falling in love with their love. I so badly want to believe in a happy ending, but in this case the ending has already been written and it can't be good. I'm sure to be heartbroken by the next ten letters. The realist in me has been terminated. I want to believe it's for a good reason.

Chapter 14

My routine is like clockwork now. After every letter I take a break. I walk the dog and do some household chores, I eat and watch some TV, and then catch up on work if need be. Just some normal things in life. I check in with the crew, who all think I'm being antisocial, and make excuses not to hang. I told everyone I have been diving into work now to take my mind off things. It's funny, I'm not sure what I will do with myself when I'm done with the letters and figure things out. It's starting to become clear I'll have to make my way to Poland. I'm getting the feeling I won't get all the answers from the letters.

I have my coffee in hand and I'm sitting down to read the letters. The attic feels gloomy; something feels different. It's dark and foggy outside as the rain starts coming down. It was sunny with not a cloud in sight just a few moments ago when I got back from walking the dog. The silence is deafening. I can see the raindrops falling, but I can't hear them. The wind blows the trees around outside, but I hear nothing. Usually when I walk upstairs into the attic, all the lights are on, but now just the light from the candles fills the room. The rest of the room turns pitch black and I can't see anything besides the table. Letter twenty-one is addressed with a red marker. When I open the letter, the handwriting is also in red. Kasia's handwriting is usually perfect, but this seems nervous and rushed. I start to read. There's no dear Charlie or any pet names they have for each other. It's straight to it.

I am so, so sorry Charlie. My biggest mistake was trusting and having faith in people, especially my family ...

There it goes: a big flash and then I'm falling in a pitch-black hole and my heart rate spikes to the point of almost making me have a heart attack. Another boom and flash and I'm sitting back up, searching for breath.

Usually I have to find them and where we are, but they are standing right in front of me. It looks like we are at a train station in the middle of nowhere. After a quick look, it seems we are at a military pick-up station or transport of goods drop-off. The sun is rising just over the train, and it's just my Grandpa Charlie and Kasia standing on the underpass. The train is carrying cargo and a few soldiers. I can see this is the last train, and it looks like they're going to shut the operation down at this location. The engine starts heating up as some of the soldiers stare at the couple waiting on the ledge.

"I'm sorry, my dear Charlie. You can't blame me or be mad at me for what happened. Again, my only mistake was trusting and believing my family and friends were human ... Charlie, I would never think they would allow Pawel to poison me!" She broke down sobbing. Poison? Damn.

"Kasia, you talk as if I blame you or I'm mad at you. I'm mad at the world, I'm mad at everyone, but mostly I'm mad at myself because I should've never put you in this situation. I should have known this was never going to work. There were so many things working against us. This is how it had to be. That baby would have come into a world of hate and we would have had everything working against us all our lives."

"You sound as if you are not mad it happened!" she screamed and hit him in the shoulder.

"You can be mad at me and take it out on me, which I understand. It's okay. You should know that my body language is

81

so I don't show weakness in front of others. Not to mention we fought for months just to keep our relationship a secret. I was tired before we found out about our gift, but now my soul is tired and I can't run or fight anymore … You know I am a spiritual man and I didn't look at the signs because love is blinding, but after hearing about you getting poisoned, I thought maybe it wasn't in God's plan."

"No, you will not do that. You will not give me this, your 'God's angel' stuff, Charlie. You know I don't understand you and will never understand this magical side, but I still feel it. You have to acknowledge this. You need to feel this like I do …"

"My sweet Kasia, you have it wrong. You see my body language right now is so I can keep the sanity I have to have on the way home. They will take advantage of me if they see me emotional, the same way I would be treated by your people if I stay. You spit on my last sentence, but God does have a plan and it does not involve you getting poisoned by your family. His plan for me, as I have told you from day one, has been to save people … The biggest disappointment for me was I could not save you. It's just not going to be our time. We will have to wait for the next lifetime."

There's a deep horn sound and the train releases itself of the brakes. The last of the cargo is being put on board.

"Charlie, come on … my *Chanuntka* … you will give up just like that? The special bond we shared is and will be like no other. It was us against the world; it's supposed to be us against the world … If anything can make this work, it's your magic." She pulls at his arms as his head drops. He looks so conflicted.

One of the men screams at Charlie that he has one more minute and he better hurry up. The soldiers continue to sit there and look at them, making the pressure even more immense.

"Kasia, all those hurdles and things we dealt with were signs to me. My love took a hit every day we tried. Then I realized my magic or my God's calling isn't love, it's saving ... All of the things we are working against I can never save us from, nor would I have been able to save the child. I prayed and prayed and really looked for a sign ...When you told me you lost the baby, it was my sign that this would just hurt more and more. It forced me to look in the mirror and admit I was wrong about who I am. You see, that's the double-edged sword. If I stay, I would not be allowed to be who I am. You're right. Our love is like no other, but it doesn't matter if it wasn't meant to be ... I love you to death, but my calling requires me to go home so I can continue to rescue and save souls and follow the destiny that was written for me ... The pain comes because I fought this destiny even though I knew it was inevitable."

"I love you, Charlie. I'm not sure what to say. I'm so lost ... my soul will be lost." I can see she feels his resolve.

"You know I love you too, and your tone and body language let me know you understand I have no choice. You are the most beautiful thing I have ever laid eyes on and will ever lay eyes on. You showed me and taught me what love is. You are my definition of love."

"My *Chanuntka* ... what do I do now? I'm not sure I can love again or have a normal love life." She seems broken; she can't stop the tears from falling.

"You must live life. You must give yourself to the world. You are an angel and special. You must be happy and get married and plant seeds of love, like you have with me. I'm being calm now but I'm dying inside. Again, *moj Kohani*, I just can't show it." A tear falls down his face and he tries to hide it from the soldiers standing by.

"I will never get over this ... My family betrayed me, my town let me down, and humanity is not fair. Please don't leave me, please ... at least write to me. Please let me know you lived.

It's killing me because you sit here bravely now, but I don't think you will be okay without me. Not just me but us. We are … we're strong enough to go against the world."

The train starts to move slowly. One of Charlie's commanders screams that he better get his ass on the train.

"This will be the last thing I can say, because I'm out of time … it will sound crazy but you know me and know there's something different. Our souls are attached. Our seed was stopped, but we are linked and our paths will come full circle. I promise before you die, the proof of my soul will come to you and complete our destiny. I love you and will always love you, and I plan to see you in heaven."

She pulls his hand back before he jumps on the train and gives him a kiss on the cheek before whispering in his ear, "I truly believe it was going to be a boy. Just so you know, I was going to call him Trevor …"

There's a flash, and I fall into the dark black hole again. My heart rate spikes and my head starts pounding. Right at the moment I feel like I can't hold my breath any longer, I pop up and I'm in the attic again.

Chapter 15

When I finally catch my breath, Kasia's last statement is stuck in my head. Obviously, by this point, I've accepted the spirits and ghost and visions, but this still blows my mind. Grandpa Charlie doesn't name any of his kids Trevor, and then my dad, who knows nothing about the past, does? I immediately call my dad, even though it's five in the morning at this point, to ask him why he named me Trevor. Of course, he thinks I'm losing my mind and emotional, but once he wakes up he tells me it just came to him—not to mention my older brothers' names both begin with the letter T, so Trevor is not too farfetched. But with everything I have witnessed recently, I don't believe in coincidences anymore. As I get over the name situation, I'm brought back to the fact that Kasia was poisoned ... another reason why I'm sitting here today. I know Charlie; if that baby were to be born there's no way he would have left. I can't believe the measures taken. I'm sure things like abortion weren't available back then, but poison? Damn. Sounded as if she trusted someone and they took advantage of her. So many questions about that last letter with no one to talk to about it.

Just as I start to pace the attic, rattling my brain trying to think of answers, I begin to smell food downstairs. I'm starving once again. The last few times this happened I was greeted with dark surprises, but it did answer a few questions. I'm anxious and scared as I run downstairs. I come around the corner of the kitchen and there she is again. Kasia is cooking in the kitchen. Once again, there's some kind of Polish song in the background as she dances and hums to the music.

"Oh, hey, Trevor. I'm glad you made it for dinner. I made you your favorite: steak and potatoes. I made the potatoes Polish style with chives and herbs. You're gonna love it." She has such a positive pull about her. I can only imagine how hard it was for Charlie to walk away.

"Thank you, I can't wait to try it … I know what happened, Kasia." We are connected and I have to get to the bottom of it. There's no more time for small talk.

"What are you talking about?"

"Do you think it would have worked out between you and Charlie had you not been poisoned?"

She freezes for second and stops what she's doing. She drops the dish she's holding in the sink. I blink and she's sitting in front of me and the room is pitch black. I can't see past the table; it's like we're sitting in space. She turns to talk to me and it's the blood-rimmed eyes again. It didn't startle me this time. I walk toward her to give her a hug and she just falls into my arms. I can feel her blood-soaked tears on my shirt. I can feel her heart beating fast as a drum. She's squeezing me so tight again. I brace myself for pain like the last time, but instead she starts talking.

"I always wanted to know what you would be like. I never got over it, Trevor. I was never able to trust anyone again … I was never able to live life to the fullest. I got married, yes, and had kids, but I knew what true love feels like and I was never able to recreate that, sadly even with my own kids, because deep down in my heart I knew my true love child wasn't allowed to come on this earth. I know that sounds horrible and I'm a horrible person for it, but it's my true feelings. I'm so sorry I didn't protect you, Trevor, or what I'm starting to believe is the soul of you. The last thing I was saying to your Charlie involved my mistake of not trusting humans."

"I understand, Kasia. I actually got a close up of that moment … What I don't understand is what is happening here. I have so many questions but one that can help out the most is … why me? Why am I seeing these things? Why do these good things keep happening to me? Why am I seeing magical things, when I've been trying to deny them? Why are you in front of me now? Why did I see all these letters in person?" She didn't let go of the hug.

"I was angry at Charlie for always saying he had a calling, and it was magic and God's word and so on, always talking the unexplainable. But every time I would think he was crazy, something magical would happen. It got to the point where I just gave up trying to understand him and instead just enjoyed him. There were a lot of questions he couldn't answer. To me he would just say 'I am an angel with a purpose, and sometimes things happen because it's God's plan.' I can only say this … everything that he promised would happen eventually did happen. If he wrote to you in a letter that something would happen, it would. Just follow the leads. I'm sorry, child. I don't have any answers for you. My advice would be to stop fighting and questioning everything. Charlie said you were put on this earth to do something, so listen to what your heart says. You will find your answers when you listen … and believe."

Instead of answering questions, this just created more. I'm supposed to believe I'm some angel, sent down to love? My grandpa told me my purpose is love, which I find very hard to believe. I have never loved anything in life other than my parents and my dog.

I try again to dislodge from the hug, but her grip gets stronger. I'm still trying to gather my thoughts as I hug this ghost … spirit

… whoever this mysterious woman is supposed to be to me. I have never loved a woman, but this connection is undeniable. I search for questions that will shake things up. The last time I was in a similar vision with Charlie around, I asked a tough question they couldn't answer and they started bleeding from the eyes. Maybe it's the only way to get answers.

"Kasia, in the letters there, you said you only told family about your pregnancy. How do you know you were poisoned? How do you know it was them?"

Her squeeze gets tighter, and it turns into pain. I try to put my arms between us but she squeezes tighter and I feel my circulation being cut off. I start to lose consciousness but then I see a big flash. My heart rate starts spiking and it feels like I'm dying again. The inside of my stomach burns like I'm drinking acid. This is similar but different from when I fall into the letters. I feel I'm on my last breath when Kasia's body turns to ashes, and I quickly sit up and catch my breath.

After a few moments of trying to get my breath back, I realize I'm no longer in my grandpa's kitchen. I recognize the place right away: we're at Kasia's family farm in the forest. I walk past the small farmhouse I saw Charlie help the family build. I walk through the horse stalls and the sheep stable when I see one of the houses lit up with smoke coming from the chimney. I walk through the wood shed wall to see Kasia sitting at the table with a group of people. It looks like family. There's small talk in Polish, but for some reason I can understand them. Their words are being translated into English in my mind. It seems like it was Kasia's parents, a few uncles, and a few girlfriends or cousins and aunts. Everyone is serious; there are no smiles. I can't get all of the conversation, but I did catch Kasia defensively say she loves Charlie. As everyone's in heated debate, a man walks through the door. Everyone greets the man and I instantly remember him from the letters. It's that guy Pawel who punched my grandpa in the stomach. The group seems happy and comfortable to see him, but Kasia tenses up a little bit.

"What are you doing here, Pawel?" She spits it out as she runs up to him.

"Your family invited me. I come in peace to help. The family told me you were in a little trouble and was in some heat, so I'm here to try and see what I can do."

"What? My family told you to come here?"

"Look, I'm sorry about what happened the last time I saw you. I was jealous, of course, and it wasn't me. I hope things can work out between you and the gentleman." I can read right through his fake demeanor, and so does Kasia, but everyone celebrates that he is there.

"Pawel, I'm not sure you understand the gravity of the situation I am in."

"Oh, I understand fully. Your dad filled me in, and I'm here to show support and work on a plan." She immediately looks at her dad in disgust, while her dad doesn't understand the problem.

They all settle in around the table in silence as tea is passed around. I didn't see if anyone else had seen it, but I did. Pawel slipped something inside the cup he passed to Kasia. Then they sit and talk, and drink up. For a brief moment, everything seems calm and everyone seems to be talking about ideas. Kasia starts feeling her forehead and squinting as if she's starting to feel queasy. After speaking to her mom for a few more moments, she excuses herself from the table, telling everyone she has to go to the next cabin for a moment because she isn't feeling well. As soon as she's out of sight and the cabin door swings closed, she collapses on the cold ground. She looks back like she didn't want anyone to see her struggle and musters up enough energy to get to the next cabin. I follow right through the wooden walls.

She falls to the kitchen floor and barely makes it to the sink, where she starts throwing up. At first it's some slimy stuff, then it turns into thick globules of blood. I'm not losing my mind, but the color of the blood is the same color that was coming out of Kasia's eyes earlier—and the black goop coming out was the same as what came out Charlie's eyes in that vision I had. She looks so sick I can see her face changing color, and I want to scream for help. She looks down and sees blood on her hands and starts crying hysterically. As she starts to fade in and out of consciousness, her father and other members of the group come running through the door. Right before she passes out, her father catches her midair and helps her to the cot in the corner of the room. She hears him whisper in her ear, "This is for the best, honey. It would have never worked the other way."

Kasia tries to take a swing at her father but is too weak and falls over on her back into the cot. She's paralyzed and tears just stream down her face. Right after she passes out cold, Kasia's mom comes running into the room.

"Are you sure she's going to be okay?" Kasia's mom cries out.

"She will be fine. Some stomach pain and in the morning we can all move on with life ... I know this was a difficult choice, but it was the only way." Kasia's father and Pawel shake hands as they look over her body.

A flash hits my eyes as the blinding light sends me falling. The longer I fall, the darker it gets, until I'm in the pitch black. My heart rate spikes and I'm unable to breathe. Right when I feel like I'm running out of air, I'm sitting up back at my Grandpa Charlie's house, gasping for air. I sit and look around the kitchen as my shirt is soaked in blood. I'm reminded of the long hug Kasia gave before showing me the vision of her pregnancy being terminated.

Chapter 16

The rain comes down harder than before. The middle of the day seems like night, the clouds are so dark. My mind matches the weather outside; I can't get past my last vision. The story is so terrible, for a moment I'm hoping it isn't true, but at this point I know better. The worst part is I'm not sure any justice was done. It was such a different time and with the war going on. I'm sure it was organized chaos. I'm sure that man Pawel knew that when he decided to poison another human being. I'm also conflicted because Charlie never even gave any hint of something like that happening. Again, I understand his reasoning for taking everything with him to the grave, but something so traumatizing and so big – how did he just keep it to himself? He didn't even give me any insight to what I was going to learn. Thought about having my mom and dad over and just spilling the beans over some drinks and sports, but the story is all so glorified I can't say it with a straight face. Again, no one would understand what I have seen.

I grab the phone and start to call Grandma Betty. For a moment I think that she had to know something; something of this magnitude Charlie had to tell his wife. But then I wonder what that conversation would be like. Would Charlie have admitted to Betty that he was going to have a baby with his true love, and if it hadn't been stopped he would have never come back? Me telling her would mean that a whole generation of family wouldn't exist. Everything is just so overwhelming I need help to cope or someone I can open up to. The only name I have is Kasia Romanowski, and I have Googled and searched every social media site and the people who pop up, I'm sure, aren't the Kasias I'm looking for. It's like finding a needle in a haystack, and that's even if she is still alive.

I pour a glass of Hennessy and settle in for what has become my Friday excitement, reading the letters. I'm not sure what to expect now. In the last letter I read, Charlie was on his way back to the States. The longest they didn't write to each other is three months. I'm not sure if it's the alcohol or not, but as I start to read this next letter my descent feels different. I can breathe instead of feeling like I'm going to drown. My heart rate doesn't spike and there's no long fall or big flash.

When my eyes open I'm back at the farm, a place and spot I have become familiar with. I'm starting to feel connected to the farm as well. Another impossibility. I see Kasia riding a horse around the farm. I follow her, halfway expecting Charlie to come jumping out of nowhere to say he stayed, but instead I just watch Kasia do some chores around the farm. I follow along with Kasia going to stores, doing everyday chores, and just having a regular life routine. I sit with her while she reads a book, American literature, and I'm waiting for something spectacular to happen but nothing. I don't know what I'm expecting, maybe something magical, but nothing happens.

When I get lost waiting for Charlie to jump out or something to happen to Kasia while she cooks her dinner, a flash goes off and the room goes bright. I start falling but not losing my breath. I can see myself falling in this black hole with nothing around me. Then suddenly I'm sitting up in the chair in Charlie's attic. Even though nothing happens, I still feel the connection to Kasia for some reason. If the rest of the letters are like this, it's just depressing. The worst part is I know I won't get any answers this way.

Chapter 17

I take a rest from the letters for a week and I continue to raise my status at work. Because I've spent the last few months finding myself in these letters, I haven't spent much money or done much travel, and my banking account seems to be bloated. What I mean is it seems like there is more than there should be, so I check back and everything seems to be legit. Shoot, my boss tells me she has loved my performance over the last two months, so I should expect big things in my future. During this week off from the letters, I also get back into my routine of life. I had a great time during Thursday night family time. There happened to be a good Bulls game on, and me, my dad, and my brothers played a good game of dominos and had a few good beers. It felt so good to just sit back and break bread with my brothers. They seemed extremely nice and were doing good. My dad was also in good spirits.

Then I go out with my crew to catch up. We did a little bowling and then hit the bar to catch up. Some of my boys are starting to settle down. One of my guys announced he is going to get engaged to his girlfriend, and we all raise our glasses to him, and then proceed to razz him for thirty minutes.

I go to breakfast with my Grandma Betty; for her age, she sure is feisty and sharp. Pushing ninety-six-years-old, she's still independent—shoot, I'm hoping I'm just walking and going to the bathroom on my own at that age. We talk about some good memories with Charlie. Again, I grew up thinking I wasn't even on Charlie's radar, but the way Betty explains it, from the day I was born he said I was special to him. All he talked about was how great I was going to be and all the people I would affect. She tells me of the moment the day my dad told Charlie he was going to name me Trevor. I freeze for a second because I know the whole story and wasn't sure where this was going. It shakes me too because I remember the last thing Kasia said in one of the letters was she was going to name her child Trevor.

Betty tells me he cried like a baby the day Dad announced he was naming me Trevor. Unlike any other grandchild, Charlie was overwhelmed at the news for some reason, she explains. She says that no one in the family knew why he acted that way, but I know why. Betty continues saying that Charlie asked Tom why he named me that, and my dad said he didn't know why; he said it just came to him. Charlie broke down at that news as well. I know Charlie was emotional because he waited for a sign all this time, and there it was, confirming all his spiritual beliefs. I know the feeling as well. I'm so caught up in Grandma Betty's story that I don't realize I'm crying.

Maybe I'm crying because during all of these simple life moments with family and friends, Kasia's there with me everywhere I go. No one can see or hear her; it's like she's a ghost stalking me, but a nice one. I could be accepting my craziness, but I'm actually getting used to her. I have learned to accept my new reality of seeing magical things happen, so I try to act normal in all the situations. Kasia is there with me as I accept an award at work and a promotion, and she sits in the back of the room clapping for me like my biggest fan. She makes me forget my speech when she just pops out of nowhere. When my brothers and father and I take a break from our domino game for a cigar smoke in the backyard, she sits with us and laughs as we joke about each other. I go on a blind date set up by one of my guys and Kasia shows up at the dinner table with us. Towards the end of the date, Kasia is shaking her no, because the girl kept looking at her phone. I agree with Kasia that this date's going nowhere. We both laugh as we shake our heads at her going to bathroom but taking her phone. Kasia tells me, "Just pay the bill and leave." It's a great idea and I hustle out.

When I go bowling with my friends, she claps for me every time I hit a strike. At one point I give her a high five, and everyone looks at me like I'm crazy for swinging at the air. She laughs so hard she starts to snort a little, and I have to play it off by making a joke. When we all grab beers and celebrate our guy getting engaged, she raises a toast and takes a chug of beer. I almost choke on my beer, spitting up half my sip, and when I look up she's gone. I'm wondering where she got the beer, and also wondered how far my mind has gone.

The most emotional visit is when she shows up at brunch with me and my Grandma Betty. When I sit down at the table and Grandma Betty grabs my hand to say thank you, Kasia sits in the seat right next to us. Betty notices I freeze for a second. I don't say anything; I just watch Kasia walk around Betty, examining her. This is weird. She seems curious. Betty asks if I'm okay and I just say I miss Grandpa Charlie. Kasia joins in as we all take a deep sigh in agreement. Kasia sits down in the chair between us with a cup of tea. At this point, I have given up on trying to figure out where she is getting her drinks from. At first we sit in silence; it's almost as if Betty could see I was nervous and confused. For a second she looks over in Kasia's direction and I feel like she knows Kasia is there or someone is there. Maybe she thinks it's Charlie.

Then out of nowhere, like she knew it would make me feel better, she starts telling stories of Charlie. Her favorite moments, good and bad. There's such an emotional pull as I watch Kasia laugh and cry at Betty's stories. There's a moment that Betty tells a funny story about how crazy Grandpa Charlie could sound and Kasia cries laughing with us. She understands as well. I lose focus of the situation and start reacting and laughing and crying with Kasia. Betty notices and I catch myself. I start rambling on, trying to save face. I'm going to get up and go, but Betty grabs my wrist and starts to tell me the story of how Charlie found out I was going to be named Trevor. There are tears, but when Betty is explaining Charlie's behavior, Kasia's sobbing uncontrollably. She can barely breathe. I'm so caught in emotions that I start crying uncontrollably. It's so hard to listen to Betty tell the story and watch Kasia react to what was an important last moment with Charlie. I can't begin to imagine the thought process she has. Maybe it's the same as Charlie's was when he first heard, but she just has a different point of view. Betty's thinking I'm caught up in emotions for Charlie, so she comes up and puts her arms around me and squeezes me tight. Kasia sees the emotional hug and comes up behind me and hugs me as well. I could barely hold myself up such an emotional moment. I feel empowered; it was a good week.

Chapter 18

Another week begins for me. I actually love Mondays; I feel like I get the most work done at the beginning of the week. It's sad to say it like this, but since Charlie's death my luck at work has skyrocketed. I just closed the biggest deal in company history; the deal was so big the president of the company called me to congratulate me on a job well done. My boss has been super nice lately and tells me to expect a big check bonus – "a life-changing bonus" are her exact words. My boss tells me to take the rest of the week off and celebrate the way I would like. Of course, I figure I'll go to Grandpa's house and finish those letters.

I pull up to Charlie's house now expecting magical things or spiritual happenings. The old lady across the street is still sitting out there. No matter what time of day, she's out there on her rocking chair. She waves and smiles like usual. I yell out my name is Trevor, but she acts like she doesn't hear me and says her name is Irene. Then she laughs and scoffs and says I should know her name by now and she calls me Charlie. I don't need to ask questions. I know right away this is some spiritual happening. I just wave and keep going.

I open the door with my eyes closed waiting for whatever is going to be waiting for me, when instead, once again, I'm hit with the smell of food. The music over the speakers is Ray Charles—that's different. I'm not sure what to expect now, and as I come around the corner there she is, dancing to the music.

I could start getting used to Kasia cooking meals when I come home. It's not weird at all that I'm getting used to a ghost. Again, there goes that indescribable connection I get to her. She jumps as she sees me walk in.

"Hi, honey, I made us a feast." She opens her arms across the island and there's a plethora of food. It looks like a Thanksgiving meal. There's turkey, stuffing, collard greens, yams, potatoes, macaroni, cornbread, Hawaiian rolls (my favorite), green beans, and an assortment of finger foods. It looks like a feast for a big group. Just like that, I feel like I'm starving.

"Kasia, this is great and all, and I am definitely going to enjoy it, but I just wish I knew what was going on."

"Well, let's discuss over our meal here. I waited up for you and I'm ready to eat." She grabs her plate and dances around the island as she picks food she plans to eat. "This Ray Charles is so good. I know why our Charlie loved him. I learned a lot from the conversation with Betty ... so many experiences and emotions that I didn't get to share with him. Sometimes I just wonder what would have happened if I would have come to the States with him." She loses herself in thought.

"Are you supposed to be haunting me? Are you a guardian angel? I'm just trying to paint a picture, because Charlie didn't exactly set me up for success," I tell her.

She pauses for a second. "I'm sorry, Trevor. Again, I know every time I see you I feel like I am apologizing. I'm still trying to figure things out myself. You see, I'm not in control of what's going on either. It started for me too when Charlie died. I was thrust into visions of your life and didn't know what was going on, if I was in a dream, or what the deal was. The real me always saw you in my dreams but never knew why. Why would I be dreaming and seeing the life of some black kid in America? After I got married and had kids I tried to move on with life and forgive and forget about me being poisoned. Then one day you were born and your dad named you Trevor, and all of a sudden I started having flashes and weird things started happening in my life. I chalked it up to weird dreams until it became a regular occurrence. I would see glimpses of your birthdays, and when you had traumatic events in your life. I would see the most important times in daydreams or dreams.

"Again, I understood you looked like Charlie, but I was so unfamiliar with your face and lifestyle and color that I wasn't sure what to think or why I was seeing these things. Of course, you have felt this feeling of being crazy too, right? I could tell no one about it because I couldn't explain it myself. You asked if I was haunting you, but I've always thought it was the other way around. For your whole upbringing I really thought, because of my mistake of not protecting you, I was being haunted and tortured with having to watch the happy life you had. But then one day I realized that you weren't the child I was supposed to have; there was something else. That something else I have yet to figure out, but you are definitely not my spirit child. Obviously with your Grandma Betty and your dad Tom and the rest of the family that idea was cemented. Your beautiful dark chocolate skin is like Charlie's, God's perfect creation. I had always loved Charlie's cocoa skin. Anyway, the visions of your life went away for a while until the day Charlie passed, and then one day during one of my visions you actually saw me and could feel me and hear me. It rocked my whole world. All these years I was thinking you were haunting me, when really there is another reason or message that is not understood yet of why we have been connected all these years.

"You aren't the child I was supposed to have, but I am connected to you in some way and just haven't figured things out just yet. The things you have seen of me and the magic popping up in your life just happens. I have no control over when I show up or what I am doing when I am there. I have gotten to the point where I just try to enjoy the moments instead of fighting them … It seems like you have reached that same point. The one time the young version of Charlie was with us was the first time I had seen him like that. I'm not sure if you could tell or not, but I was trying so hard to just enjoy the moment, but it turned dark because it wasn't what I thought it was. There is something else I need to learn as well. I believe the blood was an aggressive way to let me know I need to follow a different path. So here I'm back to ending up everywhere you are with no explanation and just trying to enjoy it, because to be honest, it's the only time I am actually happy … If it feels like I am talking fast or getting in as much information as possible it's because I am, because I don't know when this will end …" I can tell she's holding back tears.

"Wait, so that means you're … the real you is still alive and these are visions and flashbacks for the real you?!"

"Yes, the stringy, grumpy old me is hanging on still. Because of the simple life I led I remained healthy. Yes, I feel like I'm in purgatory, but I still lead a simple life. I'm healthy for now, but lately I have been sick. I started feeling sick the day Charlie died."

"This is all so surreal and crazy," I say, but I feel like a few of my questions have been answered.

"You know, in my culture we believe in spirits, but this is also crazy to me … I will say this, Trevor. It's obviously impossible you are my child that was meant to be, but we are connected in some way or another, and for both our sakes our best bet is to figure out why."

"I have been trying to answer just that for the last few months. I don't want to be redundant, but since Charlie's death …"

After a moment of silence we just start to eat. The music kicks in and we slam a bottle of wine that turns into three. We

100

eat most of the food ourselves—wow, this woman can eat! We tell stories and laugh out loud like friends. She tells me she plays Ray Charles because Betty said it was Charlie's favorite. She also cooks the Thanksgiving food because most of Charlie's favorite holiday stories revolved around Thanksgiving. After a while I tell her there's no need to explain everything; the food and company are great. I fall into tears laughing when Kasia makes a joke about all during her real life she never had Thanksgiving food or listened to soul music, but now in her spirit world she has turkey legs and listens to James Brown and the Temptations. She does a little dance and holds the turkey leg while she tells the joke. She's also very funny.

I look at the clock and start laughing again because it's two in the morning. We had so much fun that I lost track of time. I never do that. I'm feeling a little tipsy. She sees me stumble over and runs over to help. She gives me a big hug and tells me she's sorry all this is happening to me but she's glad she got the chance to know the family that Charlie built and the man I have become. I ask her how to find her in real life, then her hug gets tighter, almost to the point of pain. Again, I pull back from her and she turns to dust.

Chapter 19

I don't get to finish the letters during the rest of that week, and I have to get back to work. I spend the rest of the week listing my downtown Chicago home for sale, and moving with my dog and settling into Grandpa Charlie's house. Guess I should start calling it my home. I have been spending so much time here it just makes sense. I feel like it's what Charlie wanted in the first place. I will probably never know the carpenter, but it was built exactly the way I would have done it. My girl Maxine loves her new backyard and as I watch her running around the back the last few days, I realize I haven't spent much time with her. Not even sure when I became that big of a dog person, come to think of it. I have to build a new stairway up to the attic so Maxine can go with me. I have a feeling it will be her favorite spot.

Another week flies by and the weekend's here again, and weekends for me have meant traveling into the letters and spending time with my favorite ghost. I laugh to myself thinking if anyone heard me say that I would be committed. I hope to finish the letters this weekend. I'm on the last few and the ones previous were just Kasia doing mundane things and living a really normal, boring life. I dive in to the letters, but the magical plunder of flash-bangs and fast heart rate are gone. No more almost feeling like I was going to die from drowning. It's just a pitch-black fall and then I wake up.

I get all the way to letter thirty, the last one. The last few letters give me a look into what she's leaning towards becoming in life. I'm there when she finishes nursing school and starts her first job. I'm there when she gets her first apartment far away from her family and the family farm. The first day she gets her keys, she just sits in the middle of her empty apartment and cries. It feels like the emotions about finally being on her own, but also realizing she's actually on her own. I'm assuming it was a release of finally getting away from her past after what they did to her. None of the last letters are about her forgiving her family. I can feel the hate in her heart still. I'm there with her as she meets a new set of friends and becomes an independent woman.

Then it's time for the last letter. I pause for a second before I open the letter. Wow, I'm fighting back tears. Am I feeling emotional about not having any more letter adventures? It has been a few months since the first letter, since they met in that tent and fell in love. It feels like it has been so much longer than a few months, because time was floating, really, as I went through the letters. I have grown spiritually since finding this box of letters. Of course, I only need to look where I'm sitting to get a measure of how much my life has changed since line one of letter one. I think while fighting the emotions that I'm really going to miss Kasia in these letters. Not sure if she's supposed to be haunting me or an angel who leads me the right way and shows me signs. Whatever she was supposed or is supposed to be, she becomes a calming force when I have so many questions. I stop asking questions when she's around and our bond gets stronger. I go from not even knowing a thing about Kasia to diving into these letters and her becoming a part of my soul. At first I'm wondering why there was no mention of Kasia from Charlie growing up, but now I'm wondering how he kept it a secret all these years—not just Kasia, but the magical things that were happening to him. Then I open up that last letter …

My dear sweet Chanuntka,

> *This will be my last letter because I finally have accepted we both need to move on in our lives. For me, I have to stop writing because I wouldn't be able to get you out of my head if I kept writing. Every time I pick up this pen I'm flooded with emotions and it's a constant reminder. I have tried to move on and date and do the normal life thing but I have to be honest, I'm having difficulties …*

A flash and a bang and that feeling is back again. My breath is short and I fall fast into a dark hole. My heart rate is at max and if feels like I'm about to have a heart attack or drown. Right at my last breath, I pop back up and gasp for air. When I finally catch my breath, I look around to figure out where I am and it looks like a restaurant. It reminds me of a local steak house. It is semi-fancy and the ambiance is light and elegant. There's Kasia, sitting at a table in a beautiful red dress, her hair tied in a nice bun, wearing matching earrings and a necklace. It's a slit dress with one shoulder exposed all the way down to the middle of her back. She looks like she has been working out for her entire life—maybe the farming work is more physical than I thought. She's drop dead gorgeous. She's sitting, laughing, and, it seems, having a good time. The gentleman she's with is tall and good-looking, but very soft spoken. He seems to be interested in Kasia. They share awkward moments of talking and laughing then switching to weird silence. He grabs her hand and she let him touch her for about a second before she pulls away.

Towards the end of the date the man goes in for a kiss and Kasia turns away. After a moment of silence, Kasia removes herself from the table, and I follow her to the bathroom. She runs to the mirror and stares at herself for a moment. She screams out loud, and I'm sure someone heard it. Tears start streaming down her face as she whispers into the mirror, "I have to move on. I have to learn how to love. That doesn't mean I will ever forget, but I have to do this for me … I will always love you, Charlie."

She picks herself up, dries her tears, and heads back to her date. I'm not sure if she's talking to Charlie or just trying to convince herself. The last image I have is Kasia hugging the man but hiding the tears. By the time I get close enough to touch them, a loud bang goes off, then a bright flash. My heart rate spikes and I start to lose my breath again. The darkness appears over my body as I try to hold on to every breath.

I finally come to and I'm reaching for air. I'm lying on my back with the letter on top of my forehead. I realize the paper on my forehead isn't the letter I read. It's a blank sheet of paper with just scribbled coordinates on it. I'm not even sure if I'm reading it right because it's old and I can barely make out the numbers. I feel like I'm looking at an old treasure map or something. My big globe on the table starts spinning again. When I get close enough to touch it, it comes to a complete stop and once again a red dot sits atop Poland. No address, no city, no explanation, just Poland. I always had the feeling it was leading there, but now it's a must because spiritually everything is pointing that way.

.

"The secret to unlocking your power is falling in love."

Chapter 20

It takes me a few weeks to get my stuff together to make this trip possible. I tell my boss I need to cash in all my sick days and vacation days to take a long trip. At first she scoffs at the idea of me leaving, trying to compliment me and saying she needs her number one guy around. After a few days of negotiations and a sudden turn of events, it turns out our company is working on a project in Poland. They want to open up an office in Europe and, lo and behold, it turns out to be in Poland. I don't believe in coincidences anymore. I know what this is about and happily accept it. My boss tells me instead of taking the time off, I'll get paid for two months overseas, and I just have to do a few business meetings and some phone conferences. I check the office they want me to visit, where I'm going to start my searching, and good thing for me it's only a two-hour drive away. I agree and it pays dividends right away. The higher-ups in our company get word I'm going and think I'm being a team player and want to help the company build the brand in Europe, so they're paying for the trip, accompanied with a driver and all the amenities possible. I'm getting my own secretary for the trip and after a conference call with the president she sends me a company credit card and tells me to get whatever I want during the trip—and she makes a point to say "Anything you want …" before giving me a wink. It's so crazy. I have always wanted this kind of power at my workplace when I was coming into the workforce, and now here

I am. It happens so quickly and we all know with a little help from angels. Man, they even find a house for me to rent.

I check the pictures online of how the house looks and, wow, I will be living in luxury, complete with a Jacuzzi, a sauna, a chef's kitchen, and everything I need for a home away from home. Before the work situation is sorted out, I wasn't sure how I was going to explain to my family that I was going to Poland, but now this turn of events kills two birds with one stone and no one will question it. I was worried I wasn't going to be able to find someone to watch Maxine, and like a miracle the lady next door comes by and offers to watch her. All this time she only sat on that porch and waved, and now here she is, with no warning or no way of knowing what's going on. I wasn't sure at first. I don't know this woman and I just learned her name a few weeks ago, but soon as I open the door Maxine runs out into her arms and they start playing with each other. She never does that, especially with females. Irene, while playing with Maxine, looks up and says, "So going back to Poland, huh, Charlie?" I start to argue and say I'm not Charlie, but it seems like it wouldn't matter anyway. She's so sure I'm him. I just nod my head yes. I was going to start giving directions on what to do for food and Maxine's daily routine and medicines, but Irene just starts walking away and Maxine follows her. Maxine looks at me like she's saying goodbye, but I have to bring her back because I'm not going yet. It's good to know, though, how comfortable she is with Irene. Now I know I'm going crazy. I actually understand the dog.

I have to make sure my passport is up to date, and I have to check with work on computer situations out there and traveling. I've never left the country before so I'm getting my emergency contacts in line as well. I'm going to be in a country for two months, but I don't know the language or exactly where I'm going, and I'm not sure what I'm getting myself into. I have tons of questions in my head, but my heart keeps telling me I have to go.

My flight is early in the morning so I settle in for an early dinner. When I come out of the shower, the whole house smells like food. I can hear Maxine playing and running around with the zoomies downstairs. I walk around the corner and there's Kasia again. She's hugging and rolling around on the floor with Maxine and sees me staring at them.

"Well, Trevor, you picked an amazing dog. Throughout my whole time going through this spiritual reality no animal, or person for that matter, has been able to see me. But this cutie here sniffed me out soon as I popped up in the kitchen." Kasia squeezes Maxine's ears as she jumps into her lap.

"Hello, Kasia. I wish there was a buzzer or a bell or something that would let me know when you were going to be popping up."

"Yeah, I wish I had control over this as well, but I don't, so I'm just trying to enjoy the ride at this point. For example, how long was it from the last time I saw you and your Grandma Betty for breakfast that day?"

"It's been two weeks at least, if I remember correctly."

"You see, it felt like two hours to me. I have no control. The real me just sits around and stares at the views all day, so I actually enjoy these moments. There are a lot of questions and I've spent too many years racking my brain trying to find the answers instead of enjoying the situation that was better than my own life."

"Well, the feeling is mutual. The times we have shared together have actually been nice. I still fight the urge to not feel like I am crazy, but I too am starting to accept my side reality as well. I will say, though, if you are supposed to be haunting me, you are doing a horrible job." We both get a good laugh out of that one.

"Are you hungry? I made some grilled salmon and double-baked potatoes. I hope you like fish."

"Usually not a big fan of fish, but it smells so good, I won't mind a try, and of course for some reason whenever I see you, I'm starving all of a sudden."

"Well, my salmon is the best … so what do you have going on? I usually show up when something is about to happen. I see your bags are packed. Looks like some travel is in your future." She takes a grape and pops it in her mouth.

"Well, it's funny you should ask. I'm traveling to Poland to find you. My flight leaves early in the morning."

Kasia freezes for a second. "Wow … I'm nervous and excited at the same time. Trevor, you know it will be a long trip, and I don't mean just the plane ride. People will stare at you; my culture is not racist, just curious. The language is tough and while it might seem like people are arguing, I promise most of the time they are just talking about the weather or local news. Of course, in every culture or society there are bad people so you will encounter some bad people who want to treat you …

"It's okay, Kasia. I can tell you're nervous … I know what you and Charlie went through. I'm going into it with a different mindset. Times are different and I have to do this. I truly feel like you are sitting there, your real self, waiting with all the answers. Look, at the end of the day, Charlie's dying wish was to find you, whether I find answers or not. I will honor his last wish."

"Thank you," Kasia says, and I can feel her relax.

As we eat her delicious salmon and potatoes, she runs down all the cultural things I should look out for in Poland. I got a Polish phrase book to try and pick up on some of the common words. Not sure this book will be of any use, though, unless I take lessons, because there are a thousand different ways to say things—the Polish language is so hard. Hopefully, Kasia will pop up when I get in trouble. Or who knows? Maybe one of the magic tricks I can try is understanding and being able to speak the language. With everything that has happened, it's possible. It's weird I can understand Kasia when she speaks Polish sometimes. But it's only her that I can grab the language from; everyone else sounds like they're talking gibberish. Kasia and I have so much fun laughing at my pronunciations for sentences she wants me to try. She's actually really funny, and I'm getting used to her humor. Her English accent is also the brunt of some jokes as I make fun of the way she says the word "that." She smacks me on the shoulder every time I have her say "that."

I planned to go to bed early, but Kasia wants to listen to some more of Charlie's soul music. I'm so envious as I watch her listen to James Brown for the first time. She's in heaven. Such a joy to watch her listen to Aretha Franklin for the first time. What I wouldn't give to have that feeling of listening to these legends again for the first time. Apparently, this party is going to continue as Kasia grabs another bottle of wine and sees my grandpa's old record player. She slowly places Al Green on the record player and as soon as his voice hits the speakers Kasia melts in euphoria. She dances around the room and I can just feel how happy she is. She's really trying to enjoy every moment. What a feeling, not knowing when you will be able to have these feelings again. How would I react if I thought every move I made could be my last?

Kasia slows down from the dancing after a few songs and settles on the couch with the bottle of wine and the Johnson family album. We don't talk much as the music softens in the background. We just go through a history of pictures. It's funny, because I have no idea where this photo album came from. I'm sure it wasn't there a few days ago. She leans her head on my shoulder as I slowly explain each picture and who's who. She asks a few questions about my mom and dad and brothers, but for the most part she just slowly examines each picture. I wish I could read her mind as she soaks each picture in.

The very last picture in the booklet is a military picture of Charlie in his army gear. She pulls the picture out and just stares at it. A tear slowly drops down her cheek. She kisses the picture and I can see memories flooding through her head. She whispers out loud, "My *Chanuntka*," and just hugs the picture tight to her chest. For some reason, I feel the pain. She snuggles under my arm and we fall asleep on the couch with Maxine.

Chapter 21

Maxine's barking and the doorbell ringing startles me awake. Luckily for me I have everything packed and ready, because at the door is the limo driver sent from work. I'm able to brush my teeth, get dressed, and walk Maxine within five minutes. After leaving Maxine at the neighbor's house, I'm scrambling to make sure I have everything, when it hits me from last night. Of course Kasia is gone now, but the kitchen is clean—there's no trash, no wine bottles. Almost like nothing happened. The only thing left is Grandpa Charlie's picture on the couch. I have no time to think about it though. The driver yells out, "We're five minutes behind schedule!"

The limo was top notch; the company really went all out for me. On the way to the airport I'm able to send emails and get everything ready to be away for two months. I have traveled all over the USA, but never traveled outside the States and already the international line was different. I'm going with LOT Polish Airlines. My company wanted to put me in first class or fly me out on a jet, but I wanted to dive into the culture right away so I choose to sit economy on LOT Airlines. I can already feel the history on the plane. LOT Airlines, established in 1928, is one of the oldest airlines in the world and it's based in Poland. This is history Charlie would appreciate. If my trip is anything like my journey with LOT Airlines then I will feel like a celebrity, because everyone is staring. I guess there aren't too many dread-headed, long-haired black guys traveling to Poland by themselves.

One lady is nice enough to come up to me and ask if I need help or a guide. Thank God I learned a little Polish and I was able to say *"Dziekuje Ci,"* which is thank you, and *"Tak,"* which is yes. I use those two phrases over and over. Silly, but at least respectful. On the plane I'm seated next to two grandmas. I say hello and try to say a few words in Polish, but they just laugh and smile. My seating arrangement is for me to sit at the window, but instead the grandmas decide it's best if I sit in the middle of them. They giggle, laugh, and talk in Polish as one of them rests their head on my shoulder. In front of me, two kids, maybe five or six years old, just jump up and down in their seats and stare at me. I try playing with them but they just stare at me. This is going to be a great nine-hour flight. I'm starting to question declining the offer of the private company jet.

I'm able to catch up on a few movies and finally finish that book I wanted to read. I'm a big James Patterson fan. I believe this is my tenth book of his I have read. Airplane food is never good, but I was okay with the kielbasa served on the plane. We finally arrive, and after finding my luggage, I see a driver holding my name card waiting for me. My driver's name is Piotrek, and he's a very cool guy who tells me he wants to make sure my stay in Poland is the best ever. My hotel is in a city called Wroclaw. It's a few hours' drive away from Warsaw, so I will get some sightseeing in from the start. Warsaw is such a bustling city. With towering, beautiful high rises and such rich colors, it looks like the most progressive city in Poland. I become a tourist right away and Piotrek is nice enough to stop and explain some of the historical spots we pass. I can't get past the colors. We are definitely in Europe. I also love the different style of cars matching the rich cultural flavor. I can't wait to try some of these food places. I can't understand any of the names, but the pictures and the smells are teasing me.

As we drive out of the city and more into long roads and tall forest trees, I'm hit with the other side of Poland. We drive by a castle that was destroyed during the war days. High rises are now exchanged for big country homes and houses spread out. Reminds me of Tennessee a little. I feel like we went from big city to the middle of nowhere in just a street turn. After all this traveling I'm starving, so I ask Piotrek if we can grab some food anywhere. I look around it's just road and mountains as far as the eyes can see. Piotrek smiles and says he knows just the place coming up. I'm hoping for some home-style Polish food, but at this point I'll take whatever we can find. We take an exit that didn't even have a sign or signal on it. There's nothing on this off-the-beaten path but a small old house. I ask Piotrek about the food and he says, "Just trust me."

The house sits along a mountain line and river in the back. We park along some gravel rocks that sit next to the water. It's such a scenic place. The sun hits the water perfectly as I see some old man fishing off the dock about a hundred yards away. The mountain is so close the edge of it lays on the water. It's so big I can't see anything to the north. As I'm dipping my hand in the water a lady comes up to me and asks if I'm hungry. I have to ask her to repeat the question because her accent is so strong. She says it louder and puts her fingers to her mouth. Piotrek stays in the car on the phone and just gives me thumbs up.

The lady takes my hand and leads me into a little reception area they have right when you walk into the front door of the old house. It has the look of an old diner from the fifties. The menu board only has a few items on it with a picture of two different kinds of fish, some pierogi, and a picture of some fries. Then under the menu board are two different empty beer cans, and I'm assuming those are the two options they offer. I point at the fish on the top, though I have no idea what either fish is. She smiles and asks if I want fries with it. After agreeing, I stand there and she looks at me like I'm lost. She smiles and walks around the counter, then grabs my hand and leads me through a side door, which leads into a shaded covered porch. There are a few round tables with some plastic beach chairs to match. The lady opens the hatch window, which provides a view of the water where the man is fishing. The lady orders me to sit down. I do as I'm told and sit and enjoy the view.

Within a minute the lady comes back with a tall glass of beer. She tells me to hold the beer while she puts in some raspberry filling or something inside the beer. Never had this before; I just do as I was told. She stands there like she wants me to try the beer before she walks away. Damn, that hit the spot. It is so good. It's the tart flavor of beer with a hint of sugar from the berry syrup. I shake my head with pleasure and smack my lips, and she puts another can on the side table for me—some beer called Tyskie. I saw a whole bunch of signs for this beer on the way here, so it must be a popular Polish beer.

Now this is a slice of heaven in the middle of nowhere. I sit with my feet up on the bench, beer in hand, river and mountain view in the background, and as I'm losing myself in the moment I hear a man walking up holding a rack of fish. It looks like he just caught them. He raises his hand and says something in Polish in celebration. It seems as though he wants me to point out what fish I want. I point at the thickest one and the man laughs and gives me the thumbs up.

After the gentleman goes to the back, it sounds like he and the lady are arguing, or maybe just talking, when all of a sudden the woman comes out with a bowl of soup and places it on the table. She tells me to eat, and I've learned to do as I'm told. Some Polish music comes through the old speakers they placed on the corners of the side deck. After about ten minutes the lady comes back with a big plate of fries and my freshly caught fish. The fish is grilled and stuffed with spices, and it looks so good. The woman puts some sauce next to the fries and gives me hand signals to dip the fries in the sauce. She waits for me to take the first bite of fish and it's heaven. After she sees me enjoy it, she yells out to the man that the fish got my approval. I'm in the middle of my heavenly meal when the lady and the man both pull up a chair with their plates of food and sit down at the table with me. Nothing is said; the man just grabs his glass of beer and taps mine in cheers. What an experience! Piotrek comes and joins us at the table and we have a good meal together. Piotrek is able to translate for me and it turns out this is a couple and this is their home and they run the business out of the back. The lady, whose name I know now is Basia, makes the sides and takes the orders, while the man, whose name is Yasek, catches the fish and cooks the catch. What a genuinely beautiful and original idea. We share small talk about my visit to Poland and some history of the house and business. You would have thought I was part of the family. It's getting late so we have to get on the road, but I tell the couple I'll be back for sure. I leave a big tip, take some pictures, and leave my information. Piotrek finally gets me to Wroclaw. What a great start to my treasure hunt.

Chapter 22

After a great journey, I hit nothing but dead ends for the first three days of the trip. The address that's on the letters leads me to an old rundown building that doesn't have any tenants anymore. I can't get any help or find the owner to ask questions. Most of the time people will have to get over the initial shock of me looking like I do, looking for a lady name Kasia. I find out that Kasia is a popular name so this just adds to my finding-a-needle-in-a-haystack feeling. I stop at every shop and store that's around the building to ask questions but get nowhere. Because of the language barrier being so hard, Piotrek, my driver, has become my best friend and translator. He has been my tour guide and my historian. I wouldn't have gotten this far without him. Such a stand-up, hardworking guy, he introduces me to his wife and kids the second day after he picks me up. I feel like he has invested himself in helping more than he should and he's going above and beyond what he needs to do as a driver. He has already asked family and friends about Kasia and I can tell he's hoping I find her just as bad as I do. I will be sure to leave a lofty tip when this is said and done.

We sit down at a local coffee shop in a small town called Bielawa. Once again I can feel the rich history when I am here; this town has been around since the 1700s. There is a thousand-year-old church that sits right across the street from the coffee shop. The shop sits at the bottom of an apartment building.

The apartment building is painted in all different kinds of bright colors, again with that European flavor. As Piotrek and I look over a map and the areas we have yet to explore, Kasia appears on the couch next to us. She says hello to me and then looks around to see where we are. She smiles and whispers the word "*Bielawa.*" She seems so real to me sometimes I have adjusted to see if people see her or not. Piotrek didn't respond to her so I figure we were in the clear. I nod to Kasia as a sign to say hello.

"I used to love traveling to coffee shops like this around Poland all the time. These coffee shops just scream relax and enjoy life for a second." She talks with such joy as she sips on tea. Again, from where I don't know.

I, of course, can't respond so I just nod and smile. Piotrek looks at me awkwardly.

"My friend, are you okay? You look like you just saw a ghost." He frowns a little as I get shaken by Kasia's appearance. I laugh a little at his ghost comment.

"I'm good, Piotrek. Still getting over my jet lag, being in foreign country, and the language, you know."

He nods his head, agreeing with me. "Our language is very difficult but the culture is rich and will lead the way."

"So where are we going today?" I ask Piotrek, who has an old school map of Poland.

"Well, I figure we can try this town called Reszel. It's one of the oldest cities in Poland and not many people know about it. Maybe there's something we can dig up there and find this mystery Kasia you're looking for?"

Kasia puts down her tea, walks over to the map, and points at a spot on the map deep in the middle of nowhere. She points at a spot in the middle of a forest. It's going the opposite direction of where Piotrek just recommended. Kasia just shakes her head.

"My family farm you're searching for, and you read about in the letters, is here. Remember in the letters World War II going on and we had to hide our life and community basically because the war left uncertainty … It won't show up on any Google map or coordinates. It's probably not even on old maps due to our secrecy," Kasia somberly tells me.

"But the last letter gave me coordinates to those apartments we saw in …" I stop mid-sentence because I realize I said the comment out loud responding to Kasia. Piotrek just looks at me, perplexed.

"Okay, Trevor, but I thought we started there already and exhausted those options?" Piotrek's voice just seems confused.

"Yes, I'm sorry, Piotrek. Just thinking out loud … can you take me here now?" I point to the spot on the map that Kasia just pointed to. Right away he looks at me and frowns.

"With all due respect, Trevor, you're paying me so I will take you anywhere you want to go, but I will tell you that this place is in the middle of nowhere. Only thing you find there are old war bunkers, hermits, lots of trees and brush, and maybe a farm or two where people haven't left in centuries. I hate to say it, but I don't believe your Kasia is out there …" He seems almost scared to say it to me.

Before I speak, Kasia just shakes her head yes.

"You know what, Piotrek? I trust my gut on this one and my guardian angel is telling me this should be my next stop. Even if Kasia is not there I feel like it will lead us in the right direction."

"You are the boss." He just smiles and finishes his coffee.

Kasia puts her hand on my shoulder. "Trust me yet?"

Chapter 23

We drive for about two hours on main roads, then a good portion of our trip on one lane roads. Then we turn off into dirt roads. There's the middle of nowhere then there's the middle of absolutely alienated area. Then we come to an overpass where there are just forests and trees. It's a dense woodsy area; it feels like a maze of forest trees as far as the eyes can see. When we pull up to the coordinates pointed out by Kasia there's no road we can just pull up and drive on, at least not seen by the naked eye. Piotrek, being so thoughtful, orders us a motor buggy that he attaches to the SUV. This turns out to be a fun time as me and Piotrek do tricks and donuts as we make our way through the forest. We're laughing at the top of our lungs as we come to an opening that leads to a circle of trees and hills.

A flash hits me and the opening looks familiar. I remember in one of the letters seeing Charlie ride a horse right over this hill and through the opening in the trees. My memory is very good and I'm positive Kasia's family farm is just over the hill. I scream at Piotrek to hit the brakes. We slowly creep through the trees and over the hill. Right when we hit the top of the hill, the memories flood through my head. I see Charlie riding horses with Kasia along the hill. At the bottom of the hill is where those men jumped my grandpa, and I see many visuals of Charlie and Kasia holding hands walking up this hill. I look down and I can see the farmhouse that Charlie helped build. I can feel a pull to this place; it feels like home for some reason. It's regal to me. On top of this hill you can see about three miles in a circular view. I can feel that Kasia and Charlie spent a lot of their time hiding around this place. I'm brought back to reality when Piotrek taps me on the shoulder.

"I see you are admiring the untouched beauty of this place. Probably looked the same 100 years ago. Probably never seen something like this, huh?"

"Well, at least a hundred years before 1945, for sure." I have to stop thinking out loud. Piotrek gives me a weird look as if, how would I know?

We slowly start riding the buggies towards what looks like the center of the mini community. There's a little watering hole and garden in the middle that seems to be a centerpiece of the town. At first the place feels empty and I think we're walking into another dead end, but as we get closer to the well heads start popping out of the bushes. A few bodies start walking towards us; it feels like they're just showing up from out of the trees. We pull the buggies to a stop at the well made out of stone. This stone definitely has been built recently, and when I say recent, I mean after World War II because I don't remember this stone well in any of the letters. As we get off our buggies an old lady comes walking towards us. She has on a big dress that's green and white with big red suspenders. Her hair's tied in a bun with a white bandana that hides her forehead. It seems like traditional Polish attire. She reminds me of a female Viking. She smiles and waves as we walk closer. Right as she starts walking towards us a group of elder seniors started walking up with her. I feel like I have been taken back to the way this village lived thousands of years ago.

"Hello, my name is Trevor. I'm looking for Kasia."

They all look around at each other. Maybe it's the first time some of them have seen a black person in person. They don't say anything for a few moments until Piotrek says something in Polish. One of the ladies smiles and examines me up and down like I must be lost. After a few moments of back and forth with Piotrek, one of the ladies sends a little girl into the middle of the trees by the hill. Piotrek looks at me with excitement, like we have finally found Kasia. Not sure what I was expecting, but I have butterflies in my stomach. This woman has been in my life the last few months in such a spiritual way I'm not sure what to do. I am so nervous because it's not like I was left with a game plan once I found her. I was just told to find her. I haven't even thought far enough ahead. Not to mention the Kasia that has been haunting me is the younger version. The woman I should see now should be in her low to mid-nineties and look like my Grandma Betty's age. I almost wish the spirit of Kasia would show up now so I'd know what to do here.

There are some noises and laughs coming from a row of trees and a group of kids now joins the little girl in pulling some woman around the corner. It seems as though she came reluctantly as the group of kids drags her along. I'm disappointed at first because it's obviously not Kasia, but as they get closer I see a stunning woman. This woman is so beautiful – to say she's a beauty is an understatement. She seems to be my age. She has on a white scarf that she has tied over her head with her Indian braid hanging down to the middle of her back. Her hazel eyes are sharp as she squints to make eye contact with me. She's wearing the traditional dress that a lot of the women here have on, with the green, red, and white designs all along the dress. I can tell she's nervous through the half-smile she gives me. It takes Piotrek tapping me on my shoulder to stop me from staring at the woman for the last minute. I wish I could just tell her the whole story and she could just lead the way, but I came to find Kasia and this is not the Kasia I came to see. It's funny. This must just be wishful thinking, but this Kasia does resemble the Kasia I've been seeing in my visions. The eyes are the same and her nervous smile ... well, I feel like I've seen that in Kasia before in the letters. The walk and demeanor are what really resemble the Kasia I've been seeing.

"Hello, I'm Kasia. They said you were looking for me." Her accent is strong but her English is very good. I ignorantly expected her not to know much given the traditional attire.

"Kasia, first of all, you are beautiful. My goodness, I'm usually not this disrespectful, but I've never been at a loss for words." *Damn, what the hell is wrong with me?* She blushes but I can see her perk up a bit.

"Thank you ... I am sorry, your name again?" I would describe her demeanor as curious.

"Apologies, my name is Trevor ... I wish it was you I was looking for, but unfortunately the Kasia I'm looking for is a lot older than you ... she is a grandmother, maybe great-grandma at this point." This woman has me stuttering.

"Well, I appreciate your compliments and wish I could help," she says. I can feel her disappointment.

"Well, in a perfect world you can help me ... it's a long shot, but there was a Kasia Romanowski that used to own or work here at the farm ... it's her I'm looking for." I repeat Romanowski because everyone reacts when I mention that name. The elders gasp when I say the name while the younger generations start gossiping amongst each other. Well, at least I know there is a Kasia Romanowski, and it's another step in confirming I'm not crazy.

"I am sorry, Trevor, yes? How do you know ... how did you hear of this last name? From where did you get this?" Her aggressiveness lets me know I'm on to something. She seems confused.

"To be honest, if I told you the truth you wouldn't believe me. Let's just say my grandfather was an old friend from the war days."

Kasia turns and says something Polish to one of the elder ladies and shrugs her shoulders. She examines me thoroughly again. She keeps shaking her head no, like she doesn't believe me. Within minutes, more elders show up, and they all stare and point at me. Usually I would be uncomfortable in a situation like this, but I feel confident for some reason. I feel destined to be here. Charlie walked this land with love in his heart. I can feel it now.

"Trevor, you seem very smart and established, so I can say I have to be honest with you … my grandmother has never met a black American man. She doesn't even know English. My grandma Kasia has been in Poland all her life. She was married right after the war and lived the simple life. I'm not sure how you got your information, or how you got this location and name, but you might have the wrong information, I believe." For some reason I feel like she's putting on an act for the elders. I can feel she believed me.

Emotionally, what she said is discouraging, but I have learned not to believe in coincidences. Besides, what are the chances this is Kasia's granddaughter and she's named after her? So there is good and bad news. The good news is my trip has been validated because there is a Kasia. She must be alive; otherwise, I would have been told she's dead. All those letters that take place in the middle of nowhere are real. I know I'm in the right spot; I'm supposed to be here. Bad news, it's apparent now that I need a plan of action when I see her. I should have thought about why my family didn't know anything … it will be the same for Kasia's family. Charlie went to the grave with all the secrets from that time, and I'm sure Kasia did everything she could to remove the memory of what happened to her. No one will believe me, so I'll have to come up with a different approach just to get in front of her. I'm brought back to the group of elders and this younger Kasia is staring at me with anticipation.

"Okay, Kasia, there is a story of how I got here. It's long and personal, and I'm not sure you want me to share it with everyone around." I spread my arms out at all the eyes and people who are staring at us—there have to be at least forty at this point. She walks closer to me, out of hearing distance from everyone.

"What do you suggest?"

"Your grandmother is someone special in my life and I need to meet her here. Please allow me to take you for coffee and I can explain everything. This just isn't the time and place to say what needs to be said." It feels like every second someone else is showing up.

While she examines me one more time, one of the elder men walks over and whispers something into her ear. They proceed to chat for a few moments. It seems as though they are arguing over something. They come to some agreement as Kasia walks over and pulls me to the side.

"Trevor, I don't know who you are, or what this is about, but the information you have got the attention of the elders. No one has called my grandmother by that name in a long time ... by design, if you know what I mean. I'm afraid there are questions from a lot of them and I don't know whose heart is in the right place ... so we can have coffee, but not here and not now. If you come back here tomorrow morning at seven, I will be available to you. Right now, I have to finish my duties and figure things out. It would be disrespectful for me to just drop everything and go to coffee with you when we just met." She seems like she wants to say something to me but can't because of the people around. She's so good looking I'm having a hard time concentrating. I agree to come back at seven and walk away like a kid who just got a yes for the prom.

Chapter 24

My temporary home in the city of Wroclaw is about a two-and-a-half-hour drive away from Kasia's family farm. On the way back to the hotel, Piotrek gives me a history lesson on the area of the farm, the traditional attire, and the way the residents live. The group is called the Highlanders in American history, but to the Polish they are known as *Górale*, an indigenous mountain group who follow thousand-year-old traditional Polish traditions and rules. Between the sightseeing and getting history lessons, I'm falling in love with the country. A young black man like myself from Chicago would never think of experiences like this. The city of Wroclaw is amazing – so far my favorite. The company really took care of me with this temporary home. All the modern fixings, inside and out; they even gave me a spot that looks over the city of Wroclaw.

Piotrek drops me off says he will be back bright and early. I think about grabbing something to eat, but it looks like the airport beef jerky and the Tyskie beer I picked up from the family restaurant will be it. When I walk through the doors, the house smells like food and I can hear that familiar voice singing a Polish song. When I come around the corner, there's my favorite ghost, spirit, or whatever I should call whatever this is, Kasia. She sees me and keeps singing and dancing. She walks up, gives me a hug, and tells me to sit down.

"This meal is called *golabki*, there is rice and ground beef wrapped in cabbage. It's soaked in tomato sauce and my secret ingredient, to make it different than your traditional Polish dish, is I used garlic to add that pop. For sides, I've made some garlic bread and soup. The garlic bread isn't traditional, but I like to add different flavors. Traditionally, it's a lunch meal but it's late and you're used to big meals for dinner as an American, so we will enjoy it for dinner." She speaks as if we do this all the time.

"Hello, Kasia, it's good to see you again. Judging by the way I'm being greeted with no mention of today's events, the real you didn't get the news yet … I met your grandchild today." After I give her this news, she pauses for a second.

"Like I said the last time I saw you, I can't control when I see you or the things that happen. Which grandchild did you meet? I have three kids and they each have two kids—a total of three girls and three boys." She seems lost in thought.

"I met Kasia …"

She cuts me off before I could finish my sentence. "Oh, my sweet, pretty girl … so innocent." She stands there and looks right through me. I wave my hand in front of her face but get no response. I say, "Hello?" and she just remains still. She suddenly jumps up, runs to the liquor cabinet, and grabs two glasses and a bottle of vodka and then walks back to the table and slams the drink on the table. She fills the two glasses, passes me mine, and then proceeds to down her glass.

"Please take a shot and then eat that food. It's really good and I put my heart into making it."

"Kasia, I'm sorry I …"

"No, no, no, you don't have to do that," she tells me. "Eat and I will explain a few things while you're doing so." She takes another shot and pulls a cigarette out of nowhere.

"I'm still not sure what's going on here, or why I'm seeing you when no one else can, but you don't have to talk or say anything.

I can feel your pain right now for some reason. Obviously, something's not right about this situation."

Kasia takes a long puff on her cigarette and I cough. I can feel her heart rate spike a little. "No, Trevor, actually, I've never talked about this, and the real me is going to take it to the grave, so this is good therapy for my soul."

This is all still crazy and weird for me. I'm trying to figure out who is haunting who here. "Okay, Kasia, then I'm your therapist and I'm listening." I take a bite out of the food and she smiles and laughs a little. It's a reaction I hoped for. Damn, this food is so good.

"Oh, Trevor, Trevor, Trevor … from the letters you know the story, but I'm going to give you a piece of the story that you might not know … the story of what happened after the letters. There is a lot you might not know on my end, and it might clear up the picture for you," Kasia says before taking another shot. Can she even get drunk as a spirit? At this point, I would have been knocked out.

"Well, if your story is anywhere near as exciting as the letters, then I'm in for a treat." I'm trying to keep it light because this doesn't seem like it's going to be a fun story.

"Just like Charlie, a sense of humor even in the face of the unknown … The day your grandfather got on that train was the last day I felt love or any kind of happiness. It hurt so bad to watch him walk away, even worse than knowing my own family poisoned me. My *Chanuntka* was just different than anyone I ever came across or have come across in my life. Yes, there were magical things that happened, but he walked around with an aura that just put people at ease. He was just an angel walking the earth. The craziest part was he believed he was an angel; he truly believed it. If it were anyone else it would have come off as crazy, but when he said it, I believed it. From the time he opened those zipper doors on the tent, I could feel the difference. We spent the most amazing year and a half together, sneaking romantic moments every chance we got, horseback riding in the morning during sunrises and during sunsets. We snuck into hostels to sleep together with no questions, and some of the most amazing nights were spent with total strangers. Even simple moments of just sitting and drinking tea were made romantic by Charlie.

"Anyway, sorry, got off track … After he was taken from me—yes, taken from me was the way I saw it—I couldn't deal with it. The damage done by my family was permanent. The poisoning was so cruel. I understand, Trevor, that it was a different time so I still kept a relationship with my family, but it was dark at best. As soon as I was old enough, I ran away to Krakow and Wroclaw to get away from the small-minded villagers. I trusted no one; my heart was black. I met my now-deceased husband, Filip, a little under two years after Charlie left. The only reason my marriage worked was because Filip was weak and followed and did whatever I said. I had to fake it to make it work out, if you know what I mean. That was the curse of Charlie's love. Of course, I learned to love Filip and our beautiful kids and grandbabies, but this next comment will make me sound horrible … I never felt love for my husband or kids like I felt for Charlie. I love my kids to death, like every mother loves her children, but that's what makes it even worse. I never got to the point where I loved them as much as I loved Charlie. I tried with all my heart to match that love. I even prayed that, one day, it would equal the love I had with Charlie, but it was too much work and I was just lying to myself.

"When your heart is black, you are forced to love. The hurt just never subsided … as I say it out loud to you, I believe that is why this spirit of me was born. The real me can't die until this is laid to rest or this broken heart is mended. The hardest part in the puzzle is you. I still can't figure out why you see me and why I show up in your life events. At first I believed you were, spiritually, my unborn child, but that's impossible and it wouldn't make sense. The one thing that does make sense is I can see and feel you, as you do me, because you have some of the soul and spiritual prowess that Charlie had. It still doesn't explain the rest. I can't control this thing; I just pop up, and I wish I had more answers. I will say this: the Kasia you're looking at now is not the one you will find if you do find me. I'm grumpy and miserable. I'm very mean to people and I don't have any friends. I'm sure my family is just waiting for me to die and collect the money I'm leaving them ..."

She takes another shot and just loses herself in thought. I take a shot with her and we eat in silence for a few moments.

"So before you got going there, I mentioned I'm meeting your granddaughter Kasia for coffee tomorrow ... what got you so emotional?" She seemed fine until I mentioned Kasia's name.

"First, I'm surprised she let you call her Kasia. Everyone calls her Kasenka, because I think she doesn't want to be linked to me in any way. Like you were for Charlie, she is my last grandchild. My children and grandchildren were all raised to be more progressive. Of course, I would accept no other way because I know how closed-minded my family was. I pushed for everyone to get out to the main cities, but not just Krakow and Warsaw. I wanted them to see the world. I wanted them to know the real world, that there are other cultures and other traditions that aren't a threat to their being. Being a good person is what I preached, even though I didn't practice it.

"All the kids and grandkids followed suit and agreed with my philosophy and upbringing—all of them but Kasenka. From the time the girl could talk, we all knew she was an old soul. She was shy and timid, never really wanted any attention, and just kind of quietly went through life. By the time she was a senior in high school, she had fallen in love with the culture and the *Górale* lifestyle and way of living. She was a natural Highlander; the more we fought, the more she said it proved her point. She was set on bringing my progressive mindset to the family farm. When she turned twenty-one the farm was looking for new leadership. She jumped at the chance, and she was available at the right time. They needed someone who was young and had energy to do all the duties, but most importantly they needed someone who cared and wanted to uphold the traditions.

"Kasenka was the perfect candidate. They never used to let females in any top position in the community. She was the first. She's so smart, almost too smart for her own good. She immediately put one woman atop her governing board. Actually, it was a proud moment for me, but I couldn't show it. My son, her dad, was devastated, thinking it was a bad thing because of the way I made it seem. Kasenka has settled in nicely as leader. It's a double-edged sword for me, you see. I preached all their lives get their heads out of the forest, but it was needed for someone to keep the farm in the family, for one, but also to keep the history. I shouldn't let one mistake from my family ruin the rich, strong heritage we have in our family … Kasenka remains the only family link to the history. It's tough. She keeps the thousand-year-old traditions going but she doesn't see the world. She has no idea the beauty that is outside of those forest trees. I know what's it like to have everyone go against me, so I let her find her own path. But being stuck in that time warp comes with ignorance of other cultures and not learning how to love what you don't understand.

"You see, Trevor, that closed-minded focus they have there is the reason that my future with Charlie was destroyed. I'm sure when you were there they stared at you like you were some alien from another planet. I'm sure Kasenka was one of few who spoke English. You were, for sure, the first black man most of them have ever seen, and, no doubt, they asked questions as if you were from a tribe in Africa. Most of them have never left the forest, and I'm sure since you left you have been the talk of the town. For such a beautiful place, it has dark spirits. It would only be right that you had to go to that place to find me. The real me will only go back when I'm being buried. In the letters, you already know your grandfather helped build big portions of the farm. No one left would know anything about the dark-skinned American, the *murzynem* that helped build the foundation of that place. The irony of it all is I'm sure the two biggest places left, the two you first see when you walk over the hill, those were built by Charlie himself ..." Once again, Kasia loses herself in thought.

"Well, Kasia ... we meet tomorrow morning at seven for coffee," I tell her. She shakes her head and laughs a little.

"Trevor, you are special. They will stare and test you and give you negative body language, so be patient and let them get to know you ... we will see just how special you are tomorrow. Kasenka knows where I am and how to get to me, of course, but I must warn you she is stubborn, she is smart, and she has been taught not to trust anyone."

Chapter 25

I didn't get much sleep last night. Part of this is due to my excitement about having coffee with Kasia's granddaughter. I'm not sure if I'm excited because I'm having coffee with a beautiful woman who has something about her or if I'm excited because she is the link to find what I came for.

Last night I could feel Kasia's pain – not just the sorrow, but my heart actually ached listening to her sad life. Her hurt is for sure the reason she is supposedly haunting me. Now I just need to figure out why me. Not sure why the real Kasia can't just tell me where she is, but I guess I have to go through the hurdles. It was the same with Charlie not giving me answers. He said I have to learn the life lessons on my own.

Our drive back to the farm is as great as the first. Poland is a beautiful country with so much to see, very scenic. Piotrek is happy to see me. You can tell because he talks the whole ride to the farm. I get history lesson after history lesson of monuments and historical places. We pull up at the bend of the hill before the opening of the trees. The butterflies hit my stomach seeing Kasenka standing there waiting for us. She has such a natural beauty. She has on a pair of jeans and a brown blouse shirt, with her hair in a French braid hidden behind her bandana. Simple beauty. As we pull closer she seems nervous, a little upset. She looks around before she gets in the car. When she jumps in, she tells Piotrek to hurry and take off.

"Please just drive off," she says. No hello, no greetings, not even a courtesy head nod. She just looks around as if she's being watched. It isn't until we get to the main roads that she begins to relax. Piotrek just stares at me in the rearview mirror.

"Hello, Kasia ... are you okay?" I ask. She's shaken and mad at the same time.

"I couldn't let the elders and some in the group know I was going with you. Not sure if you would understand but my community is against outsiders. The elders believe we must not let outside influence in. They are especially particular about ... umm ... people of your skin color. It's not a racial thing. They're afraid of what they don't know and, unfortunately, you were the first, umm ..."

"You can call me a black man."

"Okay, I'm sorry. How about I just call you Trevor?" She bumps me on my shoulder and laughs. Not sure if that's a joke or she's finally saying hello.

"Look, don't let me get you in trouble with your community. I came here to find your grandmother, Kasia. Just tell me where she is and we can drop you back off at the farm and be out of your life," I tell her. She shoots me a dirty look.

"Piotrek, can you please take us to Dzierzoniow?" she asks.

Piotrek stiffened a little. "Trevor, that is almost an hour away in the other direction we came from. Are you okay with that? Sorry, Kasia, but he's writing the checks."

Man, for some reason this feels a little more serious than just coffee, I think. I figure a little coffee and I would charm her and she would tell me where her grandma is. "Whatever Kasia wants, Piotrek. I'm fine with that drive."

"Okay, Trevor," he says, tapping his forehead.

"Don't worry, Piotrek. I'll make sure to pay you for the extra drive."

We sit and drive for a moment in silence before Kasia jumps out of her seat like she couldn't sit quietly anymore.

"First, let's get a few things straight: please call me Kasenka because Kasia is my grandmother's name and I don't like people to be reminded of my grandma when they see me. I like how you just expect me to give you my grandma's address and then send you on your way. I don't know you. I don't know what you need with her. The only reason I agreed to meet with you is because not many people know that last name, Romanowski, to the point the family went lengths to not be associated with that last name."

"Did your grandmother tell you the reason?" I ask. I guess we'll jump right into the deep end.

Kasenka pauses as she thinks about my question. "Well, no, actually … She always preaches that a big portion of the family is closed-minded and not ready to be in the real world. She gave a speech one day—I believe it was her last time on the farm— saying her personality is not what it should be because of the ignorance of the farm, and her heart and joy were stolen from the stubbornness of the community to not change … she never elaborated. We just all followed … well, except me."

"The very exact reason your community stares at me as if I'm an alien is the same reason Kasia left."

"You call her Kasia with a tone as if you know her or have a relationship with her." Her accent is so strong. It's just like Kasia's, so beautiful.

"You see, if I told you I have a spiritual relationship with your grandma you'd think I was crazy, so instead I'll let you get to know me first, then I'll tell you the truth."

"Trevor, you seem like a very intellectual guy, and obviously respectable, so you will understand real conversation. I don't think you'd take offense if I said that's crazy and impossible.

I don't know how or where you got your information, but please let me know your source."

I laugh a little because she is trying to be tough, but to me she's a gentle soul. I can see right through it. "Let me ask you something. Something made you agree to actually come with me on this drive, wherever we're going … why?"

"I told you, because you knew the old family last name."

"Nah, there's more. I could've found that name on Google, like you said, and you could've just told me to get out of your life day one. You could've thought it was a lucky guess … but here you are in a car with me when, like you said, you don't know me."

"So smart and a smart ass, huh?" Kasenka replies. She is sharp.

"Now that you have called me an ass, I believe we're comfortable with each other and we can have a good conversation."

"Are you for real?"

"Kasia … sorry, I mean Kasenka. Are you a spiritual person?"

She rolls her eyes and takes a deep breath. "I am a spiritual person. It's a part of our culture, but we're from two different worlds. Your spiritual definition might be different than mine."

"You might be surprised, and if you just open your eyes to a different spirituality, I could tell you a love story that was love before its time. A love story that has led me to be sitting in front of you right now."

"So talk …"

"You know, I like Piotrek and don't mind telling him how I came here, but I'm not sure you want your family business out there. You know, since you guys are all about your privacy." It got a little uncomfortable, but I didn't come here to make friends.

She looks at Piotrek in the rearview mirror, then says, "You're right … Well, we have a little time while we drive. We'll cover things very personal to both of us, so I feel like I should know a little about you."

"Well, first you should know I consider myself a gentleman, and ladies should always go first."

"Ha, gentleman, yes, but you are also good at controlling a situation. You have a good answer for everything … okay, fair enough. I'm twenty-six-years-old. I run the family farm. I'm actually the first female to be in charge of the farm. I have big plans to upgrade the farm, not just the structure and culture, but from the nail of the first cabin to the last house around the forest. The cabins need some help. It's been a long time, maybe before I was born, that the cabins have been worked on."

"Yes, actually, since the war."

"What?!"

"Nothing, I'm sorry … Continue."

"Anyway, my community is very old and is stuck in their ways. I'm trying to bring them up to this century. They allowed a woman to be in charge, so I figure they are ready for change."

"Any hobbies? Or is life all about the farm?"

"I like to read. I do a lot of hiking. I love being out in the wilderness, and I've probably hiked every mile of my family farm and forest. I'm just a girl in the tress, and I feel like it is my calling to be in the woods." The natural beauty that she has is boosted with her love for nature. Her affinity for the forest is like my chase for the business life and money.

"Wow, much respect. I admire your passion for the life you live. You're basically living your dream. Are you married or involved with anyone?"

"Trevor, Trevor, Trevor, you call yourself a gentleman? That's not something a gentleman would ask. Now, it's your turn."

"Okay, I apologize. So where do I start? Not used to talking about myself … I can start with work. I'm in the money management and investment business. We basically buy up struggling companies, chop them up, and sell the pieces. I hold a pretty good spot within the company. I'm actually in Poland on business to close a deal. I'm like you; I'm the youngest grandchild. My brothers have kids, so there are great-grandkids now. Socially, I have a good set of friends that I get together with at least once a month. I get along with all my family for the most part. Working out is one of my hobbies I love. I read a lot because I like to read—funny, lately I was reading a whole bunch of love letters, but we'll get into that later—but yeah, that's pretty much it. I know I live the boring life."

"And are you dating someone?" she asks, smiling big and hitting me on the shoulder again.

"Well, excuse me, but that's not something ladies should ask," I respond as we both share a giggle.

"You know, Trevor," she says, "you seem sad, lost, or not really passionate about what you're doing in life, especially after I talk about mine. Please correct me if I'm wrong." Wow, this woman is definitely aggressive. She's just meeting me and already destroying my character.

"You know what, that's a fair assessment. I have everything I want and need in my life. Yet spiritually, I don't have a voice. Growing up I always believed if I got enough money to do what I wanted then I could chase my passions with no boundaries. I've spent most of life chasing money … to be honest, I believe that's why I'm here. This is something way out of my comfort zone and I'm loving every second of it. I've seen things over the last three months that have changed my mind and life forever. I'm in the middle of nowhere in Poland, a country I never ever imagined coming to. I'm here to find your grandmother based off some very, let's say, spiritual circumstances. This will sound crazy, but I've never been more passionate about finding someone in my life, if that tells you something. I've never gone this far out of my way for anything in my life."

Kasenka pauses and squints her eyes at me for a moment. "You truly believe you know my Grandma Kasia?" She seems confused.

"This might make you mad or bother you, but I'm willing to bet my life that I know her better than you do," I tell her as her face turns into a squint like she has tasted a sour lemon.

"Who are you, Trevor? You're right, that sounds absurd … You just met me and you feel you know my grandmother more than me? Of course, that sounds crazy. But crazy as that sounds, the fact is you knew her maiden name. The community leaders didn't want me to have this meeting with you—that was my first red flag. It wasn't that they were surprised or anything; no one mentioned surprise. It was how much they just wanted to destroy that name. We spend a lot of time preaching and practicing privacy, so it's almost a miracle that you not only knew where the farm was but the name. My curiosity was piqued too much not to know more."

"The only way to make you truly believe me or understand is if you let me see her. You won't believe what my last three months has been like. You won't believe what I have to say."

Chapter 26

We finally pull into the town of Dzierzoniow. Absolutely beautiful town, my favorite for sure. Big historical churches, colorful apartment buildings, trees and brush throughout the town, old mom-and-pop stores, everything is within walking distance of the middle of town. There is a big statue of Pope John Paul II in the middle of town. I see an old concentration camp right outside of the city and thousand-year-old cemeteries. I can feel the history of this town in my bones. They don't make towns like this anymore, or should I say, there aren't towns like this in the U.S.

We pull up to a security gate that lets us into what look like botanical gardens. It looks like a garden community, each lot about the size of a basketball court. We drive past about twenty, and all of them looked different. It looks like somewhere expansive, with gardens growing vegetables and fruits carrying the semblance of the Martha Stewart vineyard, while some look as if they haven't been touched in years. Kasenka tells Piotrek to stop at one of the gardens. There's a glass house in the middle of the garden. The glass room is about 500 square feet. Inside there's a little sink, a plastic table with four plastic chairs around it, a few kitchen items, and a little pond right to the side of the table. On the outside of the glass house is a plethora of vegetables, fruits, and some vines of grapes and fruits. There are raspberries, lemons, potatoes, and carrots. A corner of cabbage goes down to a pillar of grapes – there's everything here.

Kasenka looks excited as she jumps out of the car and practically runs into the glass house. She waves for me to come and tells Piotrek to come back in about three or four hours. She's so used to being a boss.

"This is very nice and tranquil, very peaceful … What is it?"

"After World War II the country was obviously in shambles and people needed help. To help families out, the government gave each family a plot of land so they could grow food and survive on their own. It was a small gesture that I'm sure they didn't think would last into this century. At first I believe it was for poor families, but as Poland progressed there wasn't a need for the majority of the gardens, but they became a part of many family tree lines. Some families let them go, but depending on what city you were from, they would dictate how well the gardens were maintained. If your city had more old people and older culture, then you would see a lot of the gardens being upheld. If you were from a more progressive city or younger town, the gardens have been let go or forgotten."

"This is great. The glass house looks so, man, I don't know what the word I'm looking for …"

"Heavenly."

"Yes, you stole the thought out of my head … It looks like your family kept up with the tradition."

"Yes, you are correct. It's so rich with history. It has been me mostly who has made sure this place stayed up to date."

"Believe it or not, I can feel the history."

"Well, I want you now to be a part of that history. Please grab that shovel over there and start digging a new hole over there near the corner barriers."

"Oh, man, you're putting me to work?" I laugh out loud.

"Did you just think you were going to grill me for information for nothing?" She smiles big.

144

We work in the garden for about an hour. We don't talk much; she just gives orders on what she wants me to do. It's just silence while working and gardening; it's very serene, actually. It's like meditation for me.

"Okay, Kasenka, why did you bring me here?" While this is very fun and relaxing, I did come here with one goal in mind.

"This was one of Kasia's favorite places to get away. This is the only place where she would ever bring me and I would see her be happy. It was only a few times, but this place is one place I felt like I had a grandma. I figured to come here to reminisce. She distanced herself from the family and this was her getaway. One day we sat here and she said to me that this place is only about the gardens. There's no hate because you can't hate fruits and veggies. It was the sense of humor I never got from her. Her obsession with being progressive sent her mad, I believe, but no one in the family ever knew why. We just followed …"

"But you?"

"It wasn't that I didn't follow. I totally agreed with her view and need for progression. I just felt it could have been done at the farm and we could be the generation that breaks that cycle. We can still keep our traditions and history but allow new age thinking."

"Okay, Kasenka. I believe now it has come to the point where I can tell you how I got here and the reason I'm here … I know why your Grandma Kasia became that obsessive about progression."

"Trevor, just in these few hours we have spent together I can tell you're a good person and not crazy or on drugs. So I'm listening, but you understand how unbelievable this seems?"

"Oh, it will sound even crazier once you hear the story, but remember I knew the name and more importantly where the farm was. It wasn't a guess."

"I'm listening with open ears and an open heart," she says as she walks over to the glass house and brings us some tea.

"This is a picture of my Grandpa Charlie. He met Kasia during his time here for the war ... World War II that is." I lay a picture of Charlie on the table. I can see I have Kasenka's full attention. Her body language changes as she examines the picture.

"Wow, very handsome man." Her accent makes me lose my thoughts sometimes.

"I feel it was love at first sight between my Charlie and your Kasia in the hospital tent where she was nursing. Charlie was a part of a battalion sent to Poland to rescue survivors from heavily occupied areas. From the start, Charlie was in love with Kasia. He risked a lot just to sneak moments with her. For a little over a year Charlie would get in trouble sneaking to see Kasia in the middle of the night. After just a few months my grandpa became a regular at your family farm. At first he blended in with the locals because the war made everyone come together. They went horseback riding, took trips to Krakow to sleep in hostels, and hid in underground bunkers together. There's a hill by the entrance of your farm I've visited many times with them holding hands. They had a spot near an apple tree where they would always meet. They just called it their spot. I'm sure you know where it is; it's where the apple trees are near your forest. Whenever things would get tough, they would meet at the apple trees just to get away. They hugged and kissed every chance they got. My heart rate spiked when you mentioned the renovations you want done at the farm. My Charlie helped build the two big houses that are in the middle of the farm, the ones with the water systems ... you're right; the renovations haven't been done since then. It still looks the same. He was so in love with your grandmother he convinced a few of his army buddies to help do some of the manual labor. I can tell you that the foundation of the farmhouse with the kitchen will go soon because back then they didn't make it to last. If you don't believe me, have some of your workers check it out right away." That last little nugget of information put it in perspective for her.

"I will admit I'm at a loss for words, and that's very hard to do, Trevor ... a smart man like yourself will predict my next question then: how do you know all of this?" she asks, and I can see her strong, confident demeanor changing.

"Umm, well, the whole way here I was trying to think of a way to tell you. I thought about telling you Charlie told me everything in a recording, but unfortunately I'm a bad liar and after meeting you, you would have seen right through me. My problem is the truth is so glorified that this will be the point that you tell me I'm crazy ... if you didn't already think so."

"You've already come this far with what I thought was a glorified chance, so fire away, cowboy."

"My Grandfather Charlie died this year ..."

"Trevor, I'm sorry for your loss. You spoke as if you'd just seen him, so I wasn't sure." She grabbed my hand with true compassion on her face.

"It's okay, Kasenka. I believe he's happy in heaven. I wasn't the most present grandchild, and I wish I would've made more time with him. It's also part of why I'm here ... You should know the last thing my grandfather said when he knew he was dying was to find Kasia. His last dying wish was for me to find her. Out of all the things this man could have wished for with his big family, he wanted just that from me."

Her face turns to stone. The compassionate face is now confused. I just told her I've seen the foundation of her life before she was even born or thought about, before her grandparents met. There might also be the realization that I'm telling the truth – or at least my reality truth.

"You understand that if your story is true this means my family history is a lie and I've been told lies, and I have so many questions ... my family is a question."

"I've been through the same mental process you're going through right now. I questioned my whole existence. After reading all the letters, I know my Grandpa Charlie's true love was Kasia. My Grandma Betty said she tried her whole life to figure out what made Charlie tick, but she never could get to the Charlie she knew was in there ... As much as it hurt, it didn't stop me from learning the truth of what happened."

"So you know this from letters? I know you truly believe what you're saying, but you have to forgive me, this sounds ... well, I don't have words for it."

"Oh, there's more. I asked you earlier if you believed in spirits."

"Yes, I thought it was a weird question before, but now in this circumstance I believe we are talking about the same definition of spirits."

"This will sound ... oh, never mind. Since the death of Charlie, the spirit of your grandmother has been visiting me. I know she's still alive but I'm being haunted by a younger version of her, if you want to call it being haunted. The version of Kasia right after the war." As I say this, Kasenka doesn't move or flinch.

"Please continue."

"When Charlie died he left his house to me, only me. He had many people in the family that I felt he was closer with, but he left it to me to the surprise of everyone. Anyway, about a week later I was at the house getting things together to sell the old home. In the attic was a box of letters, the letters I told you about already. The box of letters was labeled 'My love Kasia' ... and now back to how I know all of this. I didn't just read the letters. I experienced them ... Again, open your spiritual mind.

Every letter I read I was physically sent to that moment, right to the memories of what Kasia wrote down on the paper."

"You know, I wondered how you knew so much detail about the forest area around my farm, but I'm sorry, I'm confused. What is it you mean by experienced?"

"Kasenka, I was physically there when my grandpa walked into that tent and met your grandma. I was there when the sun was setting on their horseback rides. I was there when Charlie sat at the table with your great-grandparents and broke bread with them. I sat right next to Kasia when she and the family sang Polish hymns with Charlie being loved by all the *babcias* in the room. I was there when they ran from soldiers just to sneak a minute to be alone. I sat with them when they decided to try and be together and they were going to deal with any of the hurdles that came their way. I was there when a jealous boyfriend of your grandma brought his crew over to beat up my grandpa. Unfortunately, I was there when … let's just say I was there when things happened that made your grandma become who she is today. I was there when Charlie and Kasia stood at the station and cried together while he made the gut-wrenching decision to go back to the States.

"Kasia was never the same after Charlie left. They wrote a few letters and stayed in contact, but both agreed it was best to move on and live life. They both moved on but were never the same, could never love the same. I thought the letters would be the end of it, but things started happening in my life. Good things, but unexplainable, magical things. Along with these good things was the spirit of Kasia showing up in my life. She has made me pierogis at Charlie's house, which is now mine. She has cooked me every Polish meal possible, introduced me to food I can't even pronounce. The best part is she did it with passion. It was important for me to like the meal. But it goes beyond the food as well. She has been with me when I've gone out socially with friends. She hung out with me and my family during our traditional weekly visit. Kasia even came with me on a date. We had a good laugh when she didn't approve of the girl, and we paid the bill and ran out. I felt like I was hanging with a good friend. There was a dark moment when I got to see what it would have been like if Kasia would have come to the States with Charlie. I was there in your family's darkest hour. I witnessed your family do something terrible to Kasia. I could tell each story in more detail, but we would need more time … plus, I truly believe these stories could be told by your grandma if you let me see her."

Kasenka stands up quickly and starts pacing back and forth, staring at me. For some reason tears start falling down my face. I feel happy and okay. I guess running through all those memories again has me emotional. Kasenka stops and grabs both my hands and stands me up. She stares into my eyes. I can see sympathy for the tears, but I can also feel her searching my soul. I'm sure we have been standing holding hands for at least a minute. She keeps shaking her head no in disbelief. I know what she's going through. Questioning everything you've been told in life or thought in life is tough.

"Trevor, Trevor, Trevor … coming here was a chance for me to do something I've never done in life and have coffee and conversation with someone I didn't know from a different culture. I knew in my heart that this would be interesting, but honestly, I thought I would never see you again after today. I came here believing that you got lucky finding that information and did a little research and found my grandma by accident, but after listening to you and watching your body language I believe you truly have a relationship with my grandma in your head. I can tell you truly feel you know Kasia. It will take a little more for me to just walk you up to Kasia, but my heart and eyes are open. Look, Trevor, I need to process what you have told me, because questioning my family history that was so ingrained in me – I will need to give it some thought. Would you be able to wait another day for me to think about it? Or is your trip coming to an end soon?" She looks as if she is hoping there's more time.

"Of course there's a deadline to my hunt here, but I will not leave Poland until I can at least get in front of Kasia for a moment. She is the treasure hunt I came for." After I said that, she smiled and relaxed a little.

"Okay, let me go home and process this. If you can pick me up for dinner tomorrow, it will give me enough time to check some things."

"That's okay with me … and here is something to help you process what I have told you today. Your Grandma Kasia has a giant brown birthmark on her right butt cheek. There might only be two men who know that, Filip and Charlie. Have whoever is with her check. You'll know I'm not crazy then."

She's shocked, not because I knew about the birthmark that she didn't know about, but that I threw out her grandfather's name, which she never mentioned to me. She wants to talk about it, but Piotrek pulls up and our private moment comes to an end. We spend the whole ride back to the farm with her staring back and forth at me and the views and thinking.

Chapter 27

Of course, I can't sleep when I get back to the temp house, but it works out because I have a big lunch meeting for work tomorrow and need all night to prepare. It's the first business meeting for my company in Europe, so the higher-ups have been calling and emailing me in panic mode. Interestingly enough, I feel pretty confident, when usually I would be in a panic. Maybe it's because I have other things on my mind and this is the least of my worries.

The morning goes by in a haze because of the lack of sleep, but at the very least I'm prepared. It's a short drive because the meeting's in Wroclaw, where I'm staying. And, of course, what's an important situation without my new best friend Kasia? She gives me the biggest smile as she sits in the back of the SUV. Of course, I check to see if Piotrek can see her and he just looks up to tell me we are almost there. He pulls me up in front of the corporate building like I'm a boss, and I walk in the building as if I own it.

"You have the best timing …" I tell Kasia. I wish she would show up when Kasenka was around.

"Trevor, when will you realize and listen to me? I can't control it. I'm surprised as you are when I show up in your world."

"Well, I'm on my way into a meeting to build my company's European portfolio. It's a pretty big deal for my company, so it's important for me."

"Oh, wow, we are in Wroclaw. Ooh la la, you are big business, huh?" She smiles and I just realize that Kasenka has that same smile and strong accent. My favorite.

"Yeah, I'm excited. Hoping things go well financially. This will be big step in my life if I can make this happen."

We walk in the building together and I start to tell her about my talk with her granddaughter but I'm brought to reality when I see a few corporate guys staring at me talking to myself. I keep forgetting people can't see her, and I look crazy. I get to my floor on the elevator as Kasia talks my ear off about her history with the city of Wroclaw. When I walk in the room there's about twelve men and women talking in Polish. They all greet me and shake hands. I sit next to one of the young ladies who I believe is the translator, just in case we need one. Kasia is standing behind the group, listening to their conversation in Polish. We share pleasantries and then get right to business. Of course, there's a lot of legal mumbo jumbo, but to sum it all up this company wants our company to finance their business park and business startups. They present their pitch for about three hours. Turns out Kasia is a great ally to have in the room. The translator works for their company so she is only telling me what I want to hear and leaving small things out. Kasia gives me every single corner they tried to cut. We then come to the end of the meeting and it's time to move on or move forward. I give the expectations and numbers my company needs in return. The banter goes back and forth, then Kasia stands up and comes around the table with a determined look on her face.

"They're having a hard time trusting you. All the numbers add up and sound good. They know it will be successful but like at all levels in life they don't see or do business with black men a lot so they fear what they don't know. Unfortunately, with millions of dollars on the line for them, this is still a hurdle. You will repeat after me and we will close this deal:

"*Dajcie spokoj chlopoki, przecież wiecie, ze ten biznes ma sens. Wasza ignorancja spowoduje ze to Wam przepadnie. Wszystko się zgadza. Moja firm jest dobra, jest to korzystnie dla obu stron. Nie wspominając chłopak kocha Polska tradycje.*"

The room sits shocked thanks to Kasia's guidance. I don't even know what I'm saying at the time, but Kasia basically explains that I say "This is a great deal. Do not let your lack of trust for me make you miss out on this win-win situation," in Polish. I close by saying I love the Polish culture. I have the room at attention; even the translator couldn't hide her surprise. Kasia smiled as if she was pleased. Things are agreed to and I'm scheduled to come back at the end of the week to close things and transition. I walk out of there feeling triumphant and ready for my dinner date. I go to thank Kasia, assuming she's still with me, but she's disappeared.

Chapter 28

The meeting takes so long I don't have time to run back to the house and change, so it looks like I'll be overdressed for the dinner date with Kasenka. I get my secretary to find us a private, top-notch restaurant and it turns out there's one just thirty minutes from the farm. I know she is very private, so I aim for private and exclusive. Looks like we will both find whether or not it is out at the same time. For some reason, I catch myself going all out to make sure she has a good experience and enjoys herself. This time, instead of us picking her up from the farm, she's having us pick her up from the local bakery shop in the next town over. My breath is taken away as we pull up and see Kasenka standing there anxiously, looking stunning. She has on a beautiful, long red dress that's slit at the legs, with one strap over the shoulder, showing off her arms and figure. Damn, the farm work has treated her well. Her hair is tied up at the top as the rest of her ponytail slides down to her back. Her earrings make the hazel in her eyes sparkle. This woman is the definition of beauty. She completes the look with white platform shoes that tie around her ankle and up her calf. I'm so excited I'm compelled to get out of the car to open the door. I beat Piotrek to the door I'm moving so fast. She smiles at the gesture and lifts her hand for me to let her in.

"Forgive me for being forward, but my goodness, you look drop dead gorgeous. I mean, stop-the-room beautiful."

She smiles and tries to hide her blush. "Thank you. Oh, I feel so much better. I thought I was overdressed. I don't get a chance to go to dinners, or out at all, come to think of it. So for the occasion I wore one of my best outfits." She smiles the whole time she talks. I'm hypnotized.

"Ha, funny thing. I'm glad I wore my work suit. It, at least, allows me to fit in with you … at least as your driver," I tell her, and she giggles a little.

"First, I'm grateful for you treating me to dinner. Again, my life is the farm so this is a break from the normal for me. I actually was … am very nervous." Wow. She's a totally different person from yesterday.

"Don't thank me, because my intentions for this dinner aren't just the food. To be honest, I'm treating for dinner in the hopes you will link me with your grandma, so I'm no saint."

She laughs again. "Well, if bad intentions to you involve seeing my grandmother, you, my friend, are a saint."

On the drive to the restaurant we share small talk about her farm and what goes into a day's work running it. She's so passionate about her work and the farm. I'm envious of her passion. Piotrek pulls us up in front of the restaurant. I'm more of a beer and burgers guy, but this place is a spectacle. Before coming to the front you drive through a maze of trees and forest until you're hit with what looks like a big log cabin. It's almost like we were special guests at someone's wealthy cabin home. The walk up to the door features an overhead roofed stairway centered over a red carpet with candles riding the edge of the stairway all the way to the door. A gentleman greets us at the door and knows our names. He leads us to an open ballroom with about fifteen tables spread out. Each table has its own candle set, champagne bottles, red roses, and LED lighting. They seat us next to the window looking out over a river. There's an old man playing a piano in the middle of the room for all the guests. When I told my secretary to find something nice and private, I didn't think she would get one of the most exclusive restaurants in all of Poland. I'm feeling a little guilty because it's very romantic and I don't want Kasenka to think my mind is in the wrong place. But my nerves are quickly calmed as I catch Kasenka standing near the piano enjoying the music. She looks like she's requesting a song. She has such a good soul and aura about her. She reminds me of her Grandma Kasia. By the time I snap out of my thoughts, Kasenka is running at me.

"Trevor, Trevor, please dance with me to this song. It's one of my favorites."

So many things run through my mind as she pulls me toward the dance floor. She leaves me at the edge of the dance floor as she walks ahead of me. She slowly turns around with a little dance of the hips and waves me over. She pulls me close, snuggles up to my chest, and wraps her arms around my shoulders. I can feel her listening to my heart beat and the music. She has to notice my heart is racing. I squeeze her tight and get in a dancing rhythm with her. I start to talk but she puts her hand over my lips as a sign for me not to speak. We are the only ones dancing. I'm worried she's going to think it's too much, too romantic for just a meeting, but instead she snuggles in like we have done this before. We dance until the end of the song before finally sitting down at our table.

"Oh, my God, that was everything I had imagined it would be," she says as she jumps up in elation.

"I'm sorry. What do you mean?"

"Oh, come on, Trevor. Open your eyes. You know after being out in the great world you're lost when things are right in front of you. You have to understand the reclusive life I was brought up in. I never had a prom, as you Americans would call it. We don't do dinner dates like this in my community … To be honest, as I look around, not many people get a dinner at a spot like this. It's a different kind of dancing we do for my culture … so yes, this is like a prom for me. Thank you." Then she smiles and sits down like it's no big deal.

"I'm at a loss for words, Kasenka. To be honest, I've never done anything like this either. It's not often you slow dance in the middle of the restaurant by yourself. Thank you for letting me be a part of your first experience."

"Oh, you're a part of a lot of firsts for me in just the three times we have seen each other."

The waiter comes by to ask what we would like to drink. I'm still not sure where this dinner is going, so it's better the lady goes first. When she orders the most expensive bottle of champagne on the menu, I giggle a little.

"You look like you could afford it," she says, giving me a wink as she looks around at how glamorous the place is. She's right. I can afford it, but luckily for me the company is paying for everything so she can have whatever she wants. After being shy about what to order to eat, she tells me to go ahead order and then she tells the waiter, "I'll have what he's having." We chat over porterhouse steaks and garlic mashed potatoes with avocado toast. A girl who likes steak is a beautiful thing in itself. You would have thought we had known each other for years the way we converse. After being hidden away in that forest all these years, she sure has a worldly personality.

"Cheers to a great day. Can you celebrate with me, please? I made a deal today for my company that was big," I tell her. We clink our glasses together.

"Congratulations. A gentleman and a successful businessman? I had you all wrong … Who are you, Trevor?" Her tone changes to serious.

"You know, up until a few months ago I thought I knew who I was. I've reached my business goals and made more. I'm financially independent. I feel good health-wise. But something is missing in my life. After Charlie died, so many unexplainable things started happening in my life that made me question everything. The thing is, it hasn't been bad things happening to me that caused this. It's been magical and good. Your grandma coming into my life has actually been one of the best things. She has pulled out a piece of me that was in my grandfather that I didn't know existed. She showed me the real Charlie. They showed me what real love is."

"You're so convincing, but there has to be a different story ... You mean you've come all this way on spiritual things happening and those letters?" she asks. She still seems to be processing what I told her. I believe, at this point, she trusts me and knows I'm telling the truth, but accepting that truth would mean there were big lies in her family. It would also mean she's accepting she's a little crazy, like me.

"Yes. Again, they're not just letters. They're portals into that time period, so I can see and feel their relationship and struggles."

"Trevor ... my head, my mind, and my brain are fighting, but my heart believes you. I did call to check to see if Kasia has that birthmark on her butt and she does ... but how ..."

"Trust me, I know what you're going through. It took me a few weeks to make sense of it all before I let it happen and accepted what was happening. I'm asking you to do the same thing in a shorter amount of time. Trust me, you haven't seen anything yet. So many magical things ... this is why I have to see Kasia to hopefully get some answers."

"You sound so sure."

"Kasenka, I could smell them. I could feel their sweat in the hot sun. I could touch their cold breath in the snow. When they laughed it was pure. It was as real as me sitting in front of you right now," I tell her as I feel her start to break.

"And you believe when you see my Grandma Kasia she will recognize you and know who you are?"

"If not, then I'm crazy and all of these things were just a coincidence, but at least I got to meet you."

She sits there and plays with her fingers for a few seconds. So many thoughts are going through her head, I'm sure. "I will take you to see her ... but it will not be easy ... My family scoffed at the idea when I told them an old family friend wanted to come see her."

"Just allow me to get in front of her."

"I will also warn you that she is old and frail and has good days and bad days. She is a rude old woman that barely even lets family visit. Not to mention all my uncles will be at attention ... what I'm saying is, the odds will be stacked against you and it could blow up in your face ... mine as well." She sighs like she knows more but doesn't want to say. I believe now she is intrigued, like me, and wants a few answers herself.

"Again, I'm willing to find nothing, but I have to try and find peace."

"You can pick me up from my farm, five a.m. sharp tomorrow morning. Hopefully, we can beat the family rush in the morning."

Chapter 29

We pull up as close to the farm as we can. I'm waiting for Kasenka to run up to the car and hide in the back seat. Instead, she calmly walks over the hill from the entrance. She smiles when she sees me, once again changing my mood. I liked seeing her in that dress yesterday, but I like her more in her element. This time she's dressed in jeans and a yellow blouse with a matching yellow visor. Yellow sandals finish her look. No makeup, no jewelry, just natural beauty. I've probably said that more in the last few months than I've ever said in my whole life. Piotrek looks at me with surprise with Kasenka's demeanor compared to our first meeting.

"Hello, Piotrek. Can you take us to Krakow, please?" she asks. She seems focused.

"Yes, ma'am … Trevor, the road trip is three-and-a-half hours. Travel time and time spent there means we will not make it back in time for your conference call with your company. Is that okay?"

"I'll move the meeting until tomorrow morning. This meeting is more important right now for me. Let's hit the road."

"I hope you are ready for this," Kasenka says to me, like we're going for surgery.

"I will be fine. Will you?" I ask. She seems nervous for more reasons than just me meeting Kasia.

As soon as we pull into the main highway, she takes out a book and gets comfortable. I take note and pull out my laptop and get some work done. This SUV the company set me up with is big in the back, perfect for this road trip. Every now and then I look up from the computer at the sights. Kasenka points out historical things, cities, and places. She loves her country. Halfway through, we put our book and computer down and sit back and just enjoy the scenic drive. She actually falls asleep and snuggles up on my shoulder. Piotrek gives me a funny look in the rearview mirror and I just smile. I like Piotrek; he's a good soul, and I will be sure to stay in touch with him when this is all said and done.

When we finally reach our destination, I wake Kasenka up. She's embarrassed after seeing she left a pool of slobber all over my shirt. I just give her a smile.

"Well, sleepy head, we've made it. Sorry to have to wake you up. You were pretty out of it."

"Oh, gosh, I'm so sorry. How loud did I snore?" she asks, still groggy.

"You did snore, but it wasn't that bad. It was like a sweet snore." I give a wink and smile to ease the embarrassment.

Piotrek and I start to get out the car, but Kasenka suddenly remembers where we are and screams for us to wait. She asks Piotrek to wait in the car while we chat for a moment.

"Trevor, ahhh, I'm so nervous. I was thinking about this on the way here. We can't just walk in there and say you are an old friend. It won't work ..."

"Why not say my grandpa was an old friend from the military and I want to pay my respects and tell her my Charlie has died."

"I didn't believe you when you first told me. Part of the reason was my ignorant thoughts, thinking my grandma wouldn't have known a black man before. They will feel the same. I'm afraid maybe worse."

"Kasenka, come on. We have come this far. There's no turning back now. I just need five minutes. If we have to, we ..."

"We'll say you're my boyfriend. It's our only hope getting us through the door. I already told them I was bringing a friend. My family knows I have been very reclusive in my life, so we'll have to be creative," she says. She seemed okay on the way here, but now she seems freaked out.

"Okay, you can relax. There's no pressure. You haven't done anything wrong here. Trust me … that is, if I've earned it yet."

She puts on a half-smile. I'm starting to think there's more to the story, and it's not that she doesn't trust me – she doesn't trust her family.

The house is big and expansive. It feels like a futuristic farm, a modern day farmhouse. The long gravel driveway leads to a circular water fountain. There are about six cars parked around the fountain. There goes my idea of just peacefully meeting Kasia with no one around. The front of the house is very inviting, with tall windows all over. It almost looks like a glass house from the backyard. Of course, I'm not surprised, but it feels like we are in the middle of nowhere; the neighbors both feel about a block away. If this is where Kasia stays, I'm sure the middle of nowhere is by design. The landscaping around the house is perfect; someone takes pride in the outside of this house. As we stand at the water loop in the middle of the lot, Kasenka gives me a quick rundown of the family tree and whose cars are in the lot. She shows some disappointment in all the cars here because she originally told me usually not many family members visit because Grandma Kasia isn't so guest friendly. We tried coming during the week so no one would be here, but it didn't work, obviously. We get to the door and right before I knock, Kasenka grabs me and looks in my eyes as if she's responsible for sending me into an electric chair. She's about to speak but we hear someone coming to the door. The door opens and like a ninja Kasenka darts up and wraps her arms around my neck and places a kiss on my cheek. She leaves her lips there long enough for whomever this is to open the door and see. It was an older-looking man who I assume is one of her uncles.

"*Czesc*, Kasenka," the man says, clearing his throat.

"*Czesc Wujek*, Jacob." She actually seems happy it's him who opens the door. He goes to talk but looks at me and then looks back at Kasenka.

"I will talk English out of respect for your friend … I have not seen you since Easter of last year. Come here and give me a hug …. and your name, sir?" He reaches out his hand.

"Hello, I'm Trevor. It's nice to meet you. Thank you for allowing me into your home." We shake hands and he seems to be nice and inviting.

We walk down a long corridor into a big open living room. The living room is a big square that's sunken two stairs down into its own oasis, with a big screen TV perched atop a big fireplace. We walk past the living room and head to the kitchen. This place is so massive. When we enter the kitchen, a group of people are gathered around a big wooden table. The table looks like it seats about sixteen people. There are about twelve people at the table. When we walk up, the room falls silent and everyone looks up at us. Kasenka just freezes so I wave hello to everyone. It feels like uncles, aunts, and cousins just made their way over for breakfast. Everyone waves back. One of the women at the table gets up, comes over, and gives me a hug. That's a surprise; I didn't expect that given the atmosphere. She introduces herself as Renata, Jacob's wife. I have also learned that *Wujek* means uncle because she has called a few of the men that. Then another man comes up introduces himself, says he's Filip, and lets me know he's the brother of Kasenka's dad. I'm trying my hardest to keep track of family names, but it's impossible and their accents are so strong. It's strange. They seem like they're being nicer to me than they're

164

being to Kasenka. I'm not sure one of them, other than her uncle, has said hello other than waved.

Another woman comes over to me and she also hugs me, saying she's Filip's wife. Everyone is very welcoming to me. One of the aunts, whose name who I didn't get, comes over and pulls me to my seat. Before I could even sit down, another lady places a plate of food in front of my face. Most of the food looks like the platters of Polish food Kasia made for me before. I comment out loud, "I like *golabki*," and everyone smiles and laughs.

"Trevor, you have had Polish food like this before?" Uncle Jacob, the man who opened the door, asks me. So far it seems like he is the leader of the family.

"Yes, I have a dear friend, who is Polish, make it for me." I look at Kasenka and give a little wink to let her know it was her grandmother.

"Well, not straight from the motherland, but cooked from a Polish mamma," Jacob says, smiling and we laugh together.

"Actually, yes it was …"

Kasenka cuts me off before I finish. I was going to say some Polish grandma in Chicago, but she probably thought I was going to be emotional enough to tell the truth. I just want to get to Kasia; I can feel her. "Okay, everyone. Trevor didn't come here for all the questions now."

Everyone tenses up a little when Kasenka speaks. I can cut through the thickness of the atmosphere with a knife.

"Well, Kasenka, we will ask you the questions then." Uncle Jacob's tone switches from inviting to harsh. It's only a matter of time before I find out what's going on here.

"No need, uncle, you already know my life is basic." Kasenka's tone seems to change to defensive as well.

"Speaking of basic, how is the family farm doing? I hear you took over. How is that going?" His tone was of mockery.

"Yeah, you know nothing new. You know, cows and shit like that. You know, stuff your ancestors fought to keep alive and paid for with their lives. You know, basic shit like that. You know, stuff you never paid attention to, like how the hell you came upon all these riches. Rich Polish culture stuff that you might not know about going on as well … You know, so your grandkids can know what it's like to be Polish … You know, the usual stuff … or excuse me, maybe you don't know because you don't care about where you came from." I can feel the room start to change like everyone knew what was coming.

"Huh … still the same Kasenka, huh? Still the same Kasia, I should say, because as much as you run from the family you are just like her … miserable. Well, since I'm asking questions and you're answering, how come you're here, after a year and a half of not seeing the family, asking to see Grandma? You missed Christmas, Easter, birthdays, anniversaries, even deaths, yet no calls, no explanations, just nothing. You took over the farm and felt it was right to just cut everyone off over here? Little did you know Grandma Kasia is the only reason you're in control there … Then, wait—it gets better—you call out of the blue a few nights ago saying you're stopping by with a friend to see Grandma? Explain yourself, because this shit isn't adding up. How do you go from no contact with family, no social media, yet here you are with your boyfriend? Let's hear it, Kasenka. How did you meet this Trevor? His accent sounds American. How did you two meet?"

The room feels like it's a thousand degrees. I start feeling bad because, in just their banter back and forth, I've figured out why they're all treating Kasenka worse than me and giving her the cold shoulder. Kasenka really stuck her neck out for me. Why didn't she say anything? We could have figured out a different way. Well, now the pressure is on, and I truly hope something special happens if Kasia is here and I meet her. If not, I've just made a fool of myself and Kasenka.

"I don't think I owe you an explanation …"

Jacob slammed his hand on the table. "The hell you don't. Like I just said, the only reason the farm is in under your control is because of Grandma Kasia. She's funded everything against our wishes, so you're damn wrong. We deserve an explanation."

Kasenka starts to talk but I cut her off.

"I apologize. I don't want to get in family business or get Kasenka in trouble. We came here because of me. It was me who wanted to see Kasia Romanowski. I found Kasenka at the farm and begged her to let me see Kasia. You see, my grandfather was an old friend."

The room got smaller to go with the hot temperature. I feel so close to Kasia; I can feel her here. While everything seems like it's going downhill quickly, I'm still thinking of ways to get to her. Jacob stands up and walks around the table as he examines me up and down. He looks over at one of the other uncles in the room and whispers something in Polish.

"Kasenka, you told him our family history?"

"You see, that's why I'm here … No, it wasn't me. Come on, *Wuyek* Jacob …. out of everyone in the family I have spent my life practicing secrecy … think about it!" she yells, tears starting to fall down her cheeks. I feel so bad; she really put herself out there for me.

"Trevor, you seem like a nice man, but our family is very private and close knit. I'm not sure what Kasenka told you, or what you told her to convince her to bring you here, but this is tough. I don't know where you got that last name from, if Kasenka didn't tell you, but you better speak up now, because the only way you would know that name is if you're stalking us or if you have somehow hacked our personal files. I don't know, but it better be a good story." By the time he finishes his sentence he's standing over me, almost spitting his words on me and my food.

"You don't have to threaten me. I mean no harm to you or your family. My grandfather was a friend of Kasia's and she has something for me. If I could just see her once, I'll be out of your life forever."

Jacob looks at Kasenka and then around the table. No one wants to make eye contact. A few seconds go by before Jacob walks over to his brother Filip and whispers something in his ear. They stare at each other for a minute, then Jacob looks up to speak.

"Your claim is impossible, Trevor. I'm not sure who you are or what you're up to, but I trust no one and neither does my Grandma Kasia ... she's worse about it. So I'm afraid I will not be able to grant you your wish. She doesn't know English, and she's never met a black man in her life for sure – no offense. Again, I don't like you looking into my family like this."

Well, this has come to a point of no return. What's so sad is the very reason Kasia became the way she is now is because of how her community treated Charlie. Now flash forward and here are her kids treating me the same way. If they only knew. I have a plan that I don't want to use, but we've reached the point where I have to do something desperate. I look at Kasenka and she just throws her hands in the air. Okay, time for plan B. The problem with plan B is that I will only have a few-minute window to see her, and it could end really badly if I'm wrong.

"You know, you're right. I apologize. I do have more proof; I just don't have it with me. I know you want to know how I got the last name, not to mention how I found the farm. Will you allow me to come back with more evidence to support my claim?"

The room of people looks up at Jacob. It seems like he's conflicted over the decision.

"Kasenka, you and your guest have worn out your welcome. If you wouldn't mind, please leave."

"I understand. It's a long ride back to where I'm staying. Do you mind if I use the bathroom before we leave?"

"Sure, whatever. It's around the corner to the left at the first opening in the hall."

I jump up and quickly move towards the bathroom. As I walk out of sight, I can hear them start to argue with Kasenka, which is good. It might give me more time.

As soon as I hit the corner I start to run. I didn't come all this way for me to get this close and nothing. I can feel her close. I just start opening doors, hoping for the best. All of a sudden, after the third door, I hear an old woman's voice scream something in Polish. I run all the way down the hall to where I heard the voice. It's the end room. I swing the door open and quickly close it behind me, and there she is. I know it's her. She doesn't turn around. She just screams out again, "Who the hell is making all this noise?" in Polish. My heart rate is pounding and I'm losing my breath. After months of crazy things happening to me, with Charlie's death, the letters, my success at work, everything that has been my life for the last six months ... now I've finally reached the jackpot of my treasure hunt.

Kasia is beautiful even in her nineties. Her long gray hair falls down her back in a French braid. She's wearing a nightgown and slippers, sitting in a chair that just looks out over the view. I don't have a lot of time, so I can't play nostalgic or ease into this. I walk over to get in front of her face. I'm so nervous, almost expecting magic to happen. This could blow up in my face, because at this point I will not be able to walk out of here. I keep hearing Kasenka in my head, saying she's grumpy and mad at the world, so in my head I'm expecting this monster. But instead, I see this sweet old lady. She looks amazing and healthy. I'm frozen and

I don't know what to say as I stand behind her. She still hasn't taken her eyes off the view.

"What is all the damn noise about? It's too early for this," she says, slapping her hand on the chair. For some reason I can understand her Polish.

"Your *Chanuntka* would have loved to hear you say one word."

I hear her whisper, "Oh, my God." She doesn't turn around; she just puts her hands over her mouth. She looks perfect. I can now see her hands shaking. I walk around to sit in front of her. She takes her hands off her face and slowly starts to rub my cheeks. A tear slowly starts to come down her face. Even after all these years, those hazel eyes still look the same. The lone tear is followed by a stream of tears that pour down like rain. She tries to stop but she can't. I try fighting it, but I too start crying like a baby. It's a mix of emotions for me—tears of being tired, tears of confirmation, tears of feeling all of her pain. We embrace in a hug and all the emotions and questions from the last few months go away. Everything I went through confirms what I went through, yes, but I feel like I don't need answers anymore. The letters, the visions, the crazy good things happening in my life, not being able to tell anyone what was going on, all made worth it in this hug. I really thought I was losing my mind, then it turned into hope, then I thought I was dreaming, and now the weight that I felt on my shoulders has fallen off. It feels like I'm hugging an angel.

As I soak in this hug, I feel the old Kasia and her present self. I can feel her tears on my chest through my shirt as I'm sure she's going through the same emotions I am. My euphoric hug is coming to an end because I can hear commotion coming towards us. It sounds as if the whole table of people is coming towards us. I take a deep breath and enjoy the last few seconds of this hug. As I expect, Jacob comes kicking through the door. What I don't expect is him to be holding a gun, running at me wildly.

Chapter 30

The whole family is present in the room now. With everyone in here it puts in perspective how big this room actually is—almost twenty of us and there is plenty of room. Everyone stands in silence and just stares in shock as my hug with Kasia continues. I try to let go when Jacob screams again for me to let her go, but she just hugs me tighter. Jacob slowly walks closer to us with his gun pointing right at me. His hand is shaking and he seems very nervous, like any wrong move and this could turn tragic. I'm sure only seconds have gone by, but it feels like hours.

"I'm going to count to five. If you don't take your goddamn hands off my mom I'm afraid I'll have to start shooting ... do you hear me?" He clicks his gun and starts counting. I can hear a few cries and one of the aunts, I believe it was Beata, screams for Jacob to put the gun down.

He gets down to one when all of a sudden Kasia screams out in Polish, "Jacob *odloz teraz bron* ... Jacob *teraz!*"

"*Ale mamu ya nye moge*," Jacob responds. He shakes so hard it looks like he's going to do something stupid. He walks towards me even more as the gun gets to my head.

"Jacob ... *Twoj ojciec nigdy nie pozwoliłby ci na brak szacunku ... powiedziałem teraz!*" Once again, Kasia has my life in her hands, in more ways than one. She screams so hard the family gasps.

He begrudgingly and slowly starts putting the gun down. He makes a note to push it against my chest hard enough to make me lose my breath a little bit. He walks back slowly but keeps the gun at his side and doesn't take his eyes off me. While everyone stands in silence, Kasia just stares at me. She puts her hands on my cheeks, and the tears start falling again. I clear my throat in hopes of shaking the silence up, while Jacob still stands there with that gun, waiting for a reason to use it.

"You know what?" Kasia shockingly begins in English. "At first I was going to ask you all to leave so I can have a private moment with my boy here ... but on second thought, you all should stay here and hear about your family history ... at least the parts that were shoved under the rug for all these years."

At first I thought the gasp was because of the situation, but then I remembered that they all believed Kasia didn't know English, and now here she's talking perfect English with her perfect accent. Her English actually sounds better than I remember, like she kept studying or reading in my language. While I catch everyone in the family in shock trying to cope with the turn of events, I catch eyes with Kasenka and she has the biggest smile with tears falling down. As I'm lost in Kasenka's reaction, I'm brought back to focus when Kasia puts her hand on my cheek again.

"You look so much like Charlie. Look at that beautiful chocolate skin. In my dreams, you were a different object every time until recently. Then I saw you. You remind me so much of ... my *Chanuntka*, oh God." She falls into my arms in tears again. The family just sits in awe, on an emotional roller coaster that they all must be going through in their own way. The grumpy old grandma that didn't know English and hated everything and everyone is sitting in front of them loving and hugging on some Black American they just met. I'm about to speak but Kasia puts her hands on my lips ...

"I know, Trevor. You must be so emotionally exhausted ..."

172

Before she could finish her sentence Kasenka lets out a big sigh that shakes the room. She hadn't reacted this whole time, and I believe Kasia calling me Trevor without anyone saying anything was her trigger. No one knows the story as intimately as Kasenka does. No one knows what to do. There are too many emotions. Jacob finally puts the gun away and seems to be calming down a little. I can see his wife shaking her head in disgust. It feels like the room is settling in for story time, and Kasia and I are the main characters of the show. Kasia hugs me hard one more time and then takes a deep breath.

"Before I met your father and grandfather Filip, I had a love affair with a man named Charlie. I never really talked about the war and my time during, not because of the atrocities of the war, but because of the atrocities of my own family. For those that didn't know, I was a nurse and helped out during the war. I worked in a tent dedicated to helping the Jewish survivors that made it out of the camps. I was heavily involved towards the end of the war, so I was able to witness the darkest hour of the war. Then one day this beautiful, dark man came walking into my tent. He captured the room wherever he went. The first time we met I gave him attitude, yet he stayed calm and won me over right away. It was what we call love at first sight. He made sure at the end of our first meeting that there would be another.

"Before I knew it, we were writing letters to each other and sneaking moments to be together. We were madly in love. He would tell me he was an angel from heaven sent down to rescue people. It's what made him sign up for the war. He said out of all the people he saved, it was me who saved him. I just showed him what love was and how to love the simple farm life. I was able to show him the beauty in the forest and in the farm. Unfortunately, this beautiful love story has a very dark ending. The one person Charlie couldn't save was me. It was a much different time back then and I say this because it sets the stage for what my family did to me that could never happen now. I will also say that all of the people who were involved are dead now and aren't here to defend themselves. When I say it was a different time, I mean it was an ignorant and hateful time … Charlie and I unexpectedly got pregnant. Yes, of course against the purity of our family traditions and culture, I know. Not only that, but remember they didn't allow interracial couples to legally marry then. That could just give you a sense of what we were up against. Especially here in Europe. There were actually laws in America that prevented black and white people from being together. I laugh when I think about it now because we could be friends and work together to help people, but the moment we fell in love we were against everyone's beliefs. I say all of this to let you know Charlie and I knew what we were up against, but we thought our love would speak out for us.

"One dark night after I told the family I was pregnant and wanted to be with Charlie, the family put a plan together and we had a scheduled family meeting. They made it seem like they wanted to celebrate and help me find a way to make it work. I should have known something was up when they had my then-friend Pawel show up. You see, this is the man they wanted me to end up with. We all sat down and they let me settle down and trust and everyone made it feel like this was going to work and got me all excited. They passed around tea for everyone to drink, and Pawel handed me mine. Of course, never in your life would you think someone would poison you, and even less of a chance that you'd think your family could be a part of doing something so despicable to you. As soon as I got done drinking the tea, I knew something was wrong. I felt sick to my stomach. I can still remember the pain like it was yesterday. I tried running into the next cabin to throw up but barely made it to the door.

The last thing I remember was lying on the cot, and my mother and father asking Pawel if I was going to make it and why I was in so much pain. My father seemed satisfied, and my mother looked mortified, but it was obvious they knew the plan beforehand.

"I was sickly and bedridden for days. My mother sat next to me and kept apologizing and saying she just wanted to make sure they protected the family line. During my healing time, my heart just grew black. I put my head down and ignored everyone in life. I wanted revenge on everyone. I wanted everyone in my family to suffer. The hate I had for my family was unwavering. It developed who you see and why I raised you the way you have been raised. Once I was healthy enough two weeks later, I tried to find Charlie before he went back to America ... this is the part you might not know about, Trevor. Maybe something the letters didn't tell you, because Charlie kept it to himself ... Apparently, while I was bedridden, Charlie came back to visit and check on me. He came to the forest and farm to look for me. My mother cried as she told me the horrible story of how Pawel and some of his goons almost beat Charlie to death. They told him they took care of the monkey baby. They dragged him naked through the woods and left him for dead. My mother doesn't know how he survived. He would've had to walk at least six miles naked, bloody, and injured ... Oh, my poor angel didn't do anything to deserve that. He was such a strong soul. He didn't even bring it up when I finally chased him down before he left.

"The whole situation changed my perspective in life. I obviously could never be a part of the farm and their savage beliefs. As soon as I was old enough I ran away. Another sad layer to the story: Charlie help build the two biggest farmhouses there. I haven't been there for a while, but I'm sure to this day they're still the ones in best condition. I finally caught up to Charlie two weeks later when I found out where his unit was leaving. I could see it in his face when I caught him at the train station about to leave; he was defeated. There wasn't that sparkle in his eyes anymore. They won. I begged and pleaded for him to forgive me for trusting the family. He kissed me on my forehead and said there was nothing to forgive and that I should forgive myself and try to find happiness. I was so hurt. I wanted him to stay so badly, and I felt lost in my own country without him. The last words he spoke to me were in sadness. He told me he was still that angel that needed to save people, and he had to go back and save himself. He said he felt like a failure to God because he couldn't save me or the baby. He left me there in a pool of my tears. We kept in touch for a little while by letters, but eventually it became too difficult. The last thing I said to him was that I felt like I was going to have a boy and I was going to name him Trevor ..."

She lets that last sentence sink in so everyone can try to grasp the gravity of the situation. There's not a dry eye in the room. Silence follows the shocked looks on everyone's faces. At that moment, they are all questioning their reality and their family history. I'm so caught up in the story and staring out at the view that I don't even realize Kasia is standing right next to me, hugging me around my waist. Kasenka walks over to us and hugs her grandma. The tears flow down so hard she can barely breathe, and I hear her whisper in Polish that she's so sorry. We stand in silence for a few more moments because no one knows what to say or do next. The whole room is suddenly startled by someone ringing the doorbell. It's Piotrek, letting me know it's getting late and he's back to pick me up.

After stepping outside to let the family talk, I check in with my secretary to see if she can book three rooms at the Krakow Marriott for the night. The three-and-a-half-hour drive is not going to happen now. I get Piotrek a room and if Kasenka doesn't want to stay here with her family for the night, she has the option of a room too. I need to have a good hotel because I have my work meeting in the early morning and I need to be prepared.

I come back to the room and everyone has left but Kasenka. Kasia is lying down on the bed, and I can only imagine how emotionally exhausted she is right now. I walk over to sit by her side and hold her hand. We share a moment of staring at each other, but it's more about us being relieved that we finally met. Charlie would be so proud. She just keeps rubbing me on my cheeks as I tuck her into bed. It feels like being able to meet your fairy godmother in real life, I feel so close to her. Kasenka sits on the other side of the bed and just looks at me. It wasn't smiles, and it wasn't sadness, but something seemed to come over her. I am getting a different feeling than I've been getting from her.

"So now what?" I say to Kasia, trying to finish the story.

"My dear child, I'm exhausted. Can you please come back and see me tomorrow morning?"

Before I can answer she's fast asleep. Her smile is ear to ear as she sleeps, and my heart feels full right now.

Chapter 31

I'm just sitting in the hotel shower and letting the water run down my back. It's a beautiful hotel with a view of Krakow. In the car ride here, Kasenka doesn't say a word to me. She just stares at me the whole way. I wish I could read her mind. When she goes to her room she doesn't even say a word to me; she just walks away. There are still a few hours before my meeting. Poland is seven hours ahead of Central Standard Time in the States, so I wake up for the early morning meeting, which would be late for my Chicago office. I have about thirty minutes to kill before my meeting, and as I start to double-check to make sure I have everything I hear a knock at my door. I'm sure as I walk to the door the cleaning crew got the wrong room, but instead I see Kasenka biting her lips through the peephole.

"I can't sleep and I need someone to talk to," she tells me. She just walks past me into the room without an invite.

"Umm, okay ... I have a work meeting in a few minutes so forgive me if I have to stop."

"First, let me apologize. You spilled your personal emotions and I took you as ... I don't know ... I know it took a lot to come all the way to another country just because you started seeing things and magical, unexplainable things started happening. I'm apologizing because I didn't believe you and I questioned your motives."

"Well, Kasenka, I understand because ..."

"No, no, let me talk, Trevor. Your revelation yesterday has shaken my whole family tree. It was like a magic trick, what you did yesterday. I'm sure my uncles are still questioning their whole life. And wow, Trevor … my grandma never spoke English in front of anyone of us, including her sons, so we all just assumed, and rightfully so, that your story couldn't be true. She had to hold on to that all these years. And understand the English speaking was just the start of it; Kasia never touched anyone of us. She never showed love or affection to anyone, not to her kids … or my Grandpa Filip. The grace and love she touched your cheeks with were just so … just so … unbelievable is the only word that comes to mind. The look she gave you as she talked, well, I have never seen her eyes gleam like that. She has been the head of our family and has taught us that emotions are weaknesses and to never trust anyone. The woman I saw last night was not the grandma I have seen my whole life. That was not the grandma the whole family has seen their whole life. My soul and my heart have been turned upside-down after seeing it. Now let me talk about me because …"

There was a ring coming through on my computer.

"I'm sorry, Kasenka. That's my work calling. I have a Zoom conference I have to take now."

"It's okay, I understand … I will wait."

She does just that. She sits on the hotel couch and just watches me work as I sit there and talk with my bosses, the sales team, and some shareholders. Kasenka sits there with her knees tucked to her chest and rocks back and forth. She doesn't take her eyes off me. The Trevor of old would've been nervous and freaking out in moments like this, with bosses talking about my future and Kasenka staring a hole through me. But instead, I feel at peace. I feel empowered. I feel like I'm meant to be here. Actually, with Kasenka being in the room I feel a sense of confidence, almost like I want to show off my work. Turns out to be a blessing in disguise because the meeting is a hit. The CEO says he can feel my fire and enthusiasm. Of course, the finance industry is a bottom line industry and another lucky draw for me is that all the numbers added up. Still not sure if it's skill or luck, but since Charlie's passing my luck continues to get better at work. The company agrees with the numbers and wants me to stay and close the deal. My boss tells me a big bonus is coming my way again and that the millions I have made for the company have made us all millionaires. The meeting only lasts thirty minutes as my boss tells me to start setting up shop for the company with the remaining five weeks here.

As soon as I'm sure all the Zoom cameras are off, I burst into my happy dance. To be financially independent and create generational wealth has always been my lifelong dream. Here I sit at twenty-eight-years-old, ready for the rest of my life. I'm so lost in my jubilation that I forget Kasenka is still here. It's been at least forty minutes since she sat down and she remained in that same knee-tucked position with her eyes still locked on mine.

I grab a chair and put it right in front of her. I sit so close I can feel her breath on my neck. She doesn't move. Her eyes are the only things wavering back and forth, following my moves. I move my head back and forth just to make sure she's still here with me and she just follows me with her eyes. I move in slowly and gently wrap my arms around her. The more I squeeze, the more I can feel her relax. The more she relaxes, the more the tears come out and the harder the sobs get. I hop up and bring her some tissues and water.

"You sound very good at your job. I had no idea what anyone was saying or what you were talking about, but it sounded as though you just did something good for your company. They all seemed excited to see you either way," she says, sniffling and wiping tears.

"To be honest, half the time I don't know what they're saying either. You know what it's funny, I saw you before the two meetings I have had out here so maybe you're my good luck charm."

She giggles a little. "Trevor … I don't … I need your …"

"First off, relax. I believe you know by now I'm not here to hurt you or have some negative motive."

"I don't know what to say."

"Let's start with what you were going to say before you were cut off by my work. You mentioned let's talk about you."

"I was trying to figure out who you are. I'm looking for the flaw."

"Oh, I have many flaws. Like I've said before, the person you are seeing now wasn't the same person you would have seen if you met me before Charlie died. Or as your grandma would call him in her beautiful accent, her *Chanuntka*."

"You see, just that. You took a negative and turned it into a positive life view … you are in a country you have never been in, with a very hard language you don't know, and people have been staring at you the whole time, yet you just come and win people over and get the work done. You had to know coming here how much hatred there might be, and how difficult it was going to be to convince my family of the truth. Yet, from the moment you walked onto the farm, you have been nothing short of a gentleman."

"Would you believe that everything I'm doing now is a first? Well, at least most of what I have done over last few months have been firsts. It's strange because I feel this unbelievable calmness, like everything is happening for a reason. I feel a sense of power, a sense of fulfillment. I just can't explain the feelings or the reason behind them. Your grandma said Charlie always talked about his sense of power that led to his purpose. I feel the sense of power, and now I just need to find the purpose. Kasia told me stories of how no matter what situation they were in Charlie always felt confident because of his calling. He just knew God sent him down here to save people; he was sure of it. Since his passing I feel the sense of power as well, I just don't know my calling. Charlie said it's love, but I don't know what that means. I chalked it up to him being crazy, but he said that he couldn't answer. He told me to find Kasia and she would give me the answers."

"And you have what your grandpa had. Such grace in moments of strife. At my farm they stared and talked about you without knowing you. Today, I know you felt the awkwardness from the family, yet you would have thought you were a part of the family the way you acted ..." she says, then just stops mid-sentence.

"What?"

"Are you for real?"

"I'm sorry. What do you mean?"

"I need to know how you deal with the weight of all the information you gave us and what my grandma talked about. Since my grandma told the story of her being poisoned, I can't get that out of my head. My belief system has been turned upside-down. I have spent my whole life building this image in my head of not only the past of the farm but the future I want to represent. Now I'm not so sure ... because my belief system might not be my community's belief system ... That hatred and blind regard for life isn't what I'm about. I want no part of it. It makes me sick to my stomach to think all of my hate for my grandma growing up was baseless. I used to dismiss her thoughts of progression because she was so negative. I thought, how can we follow such a dark-hearted person, but she was bigger than all of us for not smearing the family lineage. It's a double-edged sword, as you know, because if that terrible thing didn't happen to her we wouldn't be here. I shed a tear of guilt as I think of my Grandpa Filip and how he was just the collateral damage in all this ... this all seems fake. I feel like my childhood growing up on the farm is fake. Why didn't she tell anyone?"

She falls into my arms crying. I know the feeling; it's just so overwhelming. I was never a crier, but I haven't stop crying since all the things started happening. If she could've only seen how deep their love was in the letters, this would have been even harder.

"Kasenka, your grandma couldn't say anything for the pain it would cause. Could you imagine if she told the family what happened to her? What would have happened if Kasia told Filip, 'Look, we can get married, but my heart really belongs somewhere else.' There are so many layers ..."

I planned to continue but I'm cut off by Kasenka's soft snoring. She's dead asleep. Guess I'm that boring. I'm sure it's because she hasn't slept much during this emotional week. I try to move but she snuggles up under my arm and waist. I just look at her for a moment. No makeup, tear-soaked cheeks, dead tired, hair sprawled over the other side of her face, yet she looks so beautiful. I never got the chance to say thank you. After seeing how her family treated her, I know she risked a lot just to step foot in the house, let alone come with me and let me tell my crazy stories. She never even mentions how long it's been since she has seen her family. As I get lost in thought she lays down flat on my chest and puts her arms around my waist. Her snoring gets louder, and before I know it my eyes are getting heavy and the rhythm of her snoring puts me to sleep.

Chapter 32

The alarm clock startles Kasenka so much she falls off the couch and hits her head on the end table, luckily not hard. I can see her go through the emotions of figuring out where she is.

"Here you go. The tea will help you wake up a little bit. I wasn't sure what you like to eat for breakfast so I just got us some eggs, fruit, and toast. I love orange juice so I got some of that, plus cranberry and apple juice. By the way, I know you don't have time to go home and change clothes, so I bought a few things from the thrift shop. Don't know your size—it wouldn't be gentlemanly to guess—so I just got you a few things at different sizes. I had the hotel staff put them in your room. Please eat up now so we can leave. I don't want to be late to your grandma's."

There goes that stare again. She eats breakfast but doesn't take her eyes off me. It's almost like she is waiting for me to fail.

"What time is it?" she asks. After another sip of tea, it seems she's coming to.

"It's seven and we said we would be there at nine. I wasn't sure how long you needed to get ready, hence the alarm clock. I apologize."

"My goodness, you got breakfast, a new set of clothes for me, and you're dressed and showered? How? Did you sleep? We couldn't have gone to sleep before four a.m. Was I sleeping that hard?"

"I got about thirty minutes. You were out pretty good ... it was a long day."

"You are so sweet and thoughtful. Thank you," she said. She starts to tear up a little.

"It's okay, Kasenka. It's just breakfast and making sure you feel comfortable in some clean clothes. I don't even know if you'll like them or not."

"Oh, Trevor, these are tears of joy. Another first for me is the cause of tears … no one has gotten me breakfast and topped it off with new clothes. What girl wouldn't want breakfast and new clothes? It's the care you do it with."

I laugh a little. "Well, guess what? I have never done something like this either. So this is also a first. I haven't even done this for my mom."

"It feels good."

"It does."

We sit and eat in awkward silence before I rush her off so we can go.

By the time Piotrek and I get downstairs, she's already standing by the car, once again taking my breath away with her beauty. Who would have thought she'd make a thrift store dress look like it was bought at the Gucci store? The floral print dress goes down to her knees, and she was able to put together a matching flower hat and sunglass. Even Piotrek is caught staring, and we share a good laugh together. She walks up and greets me with a hug and soft kiss on the cheek. She gives me a look of gratefulness. She has been warmer to me each time we met. During the car ride to Kasia's, she snuggles up on my lap. Piotrek gives me a little look in the rearview and I just shrug my shoulders. I can feel her relax on my shoulders.

When we pull up to the house, there are about five more cars at the house than yesterday. I'm expecting Kasenka to be nervous, but she just looks at me, smiles, and shrugs her shoulders. When we walk in we could tell there's a lot of people, but one voice stands out more than all. I can recognize Kasia's voice no matter the setting. When we walk around the corner into the kitchen, Kasia is standing with her walker at the end of the island. Everyone's sitting around listening to her talk, and they all seem to be excited to hear her stories. Kasia notices us walk in and right away we become the show. Kasia strolls over and gives me the biggest hug as we hold each other's faces and embrace. The room falls into shocked silence. I'm quickly figuring out the scenario. After me and Kasenka left yesterday, the word got out that we were coming back and the legend grew and spread like wildfire. You can hear every cough and sniff as Kasia stares at me and rubs my cheeks again.

"My *Chanuntka* used to love when I rubbed his cheeks." The whole room gasps. I have to remember some are hearing her speak English for the first time.

"Hello, Kasia. It's good to see the real you again." We both hug and share a big laugh while the room looks on in stunned silence. We know it's an inside joke and no one will get it, which makes it funnier. I can feel the room has so many questions. I know I would.

"Okay, I'm going to get straight to it because I'm old, get tired fast, and have a lot to say. I have two big things I want to talk about. Let me start by saying I'm sorry … yes, I know something you would never hear me say. Let me explain. I know it's a shock to everyone, me speaking English, hugging this beautiful black man, and maybe some of you are surprised I'm being nice. This is the real me. Let me apologize for my negativity throughout my life and pushing my narrative on you. I let my black heart dictate how I ran my family and it was wrong. I had a chance to break the cycle of our family's history; instead, I ran and I turned the focus into everyone else running away from it as well. Instead of preaching love and patience of other cultures, I just shoved protection and distrust of others down your throat. My time on this earth will be coming to an end soon and I wanted to make sure you change the legacy. Be about helping others. Honor and trust God will do the right thing in life for you. This was how I lived life once and it was stripped from me. I'm truly sorry I stripped it from you ..."

The room remains silent. I feel a few tears and some prayers. Someone begins to talk but Kasia puts her hand up.

"Let me finish now that I have apologized. I wanted everyone to hear me say this next part out loud ... because this part will take some imagination to believe. Some of you may have questions, of which there are plenty, but some may question how I carried a relationship with a black man back then when it wasn't even legal or recognized by society. You may be wondering after all these years how my English is so good, or the fact that I even know English might be a big surprise. I know some of you question how I had an endless bank account on my nursing job. How did I pay to buy the farm from the rest of the families and keep only our name on it? How in the hell did Trevor, all the way from Chicago in the U.S., find the farm and know of our family maiden name? Well, the answer can only be explained through spiritual magic. Charlie left his magic touch on my life. It was so strange – after he left Poland good things started happening to me when I didn't deserve them. Unexplainable things. My bank account mysteriously always had money, and people started treating me like I was some queen when I was a bitch to everyone. I'm positive the only reason Filip dealt with me at the beginning was because he was under some spell, because I didn't deserve a man that nice. No matter what I did, things turned out my way.

"Anyway, all this leads me to this question: how do I know it's Charlie's magic? I wanted to tell you these things to open your minds to what I am about to tell you ... One day when the word got out about me and Charlie seeing each other, my old friend Pawel, who I mentioned before, decided to send his boys to chase us around the forest. I was really scared for Charlie's life, because these men really wanted to do something bad to him. I would say they were going to kill him. We ran for about a mile through trees and hard brush. It felt so dark in the middle of the day. We finally found a little hideout spot and hoped they wouldn't find us, but they did. I was so nervous I thought I was going to throw up, but Charlie was as calm as can be. I remember feeling his heart; the beat was slow and steady. He pulled me close as they circled us. They screamed and spit at him but he kept his eyes on me. He whispered he loved me so much and whatever was to happen next would be all worth it for him. I knew he was magical, but I thought he was losing his mind. He kissed me so gently and softly, like he thought it was going to be our last kiss. All of a sudden we both started glowing. Yes, glowing like shining lights. It was like a cloud of smoke but made out of gold. The sounds of men started to get softer, but I could see them screaming louder. I could see them getting closer, but it felt like we were shrinking into each other. One of the men screamed with all his might one last time for Charlie to let me go. He was holding a pole as he slowly walked around us. I remember it like yesterday: the man looked around the room, confused, then swung with all his might. Right before he made contact, for some reason, they all froze. The pole stopped right atop Charlie's head. I could see all of them wanted to move because their eyes moved but their bodies were stuck in place. Charlie paid no attention to anything else but me. He kissed me so passionately. The harder he kissed me, the brighter the shining light got around us. The shine got so bright and then darkness surrounded us. When I opened my eyes from the kiss, we were sitting in the apple orchard just outside of the farm in the forest.

Charlie and I made love under that apple tree like there was no one else in the world. It was the greatest and scariest moment of my life.

"Charlie never said anything about what happened. We carried on our affair for another half a year or so after that night. I never questioned his majestic capabilities after that … I tell that story for a few reasons, so you know the powerful love we had, so you can understand why I became a negative, spiteful person, so you understand that there's no answer for some of the questions you may have … so you understand that Trevor standing in this kitchen amongst all of you is not a miracle, it's destiny."

She doesn't cry, she isn't emotional, and she speaks with such peace. I can feel all the different emotions in the room. I can tell her sons don't know how to emotionally process what they're hearing and seeing. I actually understand and can't imagine what my family would be thinking if they heard this story. All the aunts are crying. There are tears of joy and pain. So silent yet so loud in the room. No one is saying anything, but I can feel everyone thinking. I look over at Kasenka and she's not even looking at her grandma. She's staring at me, squinting her eyes. A tear falls down her face and she mouths the words, "Thank you." No one really wants to move or say anything.

I take a moment to just soak it all in and watch the family. I feel like this is what Charlie would have wanted and loved to see. I met these people for the first time yesterday, but they feel like family; I feel a connection. It feels amazing. I can feel the emotion in the room and it feels like healing to me. I'm lost in the healing of the room when all of a sudden Kasenka comes up and snuggles on my shoulder. There's a kiss on the cheek then a whisper in my ear.

"They will never be able to thank you enough for changing the course of their future."

I'm stuck at first because I don't know what to do. We're standing in the middle of her family. I look down at her and her eyes just scream *Hug me*. I lean down and squeeze her in a tight embrace. She snuggles her neck right against mine. She squeezes me so tight I have to tap her to ease up a little bit. I can feel the wetness from tears on my neck.

Caught in the bliss of this hug, we don't notice the silence in the room and the attention of everyone being on us. I look up to see Kasia staring at us with a puzzled look. The look didn't seem mad or happy; it seems like there is something running through her head. Kasenka finally looks up to see everyone looking at us. She kisses me on my cheek and slowly walks away. I'm frozen like a statue as I watch her walk away. *What the hell is wrong with me?* I wonder. *Are these butterflies in my stomach? I haven't had this feeling since high school football.*

Kasia breaks me out of my haze as she shouts for everyone to leave the room but me and Kasenka, saying she wants a private moment with just us two for a second. She waits for everyone to leave before she summons us to sit with her at the table.

"My dear boy, you have traveled a long way with distance, but more importantly you have come a long way emotionally. Let me apologize to you now, Trevor, because your story is still being written. Yesterday, you told me you wanted answers. Let me say this before you start firing questions: I don't have an answer for any of the magical things that are happening in your life. Charlie was an angel and when you're connected to him, good things just happen. There is no explanation for it, Trevor. It's all I know. I tried searching for answers. I researched every aspect of his life and nothing stood out. I looked up miracle happenings and got thousands of things happening in the world, but nothing that connected to Charlie. I've searched all my life for answers and my hope was almost down to zero when you walked through the door. Then I realized I was looking for the wrong thing. Instead of just enjoying life like he wanted me to, I spent time being negative for what I couldn't find. His love and his spirit were so strong there had to be an explanation, but there isn't. I've always seen visions of you but never knew why I thought they were just random dreams. Then Charlie passed and all of a sudden I saw your life clearly. I don't know why … I'm assuming your question will be based around why." Her soft, old hands drape over mine.

"My only question was, or I should say now *is* … why me?" My heart starts to race. I have come all this way for answers and feel I am about to receive some type of comfort.

"This is the part I also have yet to figure out because for all the things you're seeing and experiencing, no one else can feel or see them, so it's tough to know. I was only able to feel those things because I was connected to him, but I never was able to get answers on why I was seeing or feeling the things I did. Your situation, my child, is different. You are from his cloth and things are different for you and happening differently for you. I'm afraid I don't know why it's you … maybe you were chosen, but to be honest, I don't have answers for you."

Just as fast as my heart spikes, it crashes in pain with disappointment. "No, there has to be an explanation."

"Trevor, my child, don't you think if I had the answers that I would want nothing more than to ease your pain by answering your questions? I want nothing more than to have the answers, ease your pain, and tell you the trip was worth it. I know you're tired … but I'm a realist, as you know, and unfortunately, I have no answers."

"Do you want to know the last thing Charlie said to me?" I ask, my voice cracking a little. Guess the disappointment is bigger than I thought.

"Oh, my, I'm not sure I'm ready for that …"

"He told me I was special. Told me that I had love in my soul. Told me his power was saving people, while my power is love ... but to be honest with you, I don't know what love is. I have only ever loved myself. He said, like him, I must come find you so I can find my calling. He told me when I found you all my answers would be right in front of me ... but that's me being selfish. The real reason I'm here is that he told me if you were alive, you needed to hear that he never stopped loving you. Even after a wife, kids, and life, you still held a piece of his heart. He regretted every day getting on that train and not trying harder. He always felt the world was just not ready for your kind of love and he felt like your world was crumbling, so he had to leave so you could live a normal life. He told me we were connected and when I saw you, my power would be revealed and I would clearly see how I was supposed to finish his legacy. On his last dying days he wasn't worried about his wife, he wasn't worried about his kids, or even his grandkids, for that matter. He wasn't worried about his retirement money, will, or what he didn't get to do in life. There were no emotional goodbyes or any tears about regrets. He wasn't even worried he was about to die ... He wanted to tell me about his Kasia and the love like no other."

Kasia breaks down and tears just flow down her face. She keeps saying in her strong accent, "My *Chanuntka, moj Chanuntka.*" I hug her close and tight.

"Kasia, you're an amazing woman. I'm so glad I got to meet you. After seeing you in all those letters and spiritual moments, you are even more beautiful in person. I have kept my promise to my Grandpa Charlie and delivered my message. I'm not sure where to go from here, but I have caused a big enough stir in your family. You guys need to heal and figure things out, so I must get going now."

The satisfaction and disappointment hit me at once. I have to run to the backyard to get some air, because I don't want them to see me breakdown. I'm satisfied because I was able to complete my grandfather's last wish and deliver his message, which was well worth it. I'm disappointed because Kasia couldn't give me any answers or an explanation as to why this happened to me. I feel like running home. I walk back in to give Kasia a goodbye hug, but after I start to walk away Kasenka grabs me and give me a big hug. She pulls me back and looks at me. She doesn't say anything, but her look tells me she understood how I was feeling at the moment. She's now the one rubbing my cheeks and I can't help but start to feel better. She rubs the tears from my eyes before they start falling. She comes close, hugs me again, and puts her lips to my ear like she doesn't want her grandma to hear her. She whispers, "You are not alone." As I almost completely melt in Kasenka's arms, Kasia lets out a fake cough to get our attention.

"Trevor, can you excuse Kasenka and I for a second? It seemed like you were in need of some air, yes?" She's insistent and strong, still the Kasia they have grown to love.

"Sure, I'll go check out the view."

Kasenka doesn't even take her eyes off me or turn towards her grandma. As I walk out the back, I turn around and look through the glass sliding doors and Kasenka is still looking at me. Kasia stares at her the whole time. I'm not sure what's going on, but it seems like they're starting a serious conversation.

"*Kohani*, be careful," Kasia says, grabbing Kasenka's hand.

"Be careful with what, Grandma? I have been careful all my life and I have been living a lie."

"Yes, my child, the hurt you feel – I hoped you would never feel that … But what I meant by being careful is … well, I see the way you look at Trevor now and how you are with him. Be careful with your heart, my sweet child."

Kasenka grabs her hand tighter and takes a deep sigh. Before she speaks, she walks over to the window and watches me admire the view for a minute. When we catch eyes, I wave hello and smile. I'm clueless to what they're talking about.

"Grandma, you're right, but I can't help myself. He's different. He's … I don't know. I have …"

"Let me guess – since the moment he walked through the forest trees of the farm everything has felt different? You forget who you are in a good way around him? Random good things have started happening? You are being put in situations for the first time in your life that you are unfamiliar with and loving it? When you're around him, he makes you feel like you're the only person in the world? He has done things so caring for you that no one has ever done without you asking? Sometimes you just want to be next to him and hold him? You stare at him because you have questions, but you don't know what to ask? The best one for me … when your family and the world around you are different and crazy, it feels like nothing because he has such a calming presence? And you're wondering why you're not responding the way your brain is telling you to?"

When I look back again from the view, Kasenka has her hands on the window, looking at me with tears coming down her face. I would have been worried, but she is smiling.

"What do I do, *Bacia*?"

"There is no point in fighting it, love. There's nothing you can do. Let your heart speak and follow it. I made a mistake with Charlie, letting outside influences dictate my actions … *Kohani*, there are going to be hurdles; true love only flourishes after facing agony together. A flower must bloom only after facing the ugliness of mud."

Chapter 33

I have every intention of cutting the trip short and leaving after my business meeting at the end of the week. Kasenka basically tells me I need to stay. In her words, she's politely telling me she needs me to stay.

"You at least owe it to me to see if answers come about. You know I'm still going through mental battles about what happened ... I still need your presence to help me figure it out. Your business meeting is at the end of the week, so that gives me a week to convince you to stay longer."

She's right. She's so excited and already has a plan. She mentions she remembers me talking about how much I loved going around America, just seeing each state, and seeing the country in all its glory. She wants to show me all the wonders of her country. I'm so glad I agree, because we spend a magical week just seeing the glory of Poland. We drive all over the country and I'm now in love with Poland. Warsaw is a big metropolis city – it reminds me of a European Chicago. We eat at some great restaurants; fried pierogi just tastes different when you're sitting looking out at Lazienki Park, a historical Royal Palace. We stop by the Polin Museum of the History of the Jews, which has so much rich history that I didn't learn about in my American history books. The stops by the concentration camps are a tough dose of reality when it comes to historic places. The old town market square is actually a medieval square, which is a mini historical town rebuilt after World War II. All this history with war and I'm reminded of Charlie and his place in history.

Then we venture to the beaches. While Krynica Mosrka Beach is beautiful, it's very crowded. It seems to be much more majestic along the Baltic Sea. I would have never known this much historical water was on the shores of Poland. Then we travel around Krakow. Call me old school, but I'm a much bigger fan of Krakow than of Warsaw. While it has just as many tourists as Warsaw, it's just more old school and traditional. Warsaw is a metropolis, while Krakow is more country. We go to Wieliczka Salt Mine, where they have underground chapels and caves of majestic historical finds. It's a bucket list thing I didn't know I had to see. Who would have thought a young black man from Chicago would end up in a salt cave in Krakow, Poland?

The Wawel Cathedral is one of my favorite religious places I've ever visited. So many thousand-year-old churches. We visited Oskar Schindler's Enamel Factory where I turn into a jerk American tourist taking pictures in front of the building. After seeing the movie and learning all the history, I just feel I have to do it. This amazing museum teaches visitors of the war hero's courageous acts, but after I watched the movie and read the books about Schindler I never thought I would ever be standing in front of the actual building.

We return to the city of Wroclaw where I've been staying for the last few weeks and I automatically feel cheated because I stayed on the country side but hadn't seen the urban glory of Wroclaw. Another bucket list item is visiting a zoo in Poland. Yes, it is a very random visit but Kasenka is so happy to see the animals. I'm not even sure I've gone to the Brookfield Zoo in Chicago. Then we go to an underground water museum and science aquarium called Hydropolis. Yes, life and God are good. It's the first time I visit Poland and it's only right that I go to my first underground water museum. I keep saying I don't know what love is, but whatever this feeling is I have for Poland has to be close to love.

After having chances to reflect, I'm not sure if it's Poland or my tour guide I love. I've gotten a chance to get to know the real Kasenka and she's an amazing woman. She makes me want to do nice things for her. I'm really starting to like her. Considering my dating history in the past, this is usually where I start running because I don't know what to do, but with her I feel like I'm just beginning. This whole time I've been chasing the goal of finding her grandma to discover the answers to life, so I was blinded by my goal of the chase without taking the time to see what's in front of me. She has calmed me down, which is a hard thing to do, and I have slowed down to enjoy every moment. From the beginning I thought she was beautiful, but I really was just looking at her beauty on the outside. But her passion for her job, her culture, and her country is very strong and sexy. She has started treating me like I'm some kind of saint when I don't deserve it. For just meeting each other, we laugh and talk together like we have been friends forever. We hold hands on walks while we take pictures of the sights. Even though she has been to some of the sights we saw, she acts like it's the first she has visited those sites. We've even gone horseback riding. Kasenka told me she wanted me to experience what my Grandpa Charlie did when he was here. I'm sure he would have been embarrassed by my performance if he saw how scared I was on the horse. We also go hang gliding for the first time. I realize how much I'm not an action guy. I love the sightseeing and everything, but I'm clumsy and afraid of heights. I really like the way she looks at me like I'm important or I'm the only person around.

One of my favorite moments is when we go to her hometown and knit with grandmas. The *babcias* try to teach me how to knit and speak Polish at the same time. They talk to me as if I'm fluent in their language. Kasenka knows how to make something so simple become so much fun. We laugh and she tells jokes in English and in Polish, and even though I don't understand her I still laugh because she's funny. We dance and sing in just the simplest moments. She has taught me how to be in the moment. She reminds me so much of her grandmother. I stand there and watch her dance with the grandmas and it's like she's dancing in slow motion. As she laughs and smiles with them it's like she's having the time of her life.

We finish our trip by taking a drive to the Tatra Mountains to go hiking. The mountains serve as a border for Slovakia and Poland. There are so many nice trails and sites, but if you hike to just the right altitude you can get a good view of the forest land in Slovakia and Poland combined. There are so many different animals and species of birds. I didn't think I would be into this kind of stuff, but it's really cool to see a red fox trotting along. Kasenka is in her element out here; she loves to hike, I can tell. We share a soft moment where we just sit in silence and stare at the sunset. I feel so at peace with her. There are moments when I forget why I came here. As she snuggles up in my arms, I'm trying to think of a better time I have had traveling and I can't think of it. Another thought comes to my head as well: this feels like the ultimate date, and I can't think of a better time I have had with someone. I'm shaken out of my thought because Kasenka gets up and sits herself in my lap and puts my arms around her shoulders. My view becomes Kasenka's hair and hazel eyes shining against the sunset. My heart is racing so fast. This is usually when the lust kicks in, but this is different. I'm just trying to soak in this feeling and this moment. The great time has to come to an end as Kasenka looks at her watch, jumps up, and says, "We must get back before it's dark." The trip is so amazing I feel like I need more.

Chapter 34

It's Saturday night and time for the big work closing dinner. All the ladies and gentlemen from their company are bringing their spouses and ask if I needed a date. Luckily for me, Kasenka is my beautiful date and has become a good person to me and I'm excited about it. I have butterflies in my stomach again, another first for me. I should be focused on closing the deal and the work at hand, but I couldn't care less. I'm worried if Kasenka is going to have a good time or not. I almost fall out of my car seat when we pick her up. She looks like a celebrity. Once again, she's wearing a red dress. It's her color, but this one is different. It's so form-fitting that I can see her six-pack abs along with the lining of her chest. She's so sexy. The dress flares at the bottom with sheer fabric that you can see through. She's wearing simple red pumps that match the color of the dress. She lets her hair just flow down with a princess-style headband pulling her hair back. She also has on gleaming hoop earrings with a slim gold necklace with a cross on it. The best part of it all is she has on no makeup – no mascara, no eyeshadow, no lipstick. It's just like she woke up and threw water on her face. She's such a natural beauty, not to mention most women would never come to an event like this with no makeup on. It says something about her character. It also says to me that she's comfortable enough around me to be herself. I laugh to myself as she gets in the car and gives me a kiss on the cheek. I'm in a spell.

The night goes perfectly, and when I say perfectly I mean better than I could've planned. Someone is watching over me upstairs. I come to the restaurant all serious and thinking about business, trying to represent the company the right way, but no one wants to talk business. Instead, Kasenka and I become the topic of discussion. We tell stories and laugh like it's a family dinner. It gets so comfortable after drinks start flowing the CEO of their company pulls me to the side. I think we're going to talk about numbers or business, but instead he tells me how special Polish women are and that I have a special one in Kasenka. He tells me a joke that I better not screw it up because Polish mothers-in-law are predators. We laugh and share a shot together. This guy is the president of the company, worth millions I'm sure, and instead of talking business we take shots together and laugh. I feel like someone is playing a joke on me; this is going too well. Before the drinks get heavy, we sign the deal and I have just officially made our company millions of dollars. We tap glasses together and everyone shouts out "*Na zdrowie!*" Luckily for me, I've been getting better at Polish and I understand that means congratulations or bless you. Instead of handshakes, I get hugs from everyone. These aren't your regular women and men. These are corporate tycoons that worked hard to get to where they are, but their tough demeanor is replaced for hugging and treating me as if I am family.

Once all the business is done they bring out this drink call *Krupnik*, some kind of homemade vodka. It's so good. I have to be careful because you really can't taste the alcohol. Kasenka warns me to go slow and only have a few. I still can't believe this is business and I just made millions for myself. I should be jumping for joy inside because I have waited for this moment all my life. Instead I'm staring at Kasenka talking to the wives and businesswomen and she looks like she's in control, telling a story, making everyone laugh. She is, for sure, a part of this deal closing. We catch eyes and she just waves and smiles. When the music starts, without hesitation I grab Kasenka and we head for the dance floor. Once again it's just us, but she couldn't care less. The music starts off fast and other people start joining us. The DJ goes back and forth from old school Polska music to new age dance. Before I know it, everyone's on the dance floor sweating and singing. Once again, it's a business meeting with a family feel. I feel like I'm at a wedding. After a while the music switches to slow songs and everyone goes to sit down – everyone but us. Kasenka grabs my shoulders and pulls me closer. She wraps her arms around me and stares me in the eyes. I'm embarrassed and hoping she can't feel my erection, but instead she smiles and pulls me closer.

"Kasenka, I don't know if I am …"

Before I could finish, she places her lips on mine. Her lips are so soft. She tastes like Polish vodka and peach lip balm. She pulls back and smiles at me.

"No need to talk now. Emotions just get messed up when you try to explain them. Let's just enjoy the night."

We spend the rest of the night eating, drinking, and dancing. It's the moment we start acting like we're a serious couple. We get so lost in each other that we don't even notice we're the only ones left. The DJ has to send us off with the last song while the bartender is cleaning up.

We get in the car and Kasenka tells Piotrek to take us to my temporary home. We proceed to kiss like college kids in the backseat of the car. We don't even say bye to Piotrek and barely make it to the door before she starts pulling off my shirt. She pushes me down on the living room couch. Then she slows the mood down and smiles at me. I have never been so excited. She looks nervous at first as she slowly takes her dress off in front of me. I can't help myself; I have to just reach out and touch her stomach. Her body is as beautiful as her face. Her chest is medium-sized with the most perfect nipples, with her privates shaved perfectly into a rectangle. She is perfect from head to toe. She sits atop me naked, even though I'm still in all my clothes. She kisses me as if her life depends on it, and I get lost in her lips. She jumps up and holds her hand out to help me up. Her body is so mesmerizing. She slowly takes off my shirt and goes even slower with my pants. She looks up and gives me the most triumphant smile because she could see and feel the erection up against her chest. Then she gives me the most devilish smile as she presses up against me and she can feel my erection against her belly button now. After slowly rubbing my cheeks, she walks away slowly to the bedroom. Her butt flexes as she walks to the room, just pure perfection. The rest of the night is pure bliss. We fit perfectly together. The nervous first-time butterflies are replaced with a feeling of pure harmony and heaven, like it is meant to be.

Chapter 35

I damn near scream bloody Mary when I open my eyes. There is Kasia. The spirit of Kasia, anyway, sitting right on the edge of the bed staring at Kasenka and me. My head is pounding – must be from the homemade vodka from last night. Luckily, I don't wake up Kasenka; she snores away, again, and I'm not sure I would be able to explain my shocked look to her. Kasia just stares at Kasenka snuggled up around my waist. She just shakes her head.

"This is the most beautiful thing I have witnessed in my life … truly a blessing."

"Well, it's good to see you again, my angel … I apologize that it's in this circumstance."

"I should have known because it was right in my face. I just couldn't put two and two together."

"What are we talking about here?" I ask. I have to lower my voice as Kasenka snuggles up and kisses me on my chest.

"Oh, my God … I can feel her," Kasia says as she tears up a little watching Kasenka leave her lips on my chest.

"I can feel her too," I reply. After a few seconds we both pause and hold back our laughs.

"No, silly, I can feel her emotions. I can feel her in my soul. Her heart is so full."

"As is mine. She is an angel as well. I guess it runs in the family, huh?"

"No, Trevor, you don't understand … she is in love with you."

TODD LOVE BALL JR.

Before I could respond, Kasenka starts to wake up. She's groggy and half sleep as she kisses me on my forehead and tells me she's getting in the shower. Kasia and I both watch Kasenka walk to the shower. When I turn back around, Kasia is right in my face, looking me dead in the eyes.

"I figured it out, Trevor. I can't explain how, but I know I've figured it out. I feel it in my soul. You are looking for answers. The answer to why you're here just walked into the shower. The treasure you have been searching for is Kasenka. Think about it, Trevor: your grandfather sent you here to fulfill your destiny. He said from day one your power is love. These good things aren't happening because Charlie died, these good things are happening because you're chasing your destiny of love. It was the same with Charlie when he was saving and rescuing people; good things were happening. He saved me and that's why good things happened in my life. I was just too stubborn to accept it because I wanted Charlie in my life. He left because the first bad thing to happen to someone he saved happened to me, when my family gave me that tea. To him it was a sign from God that he must go home and save others because he couldn't save me from my family. I know it sounds crazy, but in some weird, magical way you have what Charlie had. It's just different. You must follow your heart rather than your mind …"

As we hear Kasenka getting out of the shower, Kasia continues, "I have to be quick with the next part. I can't explain to you how I know this but, the moment you fall in love is the moment I will die. Don't ask me how I know. It would be like you asking me why I'm standing here in front of you right now … I wouldn't have an answer for you. You know my true self just held on in life because I knew there was still something left from Charlie's legacy that wasn't finished. There was always something in the back of my head poking me. There were always things happening that would remind me of his magic. Just when I was losing hope and thought I was going to die without seeing proof, you walked through my door and kneeled in front of me. I knew all my life that if this moment ever came it would change the course of my family history and legacy. My happiest dreams came true ... you can finish the legacy that Charlie and I were destined to live. I know once that destiny is fulfilled I will give up and die in hopes of meeting my *Chanuntka* in the afterlife ..."

Before Kasia could finish, Kasenka comes out of the bathroom and I turn to see her. "Are you talking to yourself?" she asks, her hair still dripping from the shower.

I turn back around and Kasia is gone. I freeze and Kasenka comes around to face me.

"Are you okay? You're crying ... you look like you've seen a ghost or something."

Chapter 36

I want answers but never think about the repercussions if I don't like or believe the answers. There is still the realist in me struggling and coming to grips with this. Visions and spirits are one thing, but love is real life. I guess my mind is my own worst enemy because I have been building up this magical thing happening in my head when really I never did look right in front of me. I didn't look at the simple answers. As I sit here and watch Kasenka making breakfast in the kitchen, I can't deny there is something in me that is different. She is wearing just a small white T-shirt that barely covers her chest and boy short underwear in red. She is so perfect – I've thought that a lot. I have never said that about anyone, not even my mom. She makes something so simple, like making breakfast, seem like it's a joy to do. I must admit to myself that when I look at her I have a feeling I have never felt before. She turns around to catch me looking at her perfect bottom and she turns to look at it herself and just gives me a smile and a wink. It's rainy outside, so we put our plans on hold and instead make plans to just hang out at the temp house and watch movies. Once we decide on staying in the house, she tells me she also wants to make dinner for me, so she runs to the local stores to grab a few things. She waves bye and tells a joke about not missing her too much. This is crazy.

As soon as the door closes I'm hit with the other reality of what Kasia told me. If I fall in love, or in her words *when* I fall in love, she will pass away. I'll have a hard time knowing my love controls the start of a life together and the end of another one. A life I have come to care about. I've grown fond of Kasia, and she has become all the important women figures to me rolled into one – a mom, an aunt, a grandma, an advisor, and a good friend that I've never had. I'm so emotionally conflicted I sit here and just contemplate for the hour or so before Kasenka comes back from the store. After putting all the stuff down, Kasenka keeps looking at me funny. She grabs two tall glasses and two of those Tyskie beers, my new favorite, and walks me over to the edge of the balcony where the rain could only hit our feet.

"Okay, Trevor, you've been different since this morning. Please tell me what's wrong." She rubs my cheeks as I take a sip of the beer. I really like it when she does that.

"Oh, nothing has changed. It's just been an emotional trip, you know?"

"Trevor, Trevor, Trevor, come on. I let your body inside of my body last night. It was sexy and great and magic. Even more sexy is honesty and being real, the real you. If you can't be honest with me and tell me what's in your head, then we are wasting time."

Wow. Okay, she's right. I usually have myself to think about things, never someone to share with, so it's different for me. And she seems like she really wants to help.

"What if I told you that my destiny was to come, meet you, and fall in love – would you believe it? What if I gave you the information that the future of both of our families is dependent on me falling in love with you? Now, here is the part that makes this difficult and real ... What if I told you that when I fall in love with you, your Grandma Kasia will die?" I throw everything on the table. Another first for me, because I've never trusted anyone enough to be truthful in situations like this. Things have obviously made this situation more important than your average relationship.

Kasenka pauses for a second. She takes a deep breath as she thinks to herself. "Wow … Trevor, I must apologize because I don't want to scare you and have you running for the hills, but it's too late for me … I have fallen for you already. From the moment you showed up to my farm and those kids came and found me and said you were looking for me, I knew this was different. Something was different. From the moment I got in the backseat of the car with you, I have experienced nothing but firsts in my life. Not just firsts, but they have all been great experiences. Growing up I always knew I was different and I was destined for a different kind of love … When you smiled and shook my hand … I knew this was it. What I mean by its too late is you already have a piece of my heart. You mentioned you falling in love with me would change the course of my life. Even if I never saw you after today, you have already changed the course of my life because I would expect nothing less than the way you have treated me. You are different spiritually. I see how people change when they are around you. It's too late, Trevor. I can never change what I know about my community and my view of life, you gave me that … What I am trying to say is I barely even know you, yet I feel madly in love."

There's no flinch or hesitation. She says it with such zest that I feel it. She puts her hands to my lips as a sign for me not to say it back unless I mean it.

"Kasenka, I have feelings that I've never had before. I have a feeling when I'm around you that is like no other … but my mind has all of these hurdles. I have a life back home that you know nothing about. What if you don't like Chicago or my family and my home? You have a community here that you are in charge of and a future that you were leading before you met me. We are from two different worlds. Let me ask you something – before I walked on to your farm what were your plans in life? Because it couldn't have been me," I tell her, feeling so lost mentally.

"You can ask all the questions you want, Trevor, but here's the thing: it just doesn't matter. I'm not sure God lets us pick who we fall in love with. Everything has been different with you and I love it. I'm a different person around you and I love the person I am around you. When my grandma was telling the story of how Charlie walked into the tent and she was smitten right away, I felt that to my soul, because I felt the same way at the farm. Like Charlie, you have an aura about you that just calms everyone down. I can't explain it and I don't want it to be explained because I am on cloud nine ... I feel it in my soul like we were meant to be together ... like it's destiny."

Kasenka has the same resolve that Charlie had before he died, telling me love is my power. She has as much sureness as Kasia did telling me she loved Charlie more than her husband and kids. She has the same need her in eyes that Kasia had when Charlie was getting on the train to leave. I would be lying to say I don't feel the pull as well, but I still have questions in my heart.

"Kasenka, there are so many layers ..."

"Those are your layers you must work through. My path is clearly written for me."

"Okay, what about your Grandma Kasia dying when this moment happens?"

She pauses for a second before she answers, "You know this for sure? How do you know this for sure?" Her tone tells me she's a little confused.

"You see, this becomes the moment when I start to sound crazy, but if you want the real me I have to be honest with you ... This morning when you saw me tearing up and said it looked like I had just seen a ghost? I had seen a ghost ... it was your Grandma Kasia.

I have already told you I see a spirit of her—it's a younger version of her—and she showed up at the edge of the bed this morning. She told me in so many words that she has figured out the end game in all of this. From day one of Charlie dying, the road led to you and us meeting. Her words were 'The day you fall in love, Trevor, is the day I can let go and be with my Charlie in heaven.'"

Oh, man, what a relief to be able to tell someone out loud what I've been seeing. I feel like a crazy person who just talked to a psychologist. Kasenka just stares at me. I wish my power was mind reading. About a minute passes and she hasn't moved, blinked, or said a word. I'm not even sure she is breathing.

"It hurts. My Grandma Kasia gave up a lot so everyone in the family can live. I've had the wrong perception of her my whole life, and now I feel horrible because I know the truth. I'm sure the family will be devastated ... with that being said, I also know she told you that she was happy when she found out the truth. I'm sure she told you that she would want nothing more than to see us get together and start our own legacy. I'm sure she said that she sat there her whole life waiting for a sign and there couldn't be a happier ending for her. You see, I didn't believe you when you first told me about seeing Kasia in your visions, but that was because when you first told me I didn't know you as well and I was still processing. This relationship you have with my grandma just makes me love you more. I'm a strong Catholic woman and strong in my beliefs, and the miracles I've seen over the last few weeks make it clear what my path is. I will not stand in destiny's way ... It's too late for me, Trevor. I'm in too deep. Your question is, would I want to give my love back to keep Grandma alive? My answer is no because that's not what she would want. As when Charlie died, your life's destiny started. It will be no different for me when Kasia passes ... It's her dying last wish."

Chapter 37

We spent the rest of that day snuggling and watching movies. It's so good to watch her do things for the first time. On the farm and with her community, there isn't a lot of time for social things. She tells me she doesn't want to watch newer movies; she wants to watch old nineties movies. She wants me to find her an interesting love story, and luckily for her, one of my favorite movies of all time is *Pretty Woman*. At least it's a love story to me. I could never tell any one of my boys because they would never let me hear the end of it.

It's so fun to watch her laugh and cry during the movie. It's the joyous reactions to small things that I really enjoy about her. After the movie we sit back, eat cake, and watch old shows. We laugh at the show *Whose Line Is It Anyway*, and she copies all the skits—she's actually really funny. I get more of a laugh because her strong accent makes the jokes better. After a while we get lost in conversation and the TV just becomes background noise. We spend the night cuddling and spooning, talking favorite colors and foods, then discussing more serious stuff like political views and bucket list dreams. We relive our best childhood memories and painful memories. While I think my stories of coming up are boring, it's like Kasenka holds onto every word. Her imagination of the life I've led is bigger than what it is. But then again, it's no different when it comes time for me to hear about her upbringing. While talking about the farm life, cows, horses, and living the old school traditions bores her, I love hearing every second of it. I'm learning a lot about her as well and I keep coming back to the word I use for her: perfect.

It's getting close to the time for me to go back home, so Kasenka tells me she wants to surprise me with something – and surprise herself, because she has never told anyone this particular secret. She tells me she wants to show me something a few miles into the farm that no one knows about, not even her mom and dad or the seniors in the community. She says the family owns the property where it's located, but it's so hard to get to no one decides to venture there. At first I'm worried about her breaking barriers at her farm or getting in trouble with her elders in the community, but her childlike excitement means that she's not worried at all. Our car ride with my new brother, Piotrek, doesn't feel long at all because we all converse like we've been friends all our lives. The whole ride, Kasenka keeps saying she can't wait to show me her surprise.

As we pull up in front of the bend in the hill at the split of the forest trees, Piotrek comes to a stop. Kasenka tells him to keep driving when we come to the bend of the hill that leads into the farm. As we drive by, she shows me which cabin was the one Charlie built. I don't have the heart to tell her I already knew. There it goes, that weird connection I feel to this place again. There is something pulling me, but I can't put my finger on it. I feel a sense of home for some reason.

As we get out the car I feel the energy of the people running up to see Kasenka and her guests. A few of the little girls run up to her and smile and hug her, and then run off after she greets them. Right after that, a few of the elders walk up and ask Kasenka a few questions. It sounds like urgent business, but I can't understand Polish just yet. She barks out a few orders and sounds like she's yelling at them, but they can be talking about the weather for all I know. The language is very difficult. This is great—the first time I get to see her in boss mode—and just when I thought she couldn't get any sexier. The gentlemen get their walking orders from Kasenka and proceed to give me dirty looks on their strut away. Kasenka gives me an apologetic look for their behavior, but I give a thumbs up, because I'm getting used to the stares. I feel most of the looks I get are curiosity.

I'm just taking it all in, watching her in her element. We walk over to a side cabin that looks like a summer camp cabin; the place looks like a wooden duplex. She shows me her room, very small and modest. There are three rooms all separated by a big wooden cylinder block. Kasenka tells me she lives here with two other women. I can feel the history in this cabin. I can feel the spirit in my bones. This cabin is definitely more than 100 years old. I'm not even sure they have running water in this particular camp. Kasenka is so regal, like a princess, so I'm expecting her to be staying in a castle or something. She's so pure with such strong intelligence, and now let's add modest, because the way she talked about this place I can tell she feels blessed. Damn, listen to me obsessing over her like this.

Kasenka changes in front of me and grabs a few things. She winks and tells me she hopes I've changed my mind about leaving early. She leaves her bags by the front door as we go out the back. I'm pleasantly surprised to see the horse stable right off the back porch of her cabin. She walks up to one of the horses as it put its head down for her to kiss it. She kisses and rubs its forehead and whispers something but I can't understand. I'm gonna have to learn Polish somehow. She whistles and another horse comes running around the tree bend. She taps the harness for me to hop up on the horse as she hops up on hers. I guess she didn't get discouraged from the first time we went horseback riding, because I did.

She tells me to hold on as tight as I can; she even doubles back to make sure I'm holding on. She still isn't comfortable and gives me instruction on putting my shoulder down and keeping my head towards the wind. She tells me the horses know exactly where we are going. Before I could ask, "Why all the safety protocols?" she yells out, "Yah!" We take off so fast my shirt blows halfway up my chest and my hair flops side to side. I'm just starting to get my rhythm when we take a hard right into the thickness of the forest. The brush is so thick I can barely see anything in front of me. We ride through this thickness for at least two miles it seems. All of a sudden there's a clearing the size of a football field right in the middle of all the thickness. Right in the middle of the opening is a small cabin and around the cabin is a small pond. It's a mini getaway in the middle of nowhere. The thick brush and all the forest trees encompass this little miniature paradise. It feels like we are in a bubble that's made out of tree branches and thick forest leaves.

Little specks of sunlight peek through the trees and dot the ground, giving me the feeling we're in some other world. The pond even has fish in it. This is a paradise with its own definition because I've never seen anything like this to compare it to. The cabin looks newly built – nothing crazy, actually simple engineering, like putting together Legos. There are mini logs connecting big ones for walls and the same was done for the roof. Very small and quaint, it seems like it's just one big room, like a studio. A little deck area is located right outside the front door, which reminds me of that restaurant Piotrek and I stopped by when I first got here. Simple, clean, and original, someone did a good job of making it look rustic. I walk around amazed because she said no one knows about this, so I'm guessing on how it was built. She jumps off her horse and spreads her arms out.

"Do you like it?" she asks, smiling from ear to ear.

"I love it, actually. Very peaceful and serene. I love the deck in front of the house instead of the back, great idea. I'm sure you can spend days here just enjoying the sound of the pond."

She looks at me puzzled. "It was just completed a few weeks ago, so I haven't had the time yet to just enjoy it … until now." She walks up and holds my hand.

"It's amazing. The best part is it feels like we are on a different planet or something, it's so secluded … Whoever built this was good at keeping your secret. How did you get all of this stuff here and be discreet about it?" I ask, looking around in amazement.

"It took me four and a half years to build this." She's looking me dead in the eye to see my reaction, but I can't help but flinch.

"Wait, you mean, you and the contractor and laborers, right?"

"No, I built this with my own bare hands … piece by piece, wood log by wood log. For the last four years my free time was spent here, from early morning chopping wood to late night clearing the brush out of the way," she replies. She stands there and admires her work, but I can see the tough memories that go through her head for some reason. They come to me like flashes of visions, but I see the work she put in. This is different.

"Kasenka, you have impressed me with a lot of things but this by far is the most … definitely the most shocking."

She laughs a little. "Yeah, you didn't think a young country girl could use her hands, huh? Don't worry, I get that reaction all the time with other things I do in life," she says, beaming with pride.

"Kasenka, I don't know many guys that could pull this off, and I mean plural. You are something special." I've seen magical things happen over the last few months and this one has shocked me the most.

"It was hard work and some days I wasn't sure if I should keep going, but once I found this spot something told me to tarp the spot and build. You'll see what I mean."

"But I don't understand. You said I would be the first to see this. How is it in four years no one saw you building this? Or no one wanted to help or anything?" I'm confused.

"Oh, you are so impatient, my dear friend. I was going to try and surprise you, but you're so pushy with questions. Of course people saw me, silly. The moment I found this place I found something and covered it. I immediately told my family that since I was going to dedicate my life to the farm I wanted my own space and serenity. I tried bringing them through the bush and showing them what I wanted to do, but they didn't make it past a mile before they decided to just say go ahead and have the space. By the time anyone thought to come, I already covered the real surprise with the partial build of this cabin. They assumed I was being crazy and being an introvert, but the more I built over the surprise, the more the so-called bubble started to form. It was weird. It was like the trees and brush had started to form the way you see it now, all of a sudden, and a few months ago it turned into the majestic place you see now. My family owns about a ten-mile radius where the farm is centered, so me wanting this space on the edge was nothing to them … Anyway, there is a better treasure that no one knows about inside. Let me show you."

She grabs my hand and leads me into the cabin. It's so basic and simple, essentially a clear room with a table and chairs sitting over a rug in the middle of the floor. To one side of the room there's an old couch and what looks like an old fireplace combined with a cooking furnace. The only light coming in is from a little window she made near the door looking over the front porch. She lights a lantern and puts it on the table as we sit down. She just stares at me and doesn't say anything as the candle shines off her face. I look around in awkward silence. I'm not sure if something's supposed to happen.

"So am I supposed to guess where this big surprise is that no one knows about? This thing that I can tell is so important to you?" To be honest, I'm already surprised and impressed so I'm not sure what else there could be.

"Good." She jumps up and seems satisfied.

She smiles from ear to ear as she tells me to get up. She quickly moves the chairs and table to the side. She walks over and looks out the window before covering the window with a curtain. She then locks the doors, which have three different locks on the door frames. She removes the rug that we're on and puts it to the side. There's a swing handle sitting in the middle of the floor with what looks like a door hatch to under the cabin. She walks over and pulls the door up, and there's a stairwell that leads down to a dark hallway. She flips a switch after a few steps and a long hallway lights up. The hallway is at least 100 yards long, leading all the way to a big safe door, which looks like a bank vault door. She twists the circle lock a few times and the door makes a creaking sound as she pushes it open.

My mind is blown away when I see a beautiful open room. It has to be at least 1,500 square feet of just open space. There's a kitchen with a sink and cabinets next to an old stove. An L-shaped sectional couch is centered in the room with a nice glass table to the side of the couch. Lots of artwork and old paintings and old pottery lace the room for décor. There is an old radio that hangs with wires from the ceiling. All of a sudden I see a flash of Charlie and Kasia kissing in the middle of the room. It's only for a second, so I think maybe I'm just tired. Then as I touch the walls of the kitchen area, there's another flash of some a man screaming at Charlie.

Kasenka walks over to a cooler sitting in the kitchen area and grabs some beers. Once again that Tyskie beer is back and I'm glad. She hands me a beer and I clink my beer can with hers, then she takes a long swig.

"*Na zdrowie* … you are my first guest ever down here. I was sure someone knew about this so I waited a while. Once I knew it was hidden, I started to build over it. When I told the elders, I was halfway expecting them to tell me they knew about this old war bunker, but no one came forward. They wanted me to take it. The first thing I did was build the cabin over this spot. Like I assumed, some eventually came through the brush and saw the area but no one ever cared to venture into my cabin. Privacy is part of our community, so I took advantage of that. Again, it took me four long, grueling years, but it has been a pleasure and an escape from my duties. Obviously, someone had to build this during the war, but then like a lot of locations, once the war was over and people were liberated, it became a forgotten piece of history. There was power and water and a foundation already built here. I just had to clean it up. It's not a home yet but upgrading the water system will allow me to at least make a shower. Then I can do a TV down here and all the fixings of an upgraded home, you know, just to get away from it all." She pauses, then looks at me and asks, "What is wrong with you? Are you okay? That look of you seeing a ghost is on your face again."

"I don't know what's going on. I feel weird. My stomach hurts … I feel like I've seen this place before. Do you know what déjà vu is? I've seen this place before in my dreams or visions …"

She goes to hug me and I fall back. The room turns black and my heart rate spikes. It feels like I'm having a heart attack. My breath is short and I can't catch up. I know this feeling from the letters. There is a bang and a flash of light and I dart up, searching for my breath.

I'm still in the bunker but Kasenka is gone and so is all the furniture. There's just an army cot and a few lantern lights. As I shake off my grogginess, I can hear the door open and some voices on the other side. My Grandpa Charlie comes walking down in his army uniform, holding what looks like a picnic basket. Right behind him is Kasia, dressed in jeans and a white blouse. She's carrying a blanket and some pillows and a little basket of candles and trinkets. They light all of the lanterns on then set the blanket down. Kasia sets up a romantic display on the blanket as they sit down together and just smile at each other. They hug, kiss, and feed each other. There is no talking, just caressing and eating. At one point they laugh after Kasia accidentally puts whipped cream in Charlie's eye. But there's nothing said, no jokes made or punchlines, just pure happiness. They don't take their eyes off each other. It's so intense that I can feel the love in my heart. It's so full.

"We can drop everything and live the simple life right here."

"Oh, Kasia, I love you, but you know that's impossible."

"No, no, Charlie, think about it ... we have everything we need. The pond has fish, we can grow our own vegetables and fruits, and I know how to farm from my family history. We can have chickens and goats, we can have babies, and just live the simple life and love each other. This place is so secluded no one would find us or bother us. Even if they did, we could build a security system that would work ... Come on, *moj Chanuntka*, we deserve this, I deserve this, and I deserve you. We deserve each other. We are doing nothing wrong. I know you feel it. We were destined for this. I know how you feel. We are supposed to be here to make it work."

"My angel, that would be my dream. I would love nothing more than to just have you to myself and forget the outside world, but it's not realistic. You have family, I have family back home, and there are so many factors. How could we make it work? I take that back. We could make it work, but ... for how long?"

"I would rather have a few years with you with the hopes of the world eventually figuring it out. But even if it didn't work, I would have those years I knew what real love was about. I would rather have one year with you than a lifetime with someone else."

"You are so beautiful. I can't say no. Something is wrong with me … You're right, I would rather have six months of just you, but Kasia, you have family and friends and a life. I have a home in the U.S. that's really not a home because they hate me … If we do this, we have to tell everyone and try to make it work where we don't have to hide."

She pauses for a second after he finishes and thinks about the repercussions. In her head, society is ready and human enough to help, especially her family.

"Okay, you're right. You can stay with me here on the farm … I can tell my family. They will for sure help. I'm sure we can trust them."

Just as she finishes her sentence I remember where I saw this place. It was the first time I had a vision, and Charlie and I were playing Monopoly. This is where they have that magical moment where Charlie and Kasia become golden figures and fall in love. Just as I'm putting the story together there's a flash and a bang and a bright light. My breathing starts getting heavy and it feels like I'm falling and drowning at the same time. Everything goes black and I pass out.

Chapter 38

I bounce up and Kasenka is holding me, screaming at the top of her lungs. I'm still trying to figure out where I am but the fear in her face shakes me awake. I finally start to catch my breath and Kasenka starts pacing around the room, screaming, "*O moj Boze, O moj Boze!*" I hug her to try and calm her down. My mind is racing, and my first thought is that that was the first time someone has been around for one of my visions. I can't imagine how bad it looked. Kasenka now looks like the one who has seen a ghost.

A few moments go by and Kasenka finally stops pacing around the room. After seeing I'm okay, she grabs me by the cheeks and stares into my eyes. She looks like she has been crying really hard. Oh, boy, it must've looked really bad. I hug her tight again as I try to process what just happened. I keep going back to when Charlie started telling me things would happen and how stubborn I was. I might have listened a little more if I knew I was going to be on this emotional roller coaster. Before I'm able to get lost in my thoughts, Kasenka pushes my shoulders back from the hug and slaps me on my arm.

"Trevor, what was that?" She can't stop crying and while she calms down for a second, she is now starting to lose it again. The tears and snot come running down her nose.

"I'm so sorry you had to see that, Kasenka."

"You're sorry I had to see that?! You're sorry I had to see that, huh? What the hell was that? What just happened? Are you okay? I felt so helpless because there was no way for me to get you help out here ... Trevor, talk to me." Her hands shake, she's so emotionally overwhelmed.

"Again, we have come to the point of straight talk. That was one of my visions I was telling you about ... It's just never happened in front of anyone. How long was I out for?" I'm just starting to catch my mind up to my breathing.

"It was at least two minutes, maybe a little bit over, but no more than three minutes. It felt like three hours."

"Wow, just minutes, huh? I was with them for at least an hour."

"With them?!"

"Charlie and Kasia ..."

"Wait, what? What do you mean?"

"Hold on, because I need to know something first ... what was I doing while I was out?"

"Your eyes rolled to the back of your head. Your body kept shivering and you were talking and mumbling, but I couldn't understand anything you were saying. It felt like you were repeating a conversation that someone was having."

I'm not sure I should continue because she hasn't calmed down, but after moment I tell her, "Kasenka, that conversation I was repeating was our grandparents back during the war, talking about their plans for the future ... you weren't the only one to know about this bunker. The little items you found here most likely belonged to Kasia and Charlie. I think I know what my grandfather wants me to do. I think the legacy he wanted me to create is right here."

She starts to hyperventilate again. Maybe it's too much all at once for her. It takes me a few months to grasp the letters and visions, but she just got a crash course in it all. She just keeps shaking and trying to grasp it all. I walk up and hug her, telling her, "I understand."

Chapter 39

After two emotional months it's time for me to head back home. It's strange, I never questioned what the meaning of home is until now. I accomplished a lot on this trip but the goal I had of getting answers still eludes me. The truth is I haven't had enough of Kasenka. I have to find out if it's because Kasia and Charlie think it's my destiny, or if I do really like her for her. I haven't had enough, so much so that I need to see Kasenka with my family. My true belief is love can't be defined unless it's seen by family and those closest to you.

I have my secretary start the expedition of her passports and tickets and everything needed to be done to get her to Chicago. My secretary is really good, and she gets it done in forty-eight hours. All of these signs and all of the good things that have been happening point towards a future with this woman—and who am I to fight destiny?—but I need to see if she would work with the real me in my home and element. I'm really starting to believe that our relationship is what Kasia and Charlie's was supposed to be, but the world wasn't ready for a love like theirs. There are so many similarities – too many to be a coincidence.

I'm a little nervous because Kasenka and I haven't had a fight or an argument or anything, and that scares me about the future. I see what the pain is like if it doesn't work; Kasia changed who she was in life because of it. I felt that pain as they went through it. Yes, we are in the twenty-first century and a lot of things have changed, but we're still two different colors and from two different cultures. We are still from two different worlds and that's part of this trip. She needs to be in my world and I need to see her in my world. My family is great and my friend circle is great, but not everything is perfect and I have to assume someone will disagree. I'm hoping to see what true love is.

Already from the onset of our trip to Chicago, I can see it will be hard not to fall in love with her. Everything we do will be a first, being she barely got outside of the forest, let alone outside of Poland. She's never traveled by plane; being at the Warsaw airport made her feel like a girl at Disneyland. I have to drag her a few times throughout the terminals. She wants to take pictures at every gate, so I have to reminder her we still have a long way to go. I make sure to have us in first class, and it's so beautiful to watch her sink into her window seat and order a glass of champagne before takeoff. As we take off she grabs my arm as if we aren't going to make it alive. Once we smooth out in the sky, she starts saying Hail Marys and making the cross sign across her chest. The look in her eyes as she takes in the mountain views is so pure. I have used the words pure and beautiful a lot around her. We order filets for our meal and I love the fact she eats meats. We watch movies and nap and snuggle together. The whole process is like a great date on a plane. I'm in trouble; that's just the flight and I feel more smitten. She will be in America for two weeks so I will be melting in her arms before it's said and done.

The Uber ride back to my house takes longer than usual because Kasenka wants to take pictures and stop and ask questions. I get it because I was the same when I was in Poland. I wonder how she'll be when I take her to Chicago. We finally get to my house, or Grandpa Charlie's old house – I haven't figured out what to mentally call it yet.

I can hear Maxine barking at the top of her lungs inside the house. I turn around and there's Irene, sitting on the porch, smiling and waving again—well, at least now I know her name. I yell, "Thank you for watching the dog!" and she just waves and yells back, "Hope you found what you were looking for!"

I laugh because as she says that Kasenka gets out of the car and waves to her. I walk in the door expecting my favorite feeling of my little fur baby running up to me, but instead she runs right past me and into Kasenka's arms. They proceed to roll around on the floor together and laugh like they have known each other for years. I should be mad but I feel joy. Finally, after I clear my throat, Maxine acknowledges her dad.

Kasenka walks around the house inspecting things. She doesn't say much; she just walks around and looks. I go to put my things down in my room. Oh, my gosh, it feels so good to see my bed. Right before I'm going to lay down, Kasenka yells for me to come to the backyard.

"Wow, Trevor, you didn't tell me you had a pool!"

"I do?" When I left to go Poland, the backyard was the only thing that hadn't changed. I guess I won't be the first to see the renovation this time.

"Wow, and a hot tub," she tells me.

Oh, man, what a great surprise. I always wanted a hot tub.

I come around the corner to see not just a pool and a hot tub but a backyard paradise. There's a pool the size of a basketball court and the hot tub is placed right above the pool, looking out at the view … the view that has also changed as well. There's a slide and a cave that's built against the end of the pool. This is unbelievable! I'm not sure I could've dreamed this up. Right as I think that, Kasenka yells out, "This is my dream backyard!" By the time I come back around the bend, she is swimming in the pool, naked.

"Come, get in. It's warm and perfect. Do you have a timer or something that turns on? Because this temperature is just right," she says as she comes out of the water like she's walking in slow motion.

Her body is perfect, like a statue. She perks up her chest and walks over to me. Her hair looks amazing when its wet, as it just lays down to the middle of her back. I watch her walk up to me, and I can't say anything. She just smiles. She takes off my shirt and jeans and pulls me into the pool. We splash playfully in the pool for few moments and do handstands and naked games for a few minutes. Then she stops and starts kissing me passionately. She looks around as if someone is watching and jumps on top of me. We slide into each for a few hours.

Chapter 40

We sit in the hot tub in our post-sex glow, just letting the stars fall over us as the night fades into early morning. Kasenka sits with her legs over mine, facing me. There goes that look again. If only I could read her mind.

"Okay, I think now we're close enough that when you stare at me like this I can ask, what you are thinking?" I ask her. For the most part I feel I've shown my feelings while she just has confirmed them. I don't want this to be some kind of magical spell. I want her to feel it too.

"Well, there are many things going through my head right now."

"Okay, let's start with one."

"Well, I can't get over how magical your place is. All the details and designs, down to the fixtures you have, are exactly the way I would have done it … It's strange. It's a far cry from my humble place in the forest, but for some reason if I were able to afford such a place, this is exactly how I would have designed it. I have seen this place in my dreams, and when I say this I mean this is the place I would have put together, seriously … down to every nail. I know I don't know anything about any of this but …"

"I have to stop you there, Kasenka, because now you would not question it when I say the truth. All of this, you see, I had nothing to do with. It happened after Charlie died. Every time I read a letter or two, when I came back from the visions something would be upgraded in the house or around the house. I couldn't tell you who did it, or where the materials are from. I basically walked into each renovation … the funny part, not to freak you out, but it's the same way I would have designed it as well. Every detail and all the fixings were laid out for me. I had no say in the matter. It's almost as if someone read my mind on how I would design a house and they implemented the plans. Here is the kicker: there were a few things I liked that I wouldn't have picked … but I'm starting to get it. Those things I wouldn't have picked are the things possibly you would have. I have been fighting it, but I think the more we follow our destiny of being together the more good things happen."

I get lost in thought as Kasenka rubs up closer to me. I can see Maxine lying at the edge of the hot tub looking up at the stars. She seems more happy and relaxed than I remember.

"Can I guess why you have a thoughtful look on your face?" she asks. The cheek grab has become my weak point. I love it.

"Sure, fire away, my psychic," I tell her as I lay across her arms like a child.

"Okay, here we go … You're afraid because everything has gone perfectly between us. You're waiting for us to face a hurdle or something to go wrong. For some reason you feel like you don't deserve all the good things that have happened to you since Charlie died. Your whole life you have wanted to become a millionaire, then you did and it feels like you didn't do enough to get it or you feel you didn't earn it. I watched you after you signed the deal with that company. You made the company millions and yourself millions, yet while everyone else was celebrating the change of their life you sat back, reserved. I watched you after you found my grandma. It was the hardest puzzle of your life. You spent months researching and traveling, and you went through all of this journey to find a treasure and finally found that treasure, and yet you still questioned everything. You haven't enjoyed one step on this journey to the fullest ... You have done everything in life the right way, except answer your calling, Trevor ... or something like that? I'm just guessing ... Am I close?"

Close?! More like right on. Damn it, she has everything about me figured out. A few weeks and she spiritually knows me more than my family and friends. It's a double-edged sword because it seems everything is written for me, yet I fight. I'm afraid to mess this up. I'm so caught up in my thought process I don't notice Kasenka is sitting on top of me.

"It's okay, Trevor, nobody is pushing you to do anything. We already know I'm in love with you ... I'm here when you're ready to accept failure is part of destiny, but to be afraid to fail is not."

Chapter 41

I wake up feeling excited that Kasenka is going to meet my family, but I also wake up to an empty bed. I think something is wrong but Kasenka has already walked Maxine, cooked breakfast, and is setting up the house for the family. It's only eight in the morning. I go up for a hug and a kiss but I'm hurried out of the room so she can finish cleaning. Dressed in jeans, that brown blouse, and bandana, just a pure old school beauty look to me. She makes me a breakfast that I've never had before. It's a sausage and egg cooked together but the sausage is kielbasa and the eggs have chives and different spices in them. To complete the meal, she made some toast from homemade bread with strawberry jam and fruit on top. The good thing about dating a Polish girl is you get to date the culture as well. She schedules a honey-do list before my family comes over. Damn, she is going all out. The spread of food is amazing; it looks like it's enough food for hundreds of people. She even buys a set of outdoor lights to set the ambiance in the backyard. She makes me buy a whole new patio set—I should say, she asks me—but her body language is pretty clear that it's needed. I buy a big table that could fit about twenty people to go next to the outdoor grill.

The morning flies by. As the afternoon kicks in, the sun starts to set as my family starts trickling in. You would have thought Kasenka was in the family for years as she greets everyone at the door with hugs and kisses. I'm still waiting for someone to complain or something to go wrong. I have to relax and enjoy the moment. Instead, the theme of the night starts to become who is this mystery woman that I brought home and what has she done to me that I'm introducing her to family already. There are aunts and uncles I haven't seen in a while here, some cousins I'm meeting for the first time, and all my friends show up for the event as well. All the older uncles, aunts, and cousins come to see what I did to Grandpa Charlie's house. All the cousins and younger generation come to see the mysterious woman I brought home after one trip to Poland.

I'm expecting about sixteen people; instead, there has to be at least thirty of us. While I'm freaking out about all the extra people, Kasenka has everything in order and all that extra food I thought was too much is perfect. She smiles and entertains and keeps dinner and the night moving. I see my mom approve of the chicken Kasenka made, which is a big compliment because my mom is a food snob. The negativity that I'm fighting has melted away. I actually relax, sit back, and enjoy everything, especially seeing Kasenka taking my dad's plate and him smiling at her from ear to ear.

The night settles and everyone gets comfortable. Kasenka gets up and makes an announcement about what's for dessert, and I can see some of my family members squinting their faces, trying to understand her accent and looking at this white-skinned Polish girl standing confidently in front of my dark black American family. Everyone is smiling. She must feel uncomfortable being the only Polish girl amongst my family, but you would never know it because she keeps her grace and that smile. It's just moment after moment with my family. There is a moment when I watch all the ladies approve the food and give thumbs up. One of my aunts actually asks Kasenka her recipe for salmon and how she cooked her mashed potatoes. There is a moment when some of my younger cousins loved Kasenka's accent so much they ask her to be in one of their TikTok videos.

My brothers sit and have their meal with me while we stare at Kasenka. Tray asks me where I found her and if she has any sisters or cousins. I start to tell him the story but stop mid-sentence so I don't sound crazy. They wouldn't believe me anyway, not to mention I would have to tell them about Charlie's affair with Kasenka's grandma. Not sure that story will ever get out, to be honest. I just tell my brothers I met her at a coffee shop.

The best part of the night for me is when I catch Kasenka sitting in the corner with my Grandma Betty just talking. They seem to be having a serious conversation and Kasenka appears nervous. They seem to be getting really personal. When they finish talking, they share a long, sincere hug. Kasenka helps her get up and then they share another embrace. She walks away with a few tears in her eyes. I follow her outside to the back. I walk up and hug her from behind as she stares at the stars.

"What's wrong, beautiful? What was that about?"

"It's happy tears and hopeful tears," she says as she turns around to face me.

"Okay, talk to me. Tell me what the happy tears are about first." I hug her close.

"I'm happy that I took that leap when I first met you. I'm happy that I have nothing but firsts with you. I'm happy that I came to America to see the real you and your family. The best part is you're the same Trevor here as the Trevor I met in the forests of Poland … I'm just happy and soaking it all in. Remember, I went from never flying on a plane to flying first class. I went from never going to a prom or a dinner date to one of the most expensive restaurants in Wroclaw and had one of the most memorable nights like a princess. I went from no one ever buying me anything to someone spending money on me without me asking … again, just soaking it all in."

"Well, damn, just so you know, the feeling is mutual. It feels so good to watch you with my family ... and so now tell me, what where the tears of hope about?"

She stiffened up a little bit. "Grandma Betty was giving me her blessings and told me anyone who has come this far with her grandson is special. She also had a warning for me ... she said you're unlike any one of her children, grandchildren, or great-grandchildren, but you are the most like Charlie. She told me Charlie had a presence about him that no one understood, something magical that no one could explain. Good things just happened around him when there was love. He thrived on being needed the most, calling himself God's rescuer. The problem with that power was she felt she could never match his love or understand him to the fullest. She said she could never connect with him on a spiritual level because she could never understand his spirit. There would be moments of pure sadness in his eyes, she said, but he would still give love and give of himself. She wanted so badly to help him or understand when he was sad, but he would snap out of it and act like nothing was wrong. She told me Charlie died with those sad eyes and she is still haunted because she could never figure him out emotionally ... she warned me that you have that same look in your eyes and that you have covered your emotional distress by chasing money and power at work. She thinks you are still searching for something. She hopes you find your power and can emotionally find someone that can save you – not just save you but make you happy. She hopes it's me, but warned me not to be confused by your emotional walls ... my tears of hope are just that. That I'm the one that can reach you emotionally."

Wow, so heavy. Especially coming from Betty. There are so many layers to what was said. While Kasenka may be worried about what my grandma said, she may not be thinking about the missing link.

"Okay, Kasenka, fair enough to have tears of hope, but you are missing a big link to the story. You might not have had time to process this yet, but that sadness and missing link in Charlie's eyes was your Grandma Kasia. You see, of course he couldn't explain his sad eyes to his wife. He had to take the knowledge of knowing he wasn't with the love of his life to his grave … there is no way to tell your wife and kids 'I'm not happy because I'm not with the love of my life.' How do you tell the mother of your children that you're not happy because you lost a child and you were supposed to be with someone else? I know this because he shared this with me during one of our last conversations. I will take that with me to the grave as well; she would never understand."

I can tell that perspective hadn't crossed her mind. I can feel her ease up a little as I pull her closer. "I don't have any hurdles, there is no sadness in my eyes, and what my grandma saw is hunger in my eyes for a life that allows me to do whatever I want and feel free. It turns out, and I'm slowly figuring this out, if I follow my destiny I can get my life's dream anyway and do what I want. I think she is mistaking never falling in love for sadness …"

"And how is your chase? You see, you just said part of the reason you never found love is because you were chasing financial freedom. You have financial freedom now … so now what?"

"That's fair. Maybe I haven't opened my eyes enough. That was before I learned what love was when I found Kasia's letters. It's been nothing but new adventures with you, and since Charlie's death it has always pointed at you … his death led me to you."

We hug, kiss, and finish the night with the family. A perfect ending to a great night. I'm not sure what love is or isn't. Guess with all this magical stuff going on I'm waiting for something to hit me – a sign.

Chapter 42

It's a cold Chicago afternoon and I'm so excited to be taking Kasenka to downtown. We take the train all the way from Rockford to the downtown stop, and I get to see Kasenka look at the city for the first time. Such joyous eyes as we travel to the city. She hugs me and squeezes me tight at every stop we see. This childlike engagement never gets old. We walk along the high towers and end in the shopping district. This woman can walk; she says it's the only way she knows how to travel in Poland. We take a quick Uber ride to walk along the Navy Pier. That Chicago wind is like no other, and Kasenka walks through the wind like it's nothing, with no beanie cap or scarf. She says this is fine, like farm wintertime weather, but softer. I walk into a local shop and buy her a Chicago White Sox scarf and fluffy white beanie cap. Of course, she looks like a supermodel when she puts on the combination. The most beautiful part is she's so appreciative of the scarf and hat, like I had spent millions or something. She thanks me for not only the beanie and scarf, but she acknowledges that she hasn't pulled out her wallet since she met me, and she wants me to know how grateful she is. It actually means so much to me.

All of a sudden I feel something strange in my stomach. It goes away but I feel weird. After we finish walking around the Navy Pier, Kasenka wants to go ice skating. I've never been before but tell her I want to try it. We make it to Maggie Daley

Park Ice Skating Rink. I know I'm not good at the skating thing, and I'm terrible at first, but then all of a sudden I get the hang of it like I'm a pro. It's an out of body experience. It takes a few falls but I'm gliding now and Kasenka and I seem like we are Olympic skaters skating around the rink.

"What's happening, Trevor?" Her voice echoes like we're in some bubble.

"I'm in love with you, Kasenka."

She goes to speak but nothing comes out. I kiss her on the tear falling down her face. I can see her tear fall in slow motion. I embrace her in a hug and it starts to feel like we are floating. This feeling is so powerful. I've never felt this strongly about someone, or something, for that matter. It gives me a sense of life like I've never felt before. I squeeze her tighter as the sense of floating gets stronger. The more we squeeze each other, the brighter our glow gets. It gets so bright to the point we can only see right in front of us. We close our eyes and engage in a kiss. When we open our eyes, we are at my home in Rockford. Kasenka looks around and at first shows a little shock and surprise. but she looks up at me and sees my eyes and she doesn't ask any questions. Instead, she takes a deep breath and slowly starts to take her clothes off. Her body keeps the golden glow around it. Even though it's night out, my room shines like it's the middle of the day. We lose ourselves inside each other the rest of the night.

Chapter 43

I'm standing at my glass sliding door window in my room staring at the beautiful morning sunrise. I can't believe I have a pool and a hot tub and a view. I never even noticed the view before from this room; I'm not sure it was there before. Once again, I'm so caught up in my thoughts of last night I don't feel Kasia's presence standing behind me. I'll hope eventually these surprises come to be normal.

"Welcome back, my favorite ghost," I whisper, hoping Kasenka won't wake up.

"Hello, my child." She hugs me with the biggest smile on her face. She feels so warm.

"You seem happy," I tell her.

"I'm ... you're in love. It's destiny. It's such a beautiful thing when destiny works the way it's supposed to," she says as tears stream from her eyes.

"I would ask how you know, but there is no need to. Did you feel it or something? There was something magical that happened yesterday."

"I know because, like I promised you, the moment you fell in love I was going to die in the real world ... Unfortunately, Trevor, it has to be this way ... it's our destiny."

Her words hit me like bricks and again I'm at a loss for breath and words.

"No, no, no ... there has to be another way to make this work. You are healthy in real life, so you don't have to die." I realize as

I beg her to figure out something different how much she means to me. I realize how close I had gotten with a spirit, a person I had never met until recently in the real world. I feel like I'm losing a friend, a godmother, and an angel all in one.

"No, Trevor, you don't understand. I have waited my whole life to know there was a God … you walking through my doors, looking me in the face, and then falling in love with my granddaughter showed me there is a God and he is great … You falling in love with Kasenka and finishing the legacy Charlie and I were supposed to have is my proof. I can let go now. I'm old and tired … and more importantly, Charlie is waiting for me." There is such finality in her voice.

"Kasia, why not live to see us thrive? Why not fight to see the legacy of our kids? There are so many more things to keep living for!" Now I sound like I'm begging.

"That is not God's plan, my child … Last night, you telling Kasenka you love her was the plan. You have to understand, Trevor, I'm happy and at peace … I wanted this … I needed this."

"But I love you too," I tell her. Man, where did that come from? She even pauses for a second. I realize she's the friend, fairy godmother, mother, and sister I never had.

"My child, I love you too, and this makes me love you even more because you will carry the legacy of both our families and I will be around spiritually forever."

Before I can respond, Kasenka is up and staring at me talking to Kasia. I tried to be quiet, as did Kasia, but we both jump when Kasenka screams, "What the hell is going on here?"

I freeze because I'm not sure what Kasenka is screaming about. It's not until she starts walking at us slowly that I realize she can now see Kasia. All this time with the spirit of Kasia, no one was ever able to see her spirit. I don't know what to say or do. Kasenka walks right up to Kasia's face and goes to reach for her cheeks. Kasia just stands there, also surprised she can see her now. Kasenka gets close to Kasia so she can kiss her. She's trying to look through her soul it seems.

"Grandma Kasia?" Kasenka asks as she touches her hair.

"Yes, my child."

Kasenka almost falls out of her robe as she falls to the ground. She starts to back up like she's going to run ... like she's just seen a ghost. I grab her shoulders and hug her from behind. She tenses up and quickly turns around to look at me. I can see her eyes are lost ... the spiritual realm is not for everyone and I can see her questioning her reality. I understand. I wish I could understand why she now can see Kasia after all this time not being able to see her.

Kasenka stares into my eyes for what seems like an eternity. I can actually start to feel her relax. It's almost like she remembers what happened last night and thinks to herself that she shouldn't be surprised. It's been nothing short of magic since we met. Kasia walks over to us and puts her hand on Kasenka's shoulder. She tenses up a little and I whisper "It's okay" in her ear. She closes her eyes and turns around slowly. Kasia just smiles and looks at us together. Tears starts streaming down her face again. She touches both of our cheeks as the water works continue down her eyes.

"You two are so beautiful together. I can only hope in heaven Charlie and I share this same joyousness in your love. I'm taken back to that first moment when *moj Chanuntka* told me he loved me. You know the story, but now you know the glow and the feeling of floating and the uncontrollable feeling of pure joy. That feeling of how you can love something so much. Not many people get to share the kind of magical love you two have and will have. I have grown up to see nothing but unhappy people in their marriages. True love is hard to find but when it happens, it's magic. There is *purpose*. There is a reason you two are falling in love. Trust me when I say it's not just about you two. You two will make the world a better place and help thousands of people and show the world what love is. This is more important than you think.

"There is one part of the story that I left out when talking to the family ... That moment I started to glow was the moment everything changed in my life. It was like Charlie passed on his magic of life to me. No matter how negative I was, I still made friends. No matter how many people I turned away, people still respected me. No matter how little I made at my job, I always had more than enough. Even Filip's luck at work went well. There were good things that happened that I could not explain ... It was him, my Charlie. The family thinks it is me who paid for the farm, who took care of everyone and made sure we lived the good life, but it was all Charlie ... I've waited my whole adult life to see what Charlie predicted in God's eyes and here you are, in love."

By the time Kasia finishes talking Kasenka is on her knees, crying uncontrollably. Once again, I understand it's a lot to take in. Seeing a younger version of your grandma in the spirit realm, then hearing our similar stories connect is a lot. I pick Kasenka back up because it looks like Kasia isn't done. I ask if I should make some coffee or tea, but Kasia brushes it off and says she can feel she doesn't have much time.

"Kasenka, you must dry your eyes and listen for a second. You are only seeing me now because of Trevor's love and power. His love is allowing you to see me so I can say goodbye ..."

"What?"

"Please let me finish. Trevor warned you that when the chapter of him falling in love with you starts, the chapter of my life comes to an end. I have asked God for nothing more and it has happened. This is my power, my miracle, you understand? You probably didn't believe him when he told you, but I know you understand now. I leave you with some words of advice, my sweetie. You don't need anyone else but him. Trust when times get hard, you will figure it out together. I couldn't enjoy it to the fullest because we had to hide our love. Enjoy every moment you have, because for the rest of your life your destiny is to experience nothing but firsts in your life … All you have to do is love him."

"Grandma, you have to fight on. I never got to apologize for being so distant all this time. I didn't know …"

"My child, you will learn your destiny is still tied to that farm and you were supposed to grow up there and away from the world." Kasenka wants to talk more, but Kasia just puts her hands over her lips to be still.

Kasia looks at me as if this is going to be the last time I see her. She comes up and rubs my cheeks. I jump a little because of a chunk of her face near her forehead crumbles and falls to the ground, then turns to dust. Kasia doesn't react, but Kasenka lets out a wail of a cry, as she can't handle what's happening. I grab Kasia's hand and kiss her palm as a piece of her thumb falls down to the ground and turns to dust.

"My child, Charlie would be so proud of you following your heart and destiny. He is somewhere waiting in heaven for me, I promise you. You now see what he meant by love is your power. The more you chase her love, the stronger you become and the more you can change the world."

The ear on the left side of her face falls down and turns to dust.

"Remember, the world is still a dangerous and negative place. It won't always be easy for you and your spirit. As long as you love, the world will be a better place … you are that powerful, my child."

A piece of her shoulder falls to the ground.

"My God, Kasia, I ..."

"Don't speak, child ... just think, now I won't haunt you and pop up anymore." She laughs and her chin falls to the floor. I can't react. I have to just talk so I won't lose my emotions.

"Every time you haunted me I smiled and loved more. You and Charlie taught me what love is."

"But that's the thing you must learn. You are love ... you are a love angel. If you truly love me, and now I feel you do, you will stop searching and you will fulfill your destiny. This was my main purpose in life when Charlie left, to make sure true love really existed. You were my purpose ..."

She tries to finish her sentence but the bottom half of her mouth falls off. I hug her tightly and can't hold back tears. I feel her falling apart in my arms. I look down and her body falls apart to the ground but her eyes remain and I can feel a smile and peace in them. I stand there with just her hair in my hand as she withers away. The rest of my tears evaporate with her. The last thing left is her right hand, fully intact, holding on tight. I can feel her squeeze right before she disappears. I fall to my knees as the last of her evaporates into smoke. I'm so hurt. I've never felt this pain before. I can barely breathe.

The finality of it all hits me hard. Kasenka comes up from behind and hugs me on my knees. I can feel her tears on my forehead. As we both get lost in sorrow, Kasenka's phone brings us back to reality. She answers and we both know what the call is about. Her family calls to tell us Kasia has died.

Chapter 44

Kasenka is supposed to stay another week but, obviously, she needs to go back for the funeral proceedings and her family situation. She refuses to go unless I come with her. I feel like the family needs to grieve without me there. I also feel a little guilt because I'm sure the family feels my presence in her life has caused her death. It's not a lie, but only Kasenka and I know the truth about the circumstance. Kasenka says she needs me right now and she doesn't care what assumption the family has. My company somehow finds out my situation and pays for our first class flights back and pays for whatever costs come with the funeral.

I am back at the farm. Even in the midst of death, this place still pulls me emotionally. It's calling me home. The funeral is being held in the middle of the farm. Kasenka says the family is surprised because Kasia told them she never wanted to come back to this place, but in her will she specifically says she wants to be put in the dirt at her family farm. There are a lot of people here, at least 300 guests. As they all start filling in the seats, I can't help but think not one of them truly knows her. None of them knew how much pain her heart was in. Half of the family is dressed in their traditional *Górale* Highlander gear. Lots of green and red and beautiful assemblies of colors and flowers designs are all over the decorations. The pride and thick culture ring loudly. The other half of the guests come in suits and dresses and seem like the progressive side of the family. In such a somber situation, Kasenka still puts a smile on my face from how stunning she is in a simple black dress that flows all the way down to her ankles, with black pumps and a black corset-style hat.

The ceremony goes smoothly as everyone pays their respects. After the priest says a few words and reads a few Bible verses, everyone slowly walks by and throws a handful of dirt on Kasia's grave. As we walk by for our turn, Kasenka really doesn't have a reaction. We both throw our dirt, say our prayers, and then she looks at me and smiles. I'm surprised actually. The procession ends with everyone staying around for a special *obiad*, which I know means lunch.

Kasenka teaches me that the *obiad* is usually the bigger meal of the day, not dinner. I grew up so much different and I love our differences. There are three big tents, two of them with food and tables to sit and dine and the last one with a wooden dance floor and a DJ booth. All different styles of traditional Polish foods are being served and the live band starts to play traditional Polish songs. It feels like a family picnic to me, a celebration of Kasia's life.

I sit back and watch the family dynamic turn from sorrow to happily celebrating life. The mood has changed. Kasenka tells me she has to leave me for a second to discuss family business with the elders, and she wants to make sure I'm going to be okay. After giving my blessing, I decide to go walk around and just enjoy the celebration. The music stops and then a group of couples step on to the wooden floor as everyone else clears off. There are about five or six couples dressed in the traditional clothing. A violin sets the tone as they all start to dance in a choreographed cultural dance. I'm not sure if anyone else is seeing them dance like me, but they are dancing in slow motion. The passion and smiles in their faces are pure. The night sky starts to fall as I watch Kasenka converse with the elders. All males and another female besides Kasenka at the top – I'm sure she will change that. A few souls at the party are actually brave and nice enough to come up and introduce themselves. I see some of the girls who hugged Kasenka. They pull me on to the dance floor to dance with them. They're surprised at my moves; I picked up the traditional dances really quickly. I look around the farm and just soak it all in. This place is so serene and beautiful. I wonder if they sit back and look at it like that.

There goes that feeling again, that everything is moving in slow motion. A deep feeling of belonging falls over me as Kasenka catches eyes with me and mouths the words, "Are you okay?" I give her a thumbs up.

The crowd starts to dwindle down as Kasenka and I sit and watch the band play its last few songs.

"Kasenka, why were you smiling when we threw our dirt and said our final goodbyes?"

"Well, first, you can start calling me by my real name, Katarzyna – or Kasia. The only reason the family and everyone called me Kasenka was because it was Grandma Kasia's name and she was mean. As I said when we first met, I was trying to disassociate myself from her … but as you know, I now know the truth. I want to start my legacy, but I want it to be paid with respect to the original … so please, I would love for you to call me Kasia from now on."

"Wow … Okay, Kasia, my love … explain the smile."

"Only you and I knew this, but this is what she wanted …"

She kissed me on the forehead.

"She wanted us to be in love and that love be accepted on this farm. Look at us. It's their dream. She wanted us to have what she couldn't and didn't have with Charlie. Think about it, Trevor … she stayed alive all these years and hung on just to hear you say 'I love you' ... Damn, there is power in that. She wanted us not to just be happy, but to have a life of no worries. She wanted you to be financially set, so you could help me see the world. She wanted me to stay around the farm, so I knew the culture, traditions, and what they taught for thousands of years to pass along to the next generation. She knew you had and have a passion for this farm. I can feel it, she could feel it ... and Charlie could feel it. She wants everyone to see our love and with that change the world. She wants our life to be perfect together; they suffered so we can live. She felt the suffering they went through, and ours should match it in blessings ... The smile was because I knew she was watching us from heaven with Charlie, because all of her dreams had finally come true."

"I love you."

As we get lost in our embrace, someone taps us on the shoulder. It's her Uncle Jacob. "I have these things for you. Kasenka ... sorry, Kasia. I know you're a free spirit so I don't know when I will see you again, so I must get to business now." He hands her an envelope.

"Thank you, *voyek*. What is this?"

"It's the ownership to the farm ... you officially own the farm and the business of the farm now. You were managing and now you own. You can change the name, you change the LLC, you can fire everyone, and you do what you want with the place ... You own all of the ten-mile radius the family owned ... she put it all in your name." He seems happy for her. She seems confused and shocked.

"Thank you again, *voyek*."

"Trevor, first of all, thank you so much for paying for all of this. I know this set-up was not cheap and you went all out. The set-up was elegant. It was a great send off for my mother. Also, it is not lost on me, and some of the crew told me, you tipped the band and the food crew a lot of money. Not only does my family appreciate it, but you have helped a lot of families from your generous donations and tips."

"It was my pleasure. In return I have gotten the greatest gift." I hug Kasenka tight and kiss her on the forehead. It will take a few days for me to get used to calling her Kasia.

"Well, my mother also left you these." It was a box of letters that was labeled "From *Moj Chanuntka.*" The other item is a cylinder case with something rolled up in it. Looks like a map or something in it … but Jacob isn't done talking as he clears his throat. He starts to tear up.

"I wanted to thank you personally … I always thought my mother was a miserable person and hated the world. I don't remember as an adult seeing her smile … the moment you walked through that door was the first time I saw her really smile. I saw her smile as a kid, but something always seemed off. That smile the day I saw her look at you was a gift. It showed me my mother wasn't an evil person. I had always fought with my inner soul because I always felt like I was a positive person, but my mother always put me down. I now know there was a reason. It has done a lot for my personality and life. It has changed my marriage … it will change the course of my life. So yes, I think the least I could do is thank you … Okay, bye." He gives me an awkward hug then runs off.

I look over at Kasenka, who is immersed in the title to the business and farm. She seems to be contemplating things, already thinking of her future. I leave her to her thoughts and walk over to the nearest table to open up the container Kasia left me. I open it up and a big blue sheet falls out. It's a big blueprint of something. I can't understand what it is at first glance. There's a main sheet that had all the details and exact measurements. It looks like a futuristic box home or container, but I can't make out what it is yet. Then it hits me like rocks to my stomach and flashes of the future go through my head ... It's a blueprint for the renovation of the bunker Kasenka has been remodeling, the bunker where Charlie first told Kasia he loved her. Then I notice further down in the cylinder there are other blueprints. There's one for a bakery. There's also a blueprint for a small meat shop, a medical facility and pharmacy, a school, and a new church. The church is big and centered in the middle of the farm from this plan. There are also a few blueprints for upgrades to the buildings and farm cabins already there. But the biggest blueprint of them all is for the bunker. All new everything in the bunker, but the biggest renovation is to the cabin covering the bunker and the outside ambiance of the natural forest bubble. When I open up the blueprint all the way, a note falls out of the bottom of the cylinder ...

Dear Trev,

If you are reading this it means you have accepted your destiny and everything fell into place like it was supposed to ... you fell in love. I'm not sure a big explanation is needed. You're smart enough to understand what you have to do now— you've seen all the blueprints. Finish the projects, Trev. Put your love into that community and change all those people's views and lives for the good ... Remember, angels don't have homes, they have landing spots. You can be in both Chicago and in Poland. You have the means, and they are both your homes now. Angels don't make mistakes doing God's work ... you are an Angel of Love, never forget that. I love you.

Grandpa Charlie

P.S.: As you read this, me and Kasia are watching from heaven. So proud.

I take it literally, drop the letter, and look around to search for them. Instead, I catch eyes with Kasenka walking towards me with tears in her eyes in a panic.

"Trevor, my grandma's last wish was to change this farm to something special. How will I do that if your home is in Chicago? My home is where you are." She looks so worried.

"Come here and relax. Let's enjoy Kasia's celebration of life. I will show you the plan later. All you need to know is … I love you."

She shakes and then all of a sudden relaxes. "Trevor, you are love."

A Year and A Half Later

As I sit here on top of the church bell tower seating area, I'm so glad I made this addition on the church. This is the only place you can see the whole ten-mile radius the family farm encompasses. Up here I come to just think or think about those before me. Up here, staring at this view, I'm reminded of the world's beauty. I make my way down, out of the church and through the town—our private mini town away from it all. I walk on the beautiful new gravel road through the farm to take it all in. I wave hello to Mrs. Bak, who runs the town garden shop. So nice to drive my ATV from the cabin to pick up some fresh fruits and veggies. Two of the young girls from the local daycare come running up, give me a big hug, and tell me what they're doing in school. I stop by to see Damien at the meat shop to pick up a few steaks for dinner tonight. We catch up on the meat business and how his wife and kids are. I take my cart over to the horse stables to check in on Sabina. She runs the stable and is in control of fifty horses. Kasenka and I take our horses to her for grooming and training. I never thought I would love a horse like a dog, but Maxine and my horse Betty get along well. I make a stop by the fishermen's shop by the lake. Rafal catches the best catfish and salmon in all of Poland. He's the manager of the local fish shop. He tells me to come back later and he will have some trout for me. Of course, I have to check in on him and his wife and family.

Then comes my favorite part: it's the scenic two-mile ride to our cabin. I ride by the beautiful trees and I'm hit with the history of the place every time I drive through the brush. The newly renovated cabin looks amazing as you enter our bubble of trees. I made a new bridge that goes over the lake we have. It was a pond but somehow it has turned into a nice lake. The two-story log cabin came from what used to be Kasenka's hard work of just four cabin walls and a roof.

This is my beautiful wife Kasia and our family time with her family in Poland. Her family is from the town called Dzierzoniow, and most of the details you here about in the book are based around this city.

She had every say in how we designed the cabin; it was only right. Beautiful big wall windows let in the best lighting of darts of sun. When the sun is high, it gives a beautiful view of the house, looking as if we are in a disco ball of sun. It has the finest landscaping with a wraparound patio and a beautiful fire pit and a nice yard for Maxine and Betty to run around in. I walk through the doors and I'm greeted with a brand new kitchen. There's a new stove, sink, oven, fridge, dark tile, big print flooring, and an island to the side of the view. Of course, there's all of the technology bells and whistles for water, power, and music. We added two guest rooms to the bottom floor; I needed an in-law suite for my parents, who visit the most. My mom is so excited; she always wanted to come to Europe. The opening of the door also leads to a stairway to the upstairs rooms. There are a few more guest rooms and one big open living space, complete with a big screen TV, wraparound couch, and every toy you can want a living room to have.

I did, however, keep that old table that had covered the bunker entrance. It's sentimental and we still use it for the cover. I walk down to the edge of the bunker and just stare at my world, my miracles. Kasenka sits there with our little baby girl, Kasia the third ... our *purpose* ... as Maxine sits at their feet next to the fireplace. I walk over and kiss both of my Kasias on their foreheads. As I take a deep breath, I can feel a presence in the room. I turn around and Kasia and Charlie are hugging each other and smiling at me.

Review Requested:

We'd like to know if you enjoyed the book.
Please consider leaving a review on the platform
from which you purchased the book.

CPSIA information can be obtained
at www.ICGtesting.com
Printed in the USA
JSHW051005131022
31623JS00001B/3